Double Jeopardy

by

Carolyn Rae

The Ballard Sisters

Cover Art by *Tina Lynn Stout*

The Wild Rose Press, Inc.
PO Box 708
Adams Basin, NY 14410-0708
Visit us at www.thewildrosepress.com

Publishing History
First Edition, 2025
Trade Paperback ISBN 978-1-5092-6205-2
Digital ISBN 978-1-5092-6206-9

The Ballard Sisters
Published in the United States of America

Dedication

Dedicated to my patient husband, Jack, the DFW Writer's Workshop, and my critique partners, Pepper, Anita, Linda, Dorothy, Moira, Alberta, Jan, Bob, Randy, and Carolyn.

Chapter One

"Hot dogs! Get yours now." The eager young man waved one above his head. Jessica Ballard's stomach growled. "Smelling those makes me hungry," she told TV news director, Lawton Knight, who'd brought her to the football game.

He rose. "Come with me to the refreshment stand. I'll get us something." She followed him down the row. They paused to watch a runner score a touchdown.

Two guys, their chests painted orange and black, cheered. Down on the field, cheerleaders in orange shorts and black vests pranced along the sidelines. The one-point kick was successful, and fans around her jumped to their feet. Yelling. Clapping. Chanting cheers.

Jessica smoothed back her long blonde hair, her heartbeat drumming in rhythm with the crowd's stomping feet. If she could capture the stirring spirit of these fans for a special segment on women watching football on her twin sister's TV show, "Look Your Best," she might encourage more women to watch games on that channel. That would please Lawton, Jennifer's boss.

But most important, this was a chance to impress her own boss at the newspaper. She wanted to become a top reporter at *Metroplex News*. Wanted it with an ache that was almost painful. The energy flowing through her right before deadlines always pushed her to finish fast. The thrill of seeing her articles in print and sometimes her byline was like nothing else.

"My balloon," yelled a child a few seats beyond. He looked about six. The yellow balloon, twisted into an animal shape, floated down the row. Its string dangled out of his reach. Tears ran down his face. Trying to grab it, Jessica struggled past the last three occupants of the row, but it kept eluding her.

Reaching the aisle, she sprang up and snagged the string. She held it out to the child. The tow-headed boy smiled, showing a gap in his bottom row of teeth. "Thanks."

Jessica followed Lawton to the refreshment stand and waited behind him. The aroma of hot dogs and popcorn teased her senses. The crowd roared, and she turned toward the stairwell. She must have missed an interception. Her heart beat in rhythm with the clapping crowd.

A loud pop cracked in the air, startling her.

At first, she felt numb. A searing pain in her shoulder grabbed her. Snatched her breath away. She hurt so bad she staggered and nearly fell.

What on earth could slam into her that hard? She looked up, then down. Nothing on the floor—except a splotch of red.

People crowded around.

"Are you all right?" a woman asked.

Jessica's right shoulder throbbed. She touched it. Stared at her blood-coated fingers. They were warm, wet, and sticky. A coppery scent assaulted her nose.

Her jaw dropped. She'd been shot!

Her breath caught. Her muscles spasmed.

People crowded around. Pain sucked her voice dry.

Lawton pushed his way to her. Thank goodness.

"What happened?" He stared at her shoulder. "What the hell? You're bleeding." He yanked out his cell phone and tapped it. She hoped he was calling for help.

Some people hurried away, their footsteps shushing against the concrete floor. Others crowded so close she could hardly breathe. Dust mingled with sweat and perfume.

A woman's voice, shrill and frightened, clawed crab-like at Jessica. "I heard a shot."

"Where are the police?" a man shouted.

"I'm calling 9-1-1," Lawton said. "They should be here soon."

Her right shoulder and arm felt like she'd been hit with a 2x4. Who shot her? Would he shoot again? She scanned the crowd. Couldn't see much. Her heart beat faster. Her breaths came in gulps.

"Is there a doctor or a nurse around?" Lawton asked.

Out in the stands, fans cheered and yelled. All she could focus on was her mind-numbing pain. Her heart hammered. She could pass out any minute.

She drew in a deep breath and then wished she hadn't. Her chest throbbed. She had to keep breathing. Had to keep conscious. Had to stay alive. She didn't want to die.

Her legs gave out, and she collapsed.

On the cold floor, chills enveloped Jessica like a plunge into an icy pond. She pulled in shallow breaths.

"Where's a medic? Why hasn't someone come?" a man shouted.

Everything got fuzzy. Damn, she wanted to be alert, to remember and write this up.

A cop in a blue uniform clapped a handkerchief to her bleeding shoulder. A uniformed security guard, his thin lips clamped together, ushered onlookers away.

The cop asked questions. Dazed and afraid to move, she mumbled her name. Her throat felt like it was full of sand. She couldn't think straight. All she knew was she hurt—hurt like hell.

Moments later, paramedics appeared. Placed an oxygen mask over her nose and mouth. She could relax. They'd take care of her. Stop the pain. But they asked more questions. About allergies. About medications. Was she pregnant? She would have laughed if she didn't hurt so much.

Two men lifted her onto a gurney. Her shoulder throbbed with every movement. A security guard followed, waving people out of the way as they wheeled her out of the stadium. Every time they rolled over a crack, it jarred her. She gripped the sides. The pain was so bad she could hardly stand it. Tears ran down her cheeks.

Lawton walked beside the gurney. "Is she going to be all right? Where are you taking her?"

"Arlington General," the paramedic said.

Lawton patted her right hand. Pain shot up her shoulder. She winced.

"Don't worry," he said, "They'll take care of you." He sounded comforting, but his pale face and worried expression said she looked pretty grim.

"Call my sister," she finally got out.

"I will. Just relax." Then he was on the phone to the station, telling someone what happened, his sentences filled with sound bites. Of course—he was a newsman.

They loaded her into the ambulance. Someone slammed the back doors shut. The paramedic tapped the inside wall twice. The driver gunned the engine, and the siren blared. The gurney shook. Pain shot down her arm. She groaned. The paramedic pounded the wall behind the driver. "Hey, take it easy," he shouted over the shrieking siren. "Freaking race driver wannabe," he muttered under his breath.

What was that beeping? She craned her neck toward the monitor. The line zig-zagged, keeping pace with the rapid beep. Weak and dizzy, she panted, trying to get her breath. Then everything went black.

****

Jessica struggled to pry her eyes open. Her lids seemed stuck, like they were sealed shut with Super Glue. Somehow, she managed to open her eyes. Shadows played on cream-colored walls. It smelled of disinfectant and bleach. She wrinkled her nose. Nausea threatened.

Vaguely, she recalled Lawton's quick visit and her sister sitting beside her in the room. "I'll let you rest," he'd said and left. Her twin must have gone home as well. She remembered the doctor saying something about the bullet going almost all the way through. Thank goodness.

Bright sun streamed in the window. She must have slept a lot. Her right arm felt heavy, and her tongue felt thick. She licked her lips, wishing for a glass of water.

She'd still prepare that presentation for Lawton. She wasn't sure how, but she wouldn't miss the opportunity. However, her first-person version of the shooting might even make the front page. Now what could she use as a lead?

At the sound of footsteps, she looked up. A man built like a linebacker, dressed in a navy blazer and nice slacks, strode in. He studied her for a moment, then stepped forward. "I'm Investigator Steel, Arlington Police. I'm glad you're finally awake. Hope you're feeling better. I need to ask you a few questions about the shooting."

His husky voice made her heart skip a beat. She touched her shoulder and winced. It was still tender—even with the pain meds. She felt woozy, but at least the pain had subsided a bit. The cop would ask a bunch of questions. She sighed. No way did she feel like talking.

She studied his face. His tan contrasted with the cream-colored walls. Large, chiseled jaw and high cheek bones. His nose looked as if it might have been broken at one time. And the way that navy blazer fit his arms and shoulders—yummy—he must work out a lot.

He had an oval, silvery badge on his belt. His other job could be modeling for GQ. Just my luck to have him walk into my life when I look like a freight train ran over me.

"Damn, you're gorgeous." Omigosh, did I actually say that? She groaned and felt her face grow hot. She caught his faint smile, which quickly morphed into a solemn face.

Whatever they'd given her for pain must be scrambling her senses.

Wish I'd combed my hair. Why the devil couldn't I have met him somewhere else when I looked better. After clearing her throat, she pushed the button to raise herself up. She hoped her voice didn't sound as weak as she felt. "Steel's your last name, right? What's your first name?" she asked, going automatically into interview mode. This was better. Interviews she could do.

He opened his eyes wide, then grinned, showing dimples to die for. With that killer smile and those dimples, he could lure women without trying.

"My name's Michael, Michael Steel."

She rubbed her forehead, tried to think what to say. And now he'd noticed her indecision. "How long have you been a cop?"

His dark-eyed gaze met hers. Interest sparked in his eyes. He smiled, a warm, genuine smile.

She let out the breath she'd been holding. She didn't need to be so nervous, so aware of him.

"Five years. I've been a cop here for five years."

"Why did you become one?"

He met her gaze, his expression serious. "That's a long story." He pulled out a notepad, tapped a pen against his head, then poised it over the paper. "Now, I'll ask the questions. Tell me what happened."

She shook her head and shifted in bed. A shooting pain stabbed her shoulder. It mushroomed, making her more uncomfortable by the minute. Was the pain medication wearing off already?

It hurt worse when she sat up, so she lay back down. Now she wished he'd just go. "All I know is something slammed into me."

He didn't act like talking to her was just a job he had to do. The intent look in his brown eyes made her feel as if he really cared about what happened to her.

She took a deep breath. "At first I didn't know what happened. I don't get shot every day, you know." She gave him the best grin she could manage. "All I remember is that a bullet hit me, and it hurt really bad." She wouldn't go into detail about how it felt. She wanted to save her impressions for her article. And she had to call it in fast before it became old news.

"Did you notice anyone acting suspiciously before

or after you were shot?"

"No. Never in a million years did I think I'd be shot in a crowded football stadium." Tiredness washed over her like a tidal wave. She shut her eyes—just for a moment to catch her breath. "Was anyone else hit?"

The detective shook his head. "No one else was injured."

She opened her eyes again and caught a whiff of sandalwood aftershave. Nice. Almost covered up the hospital smells of antiseptic and bleach.

He stared at her with a puzzled expression. "Do you have any enemies who might want to harm you?"

She shook her head. "I can't think of anyone who'd want to shoot me. Did you talk to the people nearby? Anyone see anything?"

"Hold it. One question at a time. According to the report I got from an officer at the scene, only one shot was fired. He questioned several people. One mentioned a man walking awfully fast as he left the area."

"I don't suppose you got a description?"

He frowned. "Several actually. White man in his thirties, average size, average height, wearing a baseball cap that shadowed his face."

Detective Steel rubbed the back of his neck. "One person said he had a limp. Another said he walked very fast and melted into the crowd. They called in more cops and sealed the exits, but couldn't find any likely suspects, so they had to let everyone leave after the game."

"What about security cameras?"

"Nothing out of the ordinary appeared on the recordings."

"Great. You don't really have anything at all."

A frown creased his brow. He scribbled faster and pressed his pen so hard the paper tore.

"By now I'd expect you'd at least have some leads on a suspect, something you can tell me."

His frown deepened. "We haven't gotten much to go on. I was hoping you could tell me more."

"I've told you all I can remember."

"We're still tying up loose ends. We can't have a pretty woman or anyone else getting shot at football games. I'll keep working on it. I questioned several people nearby, but was anyone with you who could tell me more about what happened?"

"Lawton Knight, the director of KWIK, brought me to the game—I was researching a piece to present on his station. He was standing behind me at the concession stand when I was shot. Have you questioned him?"

"Yes, but he was facing the other direction when the shot was fired and couldn't tell me anything more."

"I want you to close your eyes and think about what you can remember about who you saw before you were shot."

Her reporter's observation skills kicked in. She was surprised at how much she could remember. "People were milling around, probably there to buy food, but I didn't see anyone with a gun.

Detective Steel seemed intent on sorting this out, but he'd called her a pretty woman. That made her feel good. Even as his questions dragged on, she couldn't help smiling. Usually, people talked about her twin, Jennifer, that way, not her. But why would anyone want to kill her?

His pants fit smoothly over well-formed thighs and long legs. He stepped closer. Seemed taller than she'd thought at first. Quickly, he jotted down her home address, got her work address and work number. "Can you think of anything more to tell me?"

She shook her head,

"Don't worry," he said. "We'll do all we can to find and apprehend the shooter."

His smile flowed over her, comforting her. She wished she had something else to say, something to keep him here, except she felt woozy. Exhausted, she laid her head back on the pillow. She needed to get a grip. He was just reassuring her while she was seeing dinner and dancing. After this, she'd probably never see him again.

He met her gaze. "Sadly, when women are attacked, it's often someone they know. Tell me about your relationships with boyfriends." Detective Steel sat patiently.

"Well, I used to date Harry Hamilton, and I've been seeing Bradley Stanton. We were supposed to meet for a drink last Tuesday night, but I had to cancel because of work. I haven't talked to him since then." She'd had heard later that he'd dated another reporter at the news on Friday. Well, she was welcome to him. If Jessica got more important stories, she'd be rushing to meet deadlines more often. She couldn't promise to meet someone right at five o'clock. Was that why she hadn't gone anywhere she could meet someone she might date? If she wanted to get ahead, that was the price she'd pay.

Her career was what made her life interesting and fulfilling. She was sure of that. It kept her going, kept her reaching for the brass ring for more interesting assignments. Work had always trumped relationships. That was more important than boyfriends, wasn't it?

He met her gaze. "Give me their phone numbers and

their addresses if you know them," Detective Gorgeous said.

She rattled off Harry and Bradley's phone numbers and addresses.

He scribbled them down, then looked up expectantly. "Anyone else?"

"No," she mumbled.

"So, tell me, was your relationship with either of them long term?" He leaned forward, waiting for her answer.

"I dated Harry most of last year. We broke up just before Christmas."

Steel's eyebrows inched closer together. "Was your breakup heated?"

She pushed the button to raise herself to a more comfortable position and to get a better look at Detective Steel. "No. We just didn't want the same things."

"Do you have a jealous co-worker at your office?"

"I don't think so."

"I'll check your boyfriends out. I really don't want you in more danger."

A stout nurse with short, slicked-back dark hair, and a name tag that said, 'Mary,' walked in and stepped close to the bed. Hands on her hips, she stared at the detective. "That's long enough. I'm taking her to get a blood test."

"I just have a few more questions I need to ask."

"You can talk with her later—during visitor hours."

"The first forty-eight hours after a shooting are critical when investigating a case. Since she was rushed to surgery soon after she got here, I didn't have a chance to talk with her."

"Well, she needed to be operated on immediately, and she took a longer than usual time coming out of anesthesia. That's why you couldn't see her then."

"I just need another fifteen minutes. Her information could be critical to finding a suspect."

"It may take half an hour to finish the blood tests, and after that she needs to rest. Come during visitor's hours, not before." Her no-nonsense expression and her stance said, no one, not even a cop, better defy me.

Obviously wanting to object, he clamped his mouth shut. He looked disappointed. Even a hint he enjoyed Jessica's company made her smile. He headed toward the door, then looked back. "See if you can remember anything else, even if it doesn't seem important. I'll be back."

At the doorway, he reached in his pocket. He walked back to her bed, smiled, and handed her a business card.

The touch of his fingers sent a brief sizzle up her arm. Seeing his slight flinch, she gripped the card and met his gaze.

"That has my office number and my cell number. If you see anyone who looks threatening, call me. I'll tell hospital security to keep a close watch on you." He smiled and headed for the door.

His walk, brisk and purposeful, kept her attention until the nurse moved to her bedside and squeezed a blood pressure cuff so tight it hurt. Trying to ignore the momentary discomfort, Jessica gripped his card.

After he left, she lay back down, but the nurse grasped her hand. "Let's get you up and off to the lab." Jessica set the card on the bedside table. She hoped she'd feel up to writing when she got back in bed. She'd do a rough draft of an article for the news about being shot. Not sure if I can write with my shoulder aching so. What if I can't think of a good lead? But I will—even if it takes all morning.

After the nurse brought her back and hurried out the door, Jessica pawed at the sheets, feeling for the call button. When someone answered, she said, "Please. I need something for the pain." She had to be able to think. She wanted to make this feature piece the best she'd ever written.

The nurse walked in and gave her something, but Jessica still felt exhausted, like she'd swum halfway across a lake with all her clothes on. She closed her eyes. Just for a few minutes. If only that pain medicine would work quickly without making her groggy, she could do this. She sat up.

"It hasn't been that long since you had surgery. Try to lie back and relax," the nurse said.

Feeling too weak to get out of bed, she begged the nurse to get her pen and spiral notebook from the closet where they'd put her things. The nurse left them on the bedside table. Reaching for them, Jessica strained her sore shoulder.

Gripping the pen and notebook, she forced her fingers to form each word. 'At the new stad—' she wrote. The pen fell from her weary fingers. Her shoulder was killing her, and she could hardly make out what she'd written. Damn.

She leaned back and closed her eyes. As soon as she had it into final form, she'd call it in. A byline would be nice, but as awful as she must look, there was no way she'd let a photographer snap her picture.

She was good with words. They'd speak for her, tell the readers how it felt to be shot out of the blue—to have people crowd around while you lay helpless on the floor. Might as well begin. She picked up the pen again.

But when she tried to write, her fingers wouldn't cooperate. Her shoulder was hurting, and she still felt fuzzy. She laid her notebook on the table. For a few minutes, she'd just lie here and think about what to put in her story—and not about Detective Gorgeous.

****

Detective Michael Steel stood outside Jessica Ballard's hospital room. He couldn't stop looking at her. She was fascinating. Her cute smile had warmed him. He would have enjoyed spending an hour talking to her, but before he got all the answers he needed, that persistent nurse kicked him out. He needed all the facts he could get to catch the shooter. He'd wanted to tell her she was obstructing justice. He trod down the hall. He needed to finish his notes.

Interviewing gunshot victims wasn't one of his favorite tasks. Usually they didn't remember much, or if they did, they didn't get the details right, but Jessica's voice had fallen on his ears like soft music. Wishing he could take her out dancing, he imagined her whispering words of endearment in his ear. Whoa, he was getting ahead of himself. He needed to take care of work first as soon as that damn nurse let him talk to Jessica.

Jessica—he should think of her as Miss Ballard— she shouldn't have seen him arguing with the nurse. Not professional. The damn nurse had won. She didn't need to waste his time with a gun-happy idiot loose. Time was of the essence. He'd be back.

Jessica had looked so frightened and alone. Touching her smooth fingers had sent a zing up his arm. Her hand felt soft, but awfully cold. He wanted to take both of her hands and warm them to make her feel better. Who was he kidding? He shouldn't get personal with a victim. He needed to be professional whether the victim was plain or beautiful, and Jessica was anything but plain.

He'd wanted to ask if any of her ex-boyfriends might have a grudge. Some guys got pretty steamed over rejection. Like the bastard who probably shot Michael's sister.

Michael swallowed. He rarely shared why he became a cop. Her ex-boyfriend had denied killing her, and there hadn't been enough proof, so he'd never been tried. "Damn." Michael gritted his teeth.

Sophia's killer could have been someone else she'd met in that bar. Michael drew in a deep breath and let it out slowly. His stomach knotted. He couldn't forgive himself for not asking where she was going with her girlfriend that night after graduation. Maybe he could have talked her out of lying her way into that club or at least gone with her.

Remembering her motionless body behind that bar with her hands crossed over her chest still gave him chills. He'd hate to see another woman lying dead in an alley. He wanted to make sure women were safe on city streets. If he prevented one beating or one death, he'd know he was making a difference.

He shouldn't be thinking about that now or the woman he'd just seen. Except he had to fill out a report on Jessica—Jessica with the beautiful smile and soft hands. Jessica, whose face had lit up when she saw him. Jessica, whose smile made him want to ask her out and get to know her better. Thoughts he shouldn't be having—especially not when he had a shooter to catch. But he couldn't help smiling. Jessica intrigued him.

****

She was dozing when the clicks of high heels alerted her to someone entering the room. Her eyes popped open.

Her sister, Jennifer, rushed to her bed. "How are you feeling now? I'm so sorry you got hurt." Jen squeezed Jessica's hand. Jen's voice, usually smooth and mellow on the air, cracked. "I've been worried about you ever since Lawton called and told me what happened. I rushed here and stayed until the doctor came out after the operation and said you'd be okay.

After they took you to a room, I waited for a while, but the nurse said it would take more time for you to completely come out of anesthesia."

Jessica stared at her sister. "I vaguely remember seeing you then."

"You were so doped up I decided I'd let you rest and come back later. The only thing you said that made sense was not to call Mom and Dad until you were better."

"You know how Mom worries. She'd think I was at death's door."

"Have you seen the doctor? Did he say your shoulder would heal okay?" Jen asked.

Jessica smiled. "Yeah, he did. I suppose I hit the evening news."

Jen nodded. "The shooting did. But they didn't mention a name. Guess the police vetoed that."

"So, how was your interview at the modeling agency?"

Jen grinned, her green eyes, just like Jessica's, sparkling. "The agency gave me a letter of recommendation for the film audition. Just think of it. I could be in the movies. I've been to so many interviews where nothing came of them, but something tells me I have a chance this time. Thanks again for going to the game with Lawton while I had the agency appointment."

"You're welcome."

A male nurse walked in and reached for the blood pressure cuff. "Stretch out your—" He glanced at Jennifer and stared, then finally turned back to Jessica. "Excuse me, miss, would you stretch out your arm please so I can take your blood pressure?"

Used to everyone staring at her glamorous sister, Jessica held out her arm. Ever since Jen discovered make-up, she'd been a showstopper. Sometimes it seemed chilly in her sister's shadow, but she was glad Jen had found success with her weekly TV show, "Look Your Best."

As the nurse fumbled with the blood pressure cuff, Jen said, "Hey, I've got some make-up in my purse. You'll look better with a little color in your face."

Jessica raised her hand to her face. That was Jen, always conscious of how she looked. "I bet you wouldn't be worrying about your looks if you'd been shot."

Jen looked contrite. "Maybe not. Knowing you look good should lift your spirits." She applied some blush to Jessica's cheeks. "Just wait and see. Did the police come here and ask you questions?"

Jessica nodded. "The cop who interviewed me asked a lot of questions."

Jen leaned forward. "You mean that good-looking man I saw writing notes in the waiting room? He was scribbling so fast, he only looked up once as I walked by."

Uh, oh. Next to Jen's fabulous looks, did Jessica stand much of a chance? Her chest constricted. She'd wanted to keep the cop's attention for herself. She'd seen

Detective Gorgeous first, but Jen picked up men without even trying. It wouldn't be the first time her sister had played up to a guy Jessica was interested in.

Jessica nodded. "That's probably whom you saw, but how'd you know he was a cop? He wasn't in uniform." Crossing her fingers, she hoped Detective Steel hadn't done more than glance at Jen.

Jen laughed. "Easy. The way he stood, straight and stiff, the alert way he assessed me, then went back to writing. Now about your hair–"

"I guess I could have it highlighted like yours, but I haven't the patience to spend all that time with a curling iron and putting on lots of make-up like I did for the game your boss took me to."

Jen pushed back long blonde curls and smiled. "But then you'd have your pick of guys to take you out."

"I don't want a man who just wants to be seen with a pretty girl on his arm. That's too much ego for me." Was Detective Steel like that?

Jen looked at her watch. "I have to run. When are they going to let you loose? I'll come pick you up."

"Not sure, but I'll let you know. Thanks."

Jennifer freshened her lipstick, then paused at the door. "Oh, I forgot to tell you about my new Sheltie puppy. He's adorable. You've just got to see him as soon as you're able." She smiled. "He showers me with kisses when I come home."

"I thought you didn't like dogs licking your face."

"Charlie's had all his shots, and I don't let him outdoors near any other dogs, so he won't catch anything. And if his paws are the least bit dirty, I wash them before I bring him inside."

Her sister seemed so excited about her puppy, but

Jessica felt exhausted—like she'd run a 5K race. She laid her head back on the pillow. She'd been working hard and worrying about pleasing her boss at the newspaper. Being shot didn't help. "When I get out, I'll stop by to see him."

Jen took Jessica's hand. "I hate to ask for a favor with you like this, but it's not until two weeks from now. You should be fine by then."

"What do you need?"

"This morning, I auditioned for that movie part, and they may want me to fly to Hollywood for a screen test. I'll ask Lawton to run filmed episodes of 'Look Your Best' while I'm gone. Could you keep my puppy for a couple of days then?"

"Sure, but what about Snowball? Most dogs don't tolerate cats."

Jen waved her hand dismissively. "He's a puppy. He won't know that."

"Well, okay, but only for a few days."

Jen squeezed her right hand. "You're a dear."

Jessica winced at the pressure on her shoulder, but it felt good to see her sister.

Jen turned back at the door. "Look, if that's too much, let me know. I can always take Charlie to a kennel. Get some rest so you can get out of here. Do you need someone to stay with you when you get out?"

"No. I'll be okay, but I need something to wear so I can leave the hospital."

"Tomorrow I'll bring you an outfit I've worn on the show before."

"Are you sure you'll be okay with me presenting what I write about spectators' love for football games on your show?"

Jennifer scrunched her face together. "Can you do it without audiences noticing you aren't me?"

Jessica raised an eyebrow. "I think I can read one page in front of the camera."

"You'll be okay then. I hope you feel better soon. Call me when you're ready to leave. Bye."

Jessica started to wave with her right hand. A sharp pain reminded her not to. She waggled her other hand as her sister strolled from the room, her hips undulating. A good-looking doctor walked by in the hall, then paused.

Of course, he stopped to speak to her. Men always did. Oh, she'd smile and flirt, but then if they asked her out, she'd say she was too busy. Maybe Jen wanted to be valued for more than her looks. Or was she hung up on her boss? They certainly spent a lot of time together. Well, Jessica wouldn't worry about that. When would Angela, her other sister, come visit? Maybe after work. Jessica felt tired. She needed to rest now, and she drifted off to sleep.

****

Jessica opened her eyes, but she couldn't see anything. Was it night? Something's pressing on my face. Can't breathe. Got to get some air. Got to push away that heavy suffocating blob—or whatever's making it hard to breathe.

Chapter Two

Jessica pushed and shoved as hard as she could. Her pulse raced, and her heart pounded. She didn't want to die. She gasped in short breaths. Forced her eyes open.

Then the pressure disappeared. In the dim light. she couldn't focus on the dark shadow bending over her.

Weak and groggy, Jessica gulped in several breaths. Finally, she could raise her head and look around. No one was in her hospital room, but her other pillow was rumpled. She must have been grabbing it while dreaming.

She glanced toward the doorway of her hospital room. Two figures stood there. Finally, she focused on the nurse, who'd been taking care of her, standing in the doorway. When the nurse switched on the light, Jessica blinked. Her short, stocky brother-in-law, Bill with his military crew cut, stood beside the nurse.

Angela's husband stepped over to her bed and patted her right arm. "Are you awake now?"

She winced and shoved his hand away. Didn't like him. Didn't like him touching her.

Still groggy, she opened her mouth to speak. Nothing came out. Had she been dreaming, or had someone really tried to smother her?

That was crazy. Whoever shot her wouldn't be dumb enough to come into her room. She was in a hospital, for heaven's sake. With lots of people around.

However, she couldn't wait until she felt strong enough to leave.

Mary her no-nonsense nurse, still stood in the doorway. "You all right, miss?"

Finally, she found her voice. "I'm okay. I'd like some water."

"I'll get it," Bill said. He grabbed the pitcher beside her bed and poured her some. "Looked like you were having some kind of nightmare. I wasn't sure whether to step in and wake you or not."

His pale blue eyes fastened on her face. "Oh, you're Jessica. I thought Angie said it was Jennifer, who got shot."

He studied her face. "I see the difference now. You don't have any make-up on. I bet Jennifer would never let anyone see her that way."

Damn brother-in-law should recognize me by now. After all the times he's put his enormous feet under Mom and Dad's dinner table—and he didn't have to make that crack about make-up. She touched her upper arm. "Jennifer didn't have a bullet rip through her shoulder. I did."

Her older sister, Angela, her dark blonde pageboy swinging, breezed into the room, carrying flowers and a vase. She rushed to the bed. "We came as soon as we could leave work." She set the vase down and placed a paperback mystery novel on the bed.

Angela was the oldest and had looked after her two sisters when their mother was out with her charity affairs. Their father, the CEO of a multibillion-dollar pharmaceutical manufacturer based in Dallas, was always busy, but he'd called to see how she was. "I brought you something to read," Angela said. "Are you all right?"

"Not really, but it's good to see family." Bill didn't count. She'd never had much use for the pompous ass. "I just had a horrible nightmare, like some weird blob was trying to swallow me whole. After all that happened, I was glad to wake up and find it wasn't real."

Angela set the flowers on a bedside table. "How long are they going to keep you here, Jessie?"

Jessica shrugged, then winced. She should have kept still. "I hope not more than a couple of days. I don't want to be cooped up here a minute longer than I have to." She squirmed on the sheets. Dry and scratchy, they smelled of bleach.

"Do you need a ride home?" Angela asked. "I can pick you up and bring you some Chinese take-out."

"Jen offered to take me home, but Chinese would be lovely," For once, since she'd grown up, Angela had offered to do something for her. That was a pleasant change.

"Jessie," Angela said, "we can't stay long. Do you want me to call Mom and tell her you're going to be okay? We haven't told her you got shot yet. She'll want to rush right over."

"Tell her not to come. I should be able to go home tomorrow or the next day. She worries so. I don't want her seeing me like this."

Angela patted Jessica's hand. "She'll worry anyway. We'll let you rest now." She turned and walked out the door with Bill.

Jessica lay back down on the pillow. Don't know what my sister sees in him, but I'm glad she's the one to work with Dad in the family business. Neither she nor Jennifer wanted to work there, although they both appreciated dividend checks at Christmas.

Her mind wandered back to her job at the paper. Hopefully, after she wrote a good article about being shot and did the TV assignment, her boss at the paper would take notice and assign her more interesting stories than obituaries and small company startups.

Had Jennifer's boss agreed to let her finish the TV segment? Jessica couldn't remember. Jennifer had talked him into letting Jessica go to the game and do a segment on women and football because the interview with the Kim Dawson Agency came up at the last minute. Jessica could write a good presentation, and after taking speech in college, reading her own words programmed into the prompter would be easy.

She'd write the script for that piece later, but now she'd concentrate on her article about her experience. It had to be good. The story should make the front page of the metro section. Was that shooter after her or someone else? Who would want to kill her? Shivers shimmied down her spine. Surely hospital security would keep out anyone with a gun.

She twisted her fingers. She hoped the cops would make an arrest before she left the hospital.

She needed to work on the article now—while it was fresh in her mind. She picked up her pen and wriggled around, trying to get comfortable. Her back hurt, her shoulder throbbed, and she could barely dredge up strength to move. She tried to write down her impressions. Now that she thought about it, she didn't exactly recall feeling the bullet tear into her shoulder. She'd felt a sudden, searing pain and seen blood.

That's it. That's the lead. She crossed out what she'd written and began again. "A quick pop and a sudden searing pain." It hurt to write, but she couldn't stop now.

Finally, after getting the rough draft of a lead paragraph down, she caught herself thinking about the handsome detective. His report would be brief and to the point.

He'd smiled when he called her a pretty woman. Did he really mean it, or did he say that to all the women he met? His charming smile drew her in like a hummingbird to nectar. It would be nice if he'd come back again. She couldn't think what else to tell him, but she sure hoped he had some leads on the shooter. If not, she'd have a constant crick in her neck from looking over her shoulder and a string of knots in her stomach whenever she went out. Would she even be safe at home?

One thing she was sure of, if Detective Gorgeous came back, she'd love to see him smile again.

She looked at the clock on the wall. Jennifer's appointment at the modeling agency was yesterday, wasn't it? She hurt so much she could hardly remember things. All the events of the last two days seemed jumbled together.

A knock sounded on her open door. "Are you up to a visitor?" Michael Steel's smooth-fitting blazer hugged his broad chest. Dark wavy hair grazed his shirt collar, and his cafe-au-lait eyes darkened when his gaze met hers.

She took in a deep breath. Oooh, yes, do come in. "Yes," she finally got out. She tried to sit up and smooth back her hair.

He stepped into the room. "I just need to ask a few more questions. I'll try not to tire you." It was good to see him again. Would his touch send the same jolt of electricity as it had before?

Hallway noise evaporated. It was just her and him … like they were all alone on a tropical island with warm waves lapping on the sand and soft breezes caressing her skin. She caught his gaze. He smiled. Hot damn.

Michael approached, his smile fading with each step. He looked serious. What now? She must have been caught up in daydreams. She'd blame it on the medication.

She swallowed. If she could just finish this discussion before she made a fool of herself, she'd push this meeting to the back of her mind—and not think of him again. Yeah, right—like she could stop breathing.

His enigmatic look held her gaze. Why didn't he say something?

Lying in her hospital bed, Jessica held her breath. Was Detective Gorgeous bringing bad news?

Chapter Three

"Hello, again, Miss Ballard," he said in that sexy voice of his. He pulled a chair up to the bed and pulled out a small notebook.

Now, she relaxed.

His deep voice fell upon her ears. "I need your cell number. I was going to get that last time, but the nurse shooed me out."

After she gave it to him, he leaned forward. "I talked to the security guard at the newspaper office. Says he asked you out, but you said you were too busy."

"I vaguely remember that. I was trying to meet a deadline and didn't have time to talk."

Detective Steel's eyebrows inched closer together. "Were you abrupt with him?"

"I might have been. He looked annoyed, but I don't think he'd attack me." She pushed the button to raise herself to a more comfortable position and to get a better look at the detective.

He met her gaze. "I'll check him out. I don't want you in more danger."

"Are there any other ex-boyfriends or anyone at your work who might want to hurt you?" He sat patiently.

She shook her head, less vigorously this time. Didn't want to chance a headache returning.

"I'll be back later." He strode from her room. Why

did he have to leave so soon?

She finished the article on being shot. Recalling the event filled her with fear again. Was she even safe here? She wished she had her laptop here so she could email her article. She tried to call it in, but they kept her on hold until she figured they'd forgotten her. Her pain meds were wearing off, and being ignored made her testy. Finally, Miss Sharp, her boss, came on the line.

"Jessica." Her boss's voice sounded cold and calculating as usual, as if she expected everyone to jump to her commands. "Can't you email your article?"

Jessica's stomach knotted. She tapped her fingers against the receiver. She wanted to snap at her boss but forced her voice to sound respectful. "I'm in the hospital, and it's too long to type on my phone. My shoulder hurts so much, I can barely read what I wrote."

"Oh, all right. Let me transfer you to someone who can type it up. We already ran a short piece on the shooting. It's not like you're somebody famous, but I am sending our photographer out to take your picture."

Jessica gritted her teeth. "I don't want a photo of me looking like this in a rumpled hospital gown."

"If you look like you're in bad shape, that will make a more newsworthy picture."

Jessica had half a mind to tell her boss to forget it, but damn it, her article was good enough for a feature, so she'd put up with that. "Okay, but please let me dictate it to Debbie." She made a mental note to notify her boss when the TV segment came on "Why female spectators love football games" would air on her sister's TV show, "Look your best."

After Jessica finished reading the article to her co-worker, Debbie said, "Wow, you must feel terrible. I'll type it up and hope it makes the front page of the metro section."

Her life-threatening experience probably wouldn't even rate the front page. "Thanks. I appreciate your help."

As Jessica hung up, she remembered the script she was supposed to write about a woman's perspective of a football game, followed by a pre-recorded clip of fashions for wearing at games.

She was glad Jennifer's weekly, thirty-minute TV show before the early evening news was doing well, but Jessica was more comfortable writing articles for the newspaper.

After filling a fresh page with her attempts at a catchy first line, she put it aside, called her father, and told him to assure her mother she was okay. Then she reached for the novel Angela had brought. It began with a woman being suffocated with a pillow. That hit too close to the nightmare she'd had. She shivered and slammed the book shut. Dare she sleep now?

****

Michael was lucky enough to find Bradley Stanton home and willing to speak. Like a typical bachelor apartment, the couch and easy chair were brown, and no pictures hung on the landlord-cream walls. Sparkling clean windows on his varnished gun case showed off two shotguns, a rifle, and a Glock. Michael asked Bradley how often he used them.

"My Glock's just like the security guard's at the paper's office building. After a busy day, I like to go to the range and blow off steam."

Michael understood. Sometimes he felt that way.

Bradley puffed out his chest. "With these, no one

will dare mess with me."

Bradley might just have a big ego, but Michael would check to see if he had a record.

He'd also retrieve the bullet removed from Jessica. The shell picked up at the stadium was the right size for a bullet used with a Glock. He held out a paper bag. "May I take your Glock to test against the bullet that hit Jessica?"

"Hey, I swear I didn't shoot her."

"So, if you're innocent, there won't be a match."

Michael spoke on the phone with Harry, who was still at work. He claimed he wasn't at the game, but he could be lying. Michael made arrangements to see him for a personal interview the next day when he'd ask him what guns if any he owned. Glad it was five o'clock, Michael walked out to his car and headed home.

Something kept nagging at him as he drove. What was it about this case that kept eluding him? After walking his dog, he shoved a frozen pizza into the microwave. He settled back in his recliner, then switched on the TV. A man announced a weekly show for women.

He was about to switch channels when he saw Jessica. Only her hair was curly and she looked well made-up. It must have been pre-recorded before the shooting. She looked glamorous, but he preferred her as she'd been in the hospital, hair tangled and bare faced, with her smile tugging at his heart.

She'd been more approachable in the hospital. When she'd moved her injured arm and then winced, he'd had to shove his hand in his pocket to keep from smoothing that lock of long blonde hair from her face. He'd wanted to tell her she'd feel better soon, but he couldn't be sure that would be true.

What was it about her that drew him in? Lots of pretty women smiled at him with come-closer glances. He'd smile back, then wait to see if their personalities lived up to those welcoming smiles. Unfortunately, few did.

Today at the hospital, Jessica hadn't even been trying to impress him. But on TV, her welcoming smiles and warm southern accent dwarfed those of her guest. However, after seeing the *before and after* views of the guest, he had to admit the make-up and different hairstyle improved the woman guest's looks, and she'd seemed more confident.

While Jessica talked to viewers, he studied her. She didn't seem as sincere as when he met her in the hospital. He'd felt surprisingly comfortable with her, except her voice hadn't been as smooth as it was on TV. Had her injury made her more vulnerable, more down to earth?

When "Look Your Best" was over, "Law and Order" came on. He clicked it off. Too much like what he saw every day.

The next day he interviewed Harry at his office. When asked, Harry admitted to having a Glock and a shotgun. Maybe Harry still had a thing for Jessica, but he seemed to be telling the truth about not attending the game, so he wasn't a likely suspect.

Michael drove to the hospital. He'd ask if she'd remembered anything else about the shooting.

At the doorway to her room, he brushed off his tan blazer and smoothed his hair back. She had a bit more color in her cheeks today. That was good. "Hello, how are you feeling?"

She smiled, showing pretty white teeth. "Much better, thank you. I bet you had a long day yesterday."

He sighed. "You're right about that, but your day at the game was a lot worse. I can't imagine how you must have felt."

Her mouth dropped open. "Like a thunderbolt hit me. I could hardly believe someone had shot me at a football game."

"Can you come up with anything more about the incident?"

"Incident?" She glared at him. "Is that what you call it? My arm could have been blown off. I'd damn sure call it more than an incident."

He took out a small notepad. "Sorry, but that's what we'll call it on the report. Can you think of anyone who'd want to kill you? Bradley Stanton mentioned the security guard at the paper's office. Bradley thinks he's in love with you."

"Bradley? Oh, he can't be. I've turned him down for dates several times."

"Since you refused him, might he be mad enough to shoot at you?

She shook her head. "He's a sweet guy. He'd never hurt me."

She focused on Michael's face. "Were there any pictures on security cameras?"

"No. The only evidence we have is a shell from his gun. It's the right size for a bullet from a Glock."

"Why do you say 'his?' It could have been a woman."

"Can you think of any females who might have a grudge against you?"

She shook her head. "My boss doesn't think much of me, but she wouldn't shoot me."

"Women seem to prefer poison. Guess they don't

like seeing all that blood."

"So, you think it was a man?"

"I'd bet on it. By the way, I saw your show last night. I don't know how you do it all. I mean write for the paper and do a short TV program as well. Have you gotten any threatening fan mail?"

"Not me. My sister has, but I haven't."

"Why your sister? Has one of your fans threatened to harm your family?"

Her laugh, unexpected, but musical rolled over him. He gripped his pen tighter. "I don't understand. I'd be outraged if someone threatened my sister."

She smiled, brightening her face like sunshine on a cloudy day. "That was my twin sister, Jennifer Ballard, you saw on TV. She's the one you should ask about threatening fans."

"Oh. I thought the segment I saw had been taped earlier. You couldn't have done a show last night. Now that I think of it, she sounds different from you." Jennifer's honeyed voice was nothing like Jessica's more matter-of-fact tones.

Her lip quivered. Then he saw it, a tiny tan mole just to the right of her mouth, one he hadn't noticed on the face on TV. "I see the difference now. You have a cute little mole near your lips. I don't remember Jennifer having one on her face."

She touched it, then smoothed out a wrinkle in the blanket. "I'll be doing a five-minute TV presentation on a woman's perspective of a football game on her show, but that's only as a favor for Jen since she couldn't make the game with Lawton."

"But you're injured. Is that wise?" He didn't want anyone else to hurt her again. His younger sister hadn't been so lucky.

"My arm hurts, but I can still write and talk. Except at the paper I work for, I have to work my way up to writing more important news."

His gaze met hers. "Your voice. I'm sure I've heard it before. Have you ever come to the police station or called in about something?"

Jessica twisted her fingers together.

Michael waited for her answer.

"I occasionally called the station to ask if anything had happened I could write about. The last time the officer who answered said in a gruff voice they'd only talk to reporters assigned to write about police news. I, uh, I may have called a few times after that asking if there were anything to report."

He raised an eyebrow. "We don't get many calls routed to my department. I must have talked to you that time I covered the front desk while the sergeant who usually mans that desk stepped out for a hamburger. When I mentioned your name, he said he'd called the paper to ask if you were actually a reporter there."

"And what did the person at *Metroplex News* tell him?"

"That you only did obits and didn't write bigger articles."

She sat up in bed, bunching a fistful of sheet in her hand. "That's a lie. I can write perfectly good articles. They just don't give me many chances to do anything but short items."

"I see. By the way, if you feel threatened, don't hesitate to call the station." He turned and strode out. Didn't even say good-bye.

****

Jessica huffed. He'd seemed so nice at first. So much for friendly relations with Detective Gorgeous. From now on he was Detective SOB.

She looked up. He was back. He stood in the doorway. "I almost forgot. I brought you the paper. I read your article."

Gripping the paper, she scanned the Metro Section he'd handed her. Good. She'd made the front page. At least now, he could see she could write well. "So, what did you think—about my article I mean?"

"It's okay, but—" He studied the paper closely, then frowned. "Why did you let them put your name at the top of the article? The shooter might see this and hunt you down to try again?"

She shook her head. Bile rose in her throat. He hadn't even noticed how well written her article was. Damn man just criticized her for allowing a byline. "Of course not. I don't go around putting myself in danger, but you don't know how hard it is for a junior reporter to get a byline.

"I can understand your ambition, but I still think it was a bad idea."

"Well, I had to put my name in the article, so what difference does it make?"

"You have a point. My name is seldom in the news. I usually deal with the aftermath after the news has hit the papers. Last week I had to investigate a missing mother. Her toddler clung to her grandmother as if she didn't want to let go. Cute little kid, though. I kept wanting to brush her dark hair away from her eyes, but I knew she'd probably be frightened if a stranger did that."

She hadn't expected him to be so perceptive about children. Maybe he actually had a heart. "Do you have kids?"

"I'm not married, but I've got a nephew about that age. He's finally warming up to me."

"Did they ever find the missing mother?"

Michael rubbed the back of his neck. "Yes, but unfortunately, she was found dead."

"Oh, that's tragic. That poor kid."

"Yes, it's sad. By the way, that TV interview you're doing—tell me when it will be on and what channel to watch. I want to see it."

"We'll tape it later this week, that is if Jen's boss will still let me do it. They were going to run it during a pre-game show."

"I'll be sure to catch it. I can tell the difference between you and your sister now. All I have to do is look for that cute little mole."

Hearing that made her smile. After he stepped out of the room, she heard him talk to a nurse about speaking to someone in security.

****

Following lunch, Jessica felt sleepy again. She let her eyes drift shut and didn't wake until they brought her supper. She went back to sleep not long after eating.

In the middle of the night, a soft click and a tug on her arm woke her. Sluggish from sleep, she blinked. In the dim light from the hall, she could barely make out a male nurse's aide with dark bushy hair doing something to her IV. Why adjust it in the middle of the night? With quiet thuds of thick-soled shoes, he strode quickly out of the room.

Breathing deeply and exhaling, she felt her arm start to tingle. A strange sensation of heat traveled up her arm. It burned. Her eyes snapped open. Her heart throbbed, its beats becoming more erratic. She glanced at the IV line, then up at the bag. Something wasn't right. Was she having an adverse reaction to something he'd added to the IV? Feeling jumpy, she yanked the bandage and IV connection from her arm and grabbed the button for the nurse.

Chapter Four

Even though Jessica had ripped off the bandage taping the IV to her arm, the burning continued.

She fumbled for the button to call the nurse. She knocked over a glass half full of water. Never mind that, she had to get someone here fast.

She tried again, finally zeroing in on the button. She pressed it, then lay back down, exhausted. A voice on the speaker asked what she wanted. All she could mutter was, "Don't feel good. Something's wrong."

Then she passed out.

The next thing Jessica knew, people were speaking in low tones near her bed. Still feeling weak, she strained to hear what they said.

"Heart rhythm's irregular, Dr. Simpson," said a woman, probably a nurse.

"Definitely." said a man. "What about allergies to medications? Has anyone checked that?"

"None were reported," said the woman.

Jessica opened her eyes. She pointed to the IV stand. "Don't know… what aide put in it. Burned my arm…made me feel strange."

The IV tubing was now disconnected, but something remained on her wrist, probably a place to hook it up again. Jessica took a deep breath and relaxed. She felt better now.

The doctor pointed to the bag of fluid. "Send that to

the lab for analysis. Don't give her anything that hasn't been checked against any known allergies she has."

At the doorway, the doctor paused. "No more medication by IV. And don't allow anyone else but a nurse to give her anything."

"Yes, Doctor Simpson," the nurse said and left her room.

Late that afternoon, Jessica woke from a nap. The blinds were closed, and light from the hall silhouetted a figure in the doorway. He was holding something behind his back. Was someone here to kill her? She reached for the call button. Warm rivulets of sweat trickled down her back.

Her heart gave a start until he said, "Hi." It was Michael Steel.

Slowly, he brought his hand from behind his back.

Finally, she saw what he held. A yellow rose, wrapped in damp tissue. She let out the breath she'd been holding. Let go of the covers she'd been clutching. Took her fingers off the call button.

Damn, she'd jumped to conclusions. If she told him what she'd been thinking. He'd probably laugh his head off. Or worse yet, regale his buddies at the station with her half-baked assumption.

He was watching. She had to act normal—concentrate on the rose. He walked closer and held it out. She took the rose, felt its velvety softness against her nose, breathed in its sweet perfume. With a drop of moisture poised on one golden petal, it was an inspiration for a painter or a poet. Her thumping heart calmed. "You'll never guess what I thought when I first caught a glimpse of you standing in the doorway with your hand behind your back. I thought it was someone with a gun."

"Oh. I apologize for scaring you. Well, I do have a gun, but I don't hold it behind my back. His smile only touched the corners of his mouth, as if he weren't sure about her reaction to the flower. "Some high school girls were selling roses to raise money for their senior trip. I always like to help teens for a good purpose. I saw this and thought you might like it." He clamped his lips together as if embarrassed.

She welcomed Michael's mellow voice. He stepped closer, wearing a beige cable knit sweater and blue jeans.

"That's sweet of you. Thanks."

Then he added, "I guess I should have gotten a vase, but I hurried here after the hospital called, because I wanted to see if you were all right."

A warm feeling coursed through her. He'd come back bearing a flower, and she'd been thinking awful thoughts about him. She pointed to the vase of flowers Angela had brought. "Just put it in there."

He stuck the rose in the vase and faced her with a warm smile. "Hello, again, Miss Ballard," he said. "How are you feeling now?"

It was good to see him again. He made her feel safer, but she shouldn't be depending on him. "Thanks for asking, but you didn't have to come. You could have called the hospital to find out how I was."

He ran his fingers through his hair and shook his head. "I wanted to see you in person and be sure you were okay."

She hadn't acted very friendly. She still felt weird, but she should make an effort. "I had a little scare. Something a nurse's assistant put in the IV bag gave me a burning sensation in my arm so the doctor told the nurse to remove the IV and only give me medications I could swallow."

"But you're okay now?"

She nodded. "I think so."

"I don't like the sound of that." He rubbed his chin. "Did someone check to see what was in there?"

"They sent it to a lab to find out."

"So, did you get a report?"

She shook her head and pushed the button for the nurse.

When the nurse came, Jessica asked what the lab report said.

"We put a rush on that. We'll check to see who attached the bag and what was supposed to be in it." She turned on her heels and walked out.

Ten minutes later the nurse hurried back. "From what you told me about your symptoms there might have been potassium in that IV. You were not supposed to have that in your medication."

Jessica swallowed. "It sounds like they don't run a tight ship here. I hope they don't mess up my meds again."

Michael rubbed the back of his neck. "What if it wasn't a mistake? What if it was added deliberately?"

Jessica gasped. "What are you getting at?"

He stepped closer to her bed. "Did you see anyone messing with your IV? What if the same person who shot you is trying to kill you here?"

She sat up. "The aide in scrubs adjusting my IV bag —"

He faced the nurse. "I want know what medications she's supposed to get and who is supposed to give them."

"If the patient gives her permission," the nurse said, "you can ask what the doctor ordered."

Jessica nodded. "Of course, I'm giving permission. I want to know what's going on."

Michael stepped closer to the nurse. "Did she get anything the doctor didn't order?"

"I can't tell you that. You'll have to speak to the supervisor."

"Then call her or him immediately. There might be a problem with the medicine she's receiving."

The nurse pushed the call button. "Yes," said a voice.

"Please ask Ms. Johnson to come to room 256 as soon as it's convenient." She turned to Michael. "She should be here shortly."

He pulled a chair close to the bed. "I'm not leaving until we find out what happened."

A few minutes later the supervisor appeared, prim and proper in her well-pressed, teal scrubs and starched attitude. Michael said, "It looks as if there's been some irregularity here."

The supervisor raised her eyebrows. "What do you mean?"

"Was there supposed to be potassium in her IV bag?"

The woman stared at Michael. "I'd have to check her chart."

"I'd expect a little more care with the way medications are dispensed."

The supervisor glared at him. "We make it a point to be very careful. It's important that the patient get exactly what the doctor ordered and nothing else."

Jessica pointed to the IV stand. "A male aide in scrubs came and adjusted my bag. Are they supposed to do that?"

The supervisor stepped closer, her expression stern. "Did you notice a name on his badge?"

"I didn't see a badge."

"All our aides wear one. You might have missed it." She pushed her glasses higher on her nose, then strode to the door.

"I know what I saw, and he didn't have a badge."

The supervisor faced Jessica. "What did he look like? I'll ask the staff who might have come in here." Her no-nonsense attitude said her subordinates better have answers.

Jessica gave a detailed description. After all, she was a reporter and used to remembering what she saw.

Michael pulled the chair back into the corner facing the door. "I'm not leaving until they get to the bottom of this." He held up a book. "I see you already have a mystery novel. I brought you another, but I think I'll check out this one myself while you finish that. Wouldn't want to give you nightmares if this one's too scary." He settled back in the chair and flipped it open.

Jessica stared at him. "Don't be ridiculous. I like thrillers. Are you staying because you think I'm in danger?"

"I'm not taking any chances. I want to see that lab report. I don't trust their practices or the security around here."

"I can't expect you to stand watch over me until I'm discharged."

"I'm staying. The staff here are not trained to disarm someone intent on murder."

She stared at him. "Murder?" Chills shimmied down her back.

"My gut says things aren't right here. You rest. I'll

be here and keep an eye out for you."

His words should have made her feel better, but what might happen when he left? Better sleep now while he was here. She shut her eyes and tried to relax.

Sometime later she opened her eyes. Michael slouched in the chair near her hospital bed, his attention apparently glued to the pages of the thriller novel. Still sleepy, she watched this detective who seemed determined to play bodyguard. Large hands with strong masculine fingers gripped the book. His foot tapped softly. He periodically glanced at the door, alert and watchful to the nth degree.

Was she in danger or just the victim of an incompetent aide? Her pulse pranced, increasing its pace. An eerie feeling swirled in her stomach. "Michael, please, tell me what you're afraid of."

Slapping the book shut, he focused on her face. His brows moved together. Straightening his shoulders, he seemed to expand his chest as if to form a wall of opposition like a football linebacker. He leaned forward in the chair, his elbows jammed onto his thighs. "The mishap with your IV was intentional."

Someone was out to get her.

"Whoever did it could have stolen scrubs from the laundry cart or bought them and sneaked in to tamper with your IV." He pounded a fist on his knee. "No one else is going to harm you on my watch."

She swallowed, fully awake now—and apprehensive. "So, you've been assigned to watch over me?"

"Not exactly. We don't have the manpower to stand guard over everyone that's threatened. I'm staying until I'm sure the staff has found the person responsible and dealt with him or reported him to the authorities."

"I don't know what to say except I really appreciate that. I feel safer with you here."

"You're welcome. Besides, I'm off the clock now. Hey, I'm single, got no kids, and nobody's waiting at home for me except my dog." He grinned. "And he'll lick my hand and wag his tail no matter how long I'm gone." He held up the book. "Besides, this is a good story."

"What kind of dog do you have?"

"An Irish setter."

"What's his name?"

"Dog."

She frowned. "I mean what do you call him."

"Dog. That's it."

"Everyone gives their dogs names. Why don't you?"

"I don't want to get too attached. He might run off or get run over. I had a dog I loved when I was a kid. When he got sick, Mom took him to the vet and had him put to sleep." His voice was gruff, but his eyes looked sad.

"That's awful—unless he was so sick he would have died anyway."

"That wasn't it. She wouldn't spend the money for the expensive operation he needed."

"That's too bad. Did they get you another dog?"

He shook his head. "Mom insisted she didn't have time to housebreak a puppy and clean up after it. Said we couldn't afford to pay for shots."

"What about your dad?"

"He and my mom were divorced by then. I had to do what she said."

Jessica shifted in the bed, imagining a little boy with

a tear-streaked face. "I'm sorry. You must have felt really bad."

He shrugged. "I got over it." He leaned back. "I've seen a lot worse since I became a cop."

"Being a cop must be pretty risky. I mean, you could lose your life or your partner any day."

"I don't have one. Investigators work alone. In Arlington, even the patrol guys drive alone. They can call for back-up when they need it."

"Do you prefer being a loner?"

He shook his head. "I'm not a loner. I have friends. The guys at work are buds. Some of us go out for a beer about once a month."

It didn't sound like he had any real friends. Jennifer was her twin and best friend, and her sister, Angela, was a close second, but she had others too. Friends that made life worth living. Friends she'd do most anything for.

Michael frowned. "Speaking of friends. I want to talk with Bradley again. In the meantime, I'm staying." He turned his attention back to the book.

Was he right? Was she still in danger?"

****

Michael caught Jessica's gaze focused on him and raised his eyes to meet hers. She looked so vulnerable. Why couldn't she accept that he was just being careful, like any good investigator—well that was pushing it, but he enjoyed watching over her?

He shifted on the chair but couldn't get comfortable. He tried to concentrate on the story, but he kept seeing his sister's bruised face and battered body lying in an alley. Okay, so it wasn't part of his job to watch over Jessica, but he'd be damned if he'd let another woman become a victim like Sophia.

He blinked away the tell-tale wetness from his eyes, hoping Jessica hadn't noticed. Tears wouldn't bring his sister back. Even with several eye-witness descriptions, they'd never caught the guy who killed Sophia. But Michael would be damned if he'd give up on finding her killer. The following week he'd begun training as a cop. His sister's tragic death made him realize that law enforcement was a job that he needed almost as much as the citizens needed another good cop.

He'd read over copies of the cold case. Could the same man be stalking Jessica? Not likely, but that killer was still at large. Michael slammed the book shut. No use trying to concentrate. Jessica was awake now. Might as well ask more questions.

"Jessica, you said your sister might have evidence that someone's stalking her. Has she kept any threatening letters?"

She nodded. "Jen mentioned one weird note to me but didn't seem worried. Said it comes with the territory."

"Did she show it to you?"

Jessica nodded.

"What was it like?"

"It was on fancy paper in a pale shade of magenta."

"Magenta, what's that."

"Sort of pink shading into purple."

"Did she get any other notes like that?"

"She got one earlier with the same flowery background, but she figured a man wrote it because the writing had thick, bold strokes, like someone was pressing down hard."

"The note you saw—what did it say?"

"A bitch dressed up in fancy clothes is still a bitch.

All you care about is showing off to men."

He frowned. "Not exactly a fan note."

"Her show's not for men. It's for women who need the right make-up and clothes to make the most of their looks."

She rubbed her forehead. "Every time I move my head, it throbs even worse."

His gaze met hers. "Ask them to give you something."

Her gaze shot to the open door to the hall, then focused on him. "I don't want anything that makes me less alert."

She seemed haunted. She wasn't admitting it, but he could tell she was scared. He'd be sure to contact Jennifer about those notes. He leaned forward. "You'll feel better once you get home." He hoped she'd be safe there. "Do you know when you'll be released?"

"No." Her voice was quiet. She sounded down.

"Want me to find out?" He'd check at the nurse's station. See if anyone besides her family were asking about her.

"I'd appreciate it."

At the doorway he scanned the hallway. No one looked suspicious. A pink-clad nurse with every blonde hair in place and her ponytail fastened at the nape, stood behind the counter checking monitors. He waited until she acknowledged him with a smile.

"May I help you?"

He showed his badge, then asked about visitors to Jessica's room. He left a business card on which he'd scrawled his cell phone number. "Don't let anyone but her family or me visit her. I'm not sure the person who shot her won't try something."

The nurse looked taken aback but took the card. "I'll tell that to all the staff."

"Have they found the aide or whatever you call them, the guy who messed up her IV? If it wasn't an accident, I want her moved to another room with no name posted at the door as soon as possible."

The nurse shifted her gaze to the bank of monitors, then looked up. "I'll notify security and arrange that as soon as I check the patients' monitored reports on my computer. I'm the only one at the desk here."

"I'll wait."

Michael drummed his fingers on the white laminated counter until the nurse shot him a look of irritation. What was taking so damn long? Didn't monitors beep if something was wrong?

A loud beeping noise sounded. The nurse glanced at the monitor. "Uh, oh." She grabbed the phone and pushed buttons. Over the speaker she announced, Code blue, Room 252. Doctor Brown, paging Doctor Brown."

Was that Jessica's room? No, her room number was 256. Nurses and aides hurried past him, pushing a cart loaded with instruments down the hall.

The nurse looked up. "There's a medical emergency. Please stay out of the way."

Michael headed back toward Jessica's room, but all the staff and the equipment cart blocked his way. Easing against the wall, he slid past, trying to stay out of the way.

A man, dressed in scrubs like a nurse slipped into Jessica's room. Michael followed. Sunlight shone through the fluid in the IV bag connected to Jessica by a thin plastic tube. The man reached up to attach another bag to the IV stand.

Standing in the doorway, Michael cleared his throat, startling the man. "Don't touch that IV unless you can show me written orders."

The man with dark eyebrows, long unkempt hair, and a bushy mustache, still holding the bag he'd brought, bumped Michael against the wall and rushed past.

"Stop. Arlington police," Michael called after him. He'd be damned if he'd let anyone threaten her.

In an instant, Michael took off after the suspect, now heading for the exit door for the stairs. He wished he had another cop here to watch Jessica. The man might have an accomplice. The guy took the stairs, and Michael hurried after him. At the next flight down, the man yanked a door open, ran through and slammed the door after him. Michael pulled the door open and looked both ways.

The man was gone.

Michael hurried back to Jessica's room. Thank goodness, she looked all right. He grasped her hand. "Did that man do anything to the IV?"

"I don't think so. I was dozing. I saw someone take hold of the IV stand, but it's not connected to my arm right now."

"Was it the same guy who fiddled with your IV before."

"I didn't get a good look. He had dark, shaggy hair. "How old was he?"

"I couldn't tell. It was dim in the room."

Michael frowned. "I don't like this. Have you gotten any threatening notes?"

She shook her head.

"Do you still plan to do your story about women and football games live on TV or will Jennifer read your words?"

She nodded. "Jen says she'll make me up to look like her. I can wear one of the outfits she's worn recently. She's curious to see if anyone will notice the difference. Somehow, I get the feeling she's afraid I'll sound as good as she does."

"Why?"

"Some days she acts as if she doesn't feel secure in her job. From time to time, they poll customers to see which programs they watch. Once Jen said she was afraid they'd cut out her spot in favor of more sports coverage."

"Surely, letting you appear once won't jeopardize her job."

"I told her she had nothing to worry about. I can write a script, but I can't do what she does every week."

He frowned. "What if that guy who shot you thinks you and she are the same person?"

She swallowed. "That would put us both in danger."

He shot her a look. "You need to be careful when you leave the hospital."

She waved a hand in his direction. "Don't worry. I won't do anything foolish. I don't go out alone at night. I'll tell Jennifer to be careful too."

"I sure as hell don't want to see either of you in the morgue."

A shudder shook her. "Do you have to look at dead bodies a lot?"

"Unfortunately, it's part of the job. It's bad if it's someone I knew. It breaks my heart to see someone I last saw laughing and talking laid out ... ." He blinked as if to clear his eyes. "Like my sister Sophia."

She met his gaze. Her eyes seemed to mirror

concern. "I'm sorry. That must have been awful."

He swallowed the lump in his throat and nodded.

"How long ago was she killed?"

"Let's see. Probably five years, but it seems like yesterday."

He clenched his hands into fists, wishing he could beat the murderer to a pulp. "That night, my mother called me at two-thirty in the morning to say that Sophia never came home. 'It's not like her,' my mother said. Her voice sounded tight and anxious. 'She's a good girl,' Mom insisted. 'She doesn't sleep around. She wouldn't dare disgrace us that way or take a chance on getting pregnant.'"

"So, how did you find her?"

He rubbed the back of his neck. "I finally managed to get through my mother's ramblings—learn the name of the girlfriend my sister went out with. I called the friend. Apparently, Louise and Sophia had gone to a club on lower Greenville in Dallas, one that didn't ask for ID. Louise said my sister spent a long time talking to a guy and finally left with him."

"I took my sister's picture to that bar and talked to a female bartender. She claimed Sophia had left with a good-looking man, who seemed taken with her.

"The bartender claimed that guy was putting the moves on Sophia, but she acted reluctant at first. Finally, she finally left with him."

Michael knew in his gut, that man had been her killer. "Surely, she had better sense than to go with him. Trying not to imagine the worst, I scanned the parking lot, then walked around to the back of the building."

He swallowed and rubbed his eye. "That's when I found her body."

"Did the police catch the guy who did it?"

Michael shook his head. "Even though I got a description of the man, we never caught him."

"That's terrible. That must be a hard thing to live with. Are there many cases like that?"

"Too many. We do all we can to apprehend them, but unfortunately some get away scot free."

She snuggled under the covers. Her eyes drooped. He'd better stop talking and let her rest. Michael focused on the novel he was reading but made sure to look up every few minutes. At least in books the bad guy got what he deserved.

****

Jessica lay there, thinking about her sisters. She'd sure miss Jennifer and Angela if something happened to either of them.

When Jen came to see her again, she'd remind her to double-check windows and doors to be sure they were locked. She was glad her sister lived in an apartment building where one had to be buzzed in, and a security guard kept watch at night. Maybe she'd move to one like that, too.

Having a policeman here now made her feel safe, but she couldn't expect him to give up his free time out of a misguided sense of loyalty to his dead sister. She felt sleepy but forced her eyes open. "Don't feel you need to stay all day. You need to get some rest too."

He shook his head. "I'm not leaving until I'm sure you'll be safe here."

"I have nurses to keep an eye on me. I'll be fine."

"I'm staying."

A female aide walked in, her steps quiet but steady, and set supper on the movable tray table. Although not very hungry, Jessica needed to eat to keep her strength up. She couldn't wait to get out of here. She lifted the plate cover. Beef stew, redolent with the smell of gravy, carrots, and onions beckoned.

Then she glanced at Michael. "I hate to eat in front of you. Why don't you go get a bite to eat?"

He glanced out the door. "Maybe I'll just grab a sandwich and come back. I won't take long." He strode from the room, his steps smooth and sure, his body moving with an easy grace.

The room seemed much cooler now. A strong rose smell emanated from the bouquet on the table beside the bed. Strange she hadn't noticed the strong fragrance before. The yellow rose Michael had brought had a nice smell. She moved the yellow one to the front.

She took a bite of the stew. It tasted greasy and watery. She pushed the tray aside.

Hospital noises had settled down into a quiet hum. Footsteps paused by her door. A man she'd never seen before stood there. Wearing a grimy T-shirt, faded jeans, a baseball cap with streaked blond hair sticking out and sunglasses, he just stood, watching her. She clamped her lips together.

Why did he keep staring at her?

He stepped closer. Stood just inside the doorway. His eyes focused on her, his intense look setting her on edge. Uneasiness roiled inside. She reached for the call button.

Chapter Five

The eyes of the man at the door to Jessica's hospital room bored into hers. She heard him say, "beautiful bitch."

The intense look in his dark eyes scared her. She pressed the button.

No voice came from the speaker above her head. No nurse came to check on her. Michael had been gone quite a while. He should be back by now, but he wasn't.

The man at the door stepped farther into her room. A frisson of fear nearly paralyzed her, chilling her all over. She jabbed the button again.

The speaker crackled to life. "Dr. Smith, report to the emergency room, STAT. Dr. Smith, report to emergency STAT."

People scurried about in the hall. Someone pushed a cart with machinery on it past her room.

Still, the guy stood there, his eyes fastened on her face. Afraid to look away, she stared right back. She wouldn't let him intimidate her. She pushed the button again.

"Yes, Miss Ballard. Do you need assistance?"

"There's a strange man in my room."

"We'll send someone to check."

The man at the door looked both ways, as if to see if anyone were coming. He shot a venomous look her way, then strode into the hall.

She shivered. A moment later, a nurse appeared at the door wearing a stern expression. "Is there a problem, miss?" Her clipped tones reinforced her no-nonsense demeanor. Her name tag said "Dorothy." No doubt they used first names to encourage a friendlier atmosphere, but Dorothy's manner made Jessica want to speak to her as little as possible.

"There was a man here, staring at me."

"Did he come into the room?"

"He only took two steps inside, but he just stood there, looking as if he hated me."

"Have you seen him before?" the nurse asked. "Could he be man who tried to mess with your IV earlier?"

"I don't think so. His hair was different." Jessica swallowed. "What if he doesn't belong here. He might hurt me."

"Maybe he was just looking for someone else and stopped at your room. Could be you remind him of someone he dislikes. We'll look into it," said the nurse, the tight firm line of her lips bisecting her face. "Now, is there anything else you need?"

"No, but would you please report what I saw?"

"Yes. I'll notify security." The nurse pivoted on her heel and strode toward the hall. At the doorway she paused. "I'll shut the door."

"No, leave it open. If I scream, I want to be sure someone hears."

The nurse frowned. "We don't allow people to bother our patients." Her quick footsteps soon faded away, leaving Jessica feeling even more uneasy.

Feeling anxious, she studied everyone who passed her door. That guy could wait until no one was watching, then slip in to attack her. If that happened, would anyone check on her before it was too late?

She read over her script for the TV spot about the football game, changed a few words, and then dialed the news director at KWIK TV.

After several minutes, Lawton Knight's raspy voice finally came on the line. He coughed. "Caught a damn cold sitting in the bleachers at a soccer game last night watching my nephew play."

"Sorry to hear that. Feeling better now?"

"A little. Thanks for asking. Hope you're doing okay. I need to film what you've written. I want to air it during the pre-game show Thursday."

She'd hoped he'd wait until next week. "You're going to use it that soon? "

"I planned to use it this week, but you're in no shape to do it. E-mail me what you've written. I'll have someone else read it live on Thursday night."

"Why not film me here against a wall ahead of time? My sister brought me a long- sleeved blouse so the bandages won't show."

"I hate hospitals. I'm not coming there or making my camera crew lug in all their stuff."

She frowned. She couldn't miss this opportunity to show her editor how well she could write about something besides small entrepreneurs. "I can come there tomorrow afternoon." By then she should be released.

"I need that tonight. We're too jammed up to handle it later."

"If I come tonight, will you do it?"

"If you can get here before eight o'clock."

Jessica left Jen a voice mail and text messaged her.

But her twin didn't answer. Then she called Angela.

"It's been crazy at work," her sister said. "Bill and I are on our way out to eat. See if Jennie can do it. Bill's honking the horn. I've got to go."

Ten minutes passed. Jessica tried Jen again. Still nothing. Damn. What could she do without a car?

A taxi or an uber. She searched on her phone.

A uniformed woman stood in the doorway. Damn. Nurse Dorothy again.

You need to rest instead of calling someone," she said, turned on her heel and left.

Detective Steel walked back in with a cup of coffee. "They didn't have anything that looked good to me. I can eat later.

He had a smile on his face. Why did he make her feel so good? Must be because, unlike Nurse Prim, he seemed to care how she felt. Wait a minute. She could ask him to take her to the TV station. Seemed like a lot to ask a public servant, but she'd offer to buy him dinner later. That would be a good excuse to see him again.

She twisted her fingers. Maybe she should forget the whole thing and let Jen do it. Except she really wanted to do it and get her boss to watch it. If he didn't want to take her, all he had to do was say, "No."

"How are you feeling?" His smile buoyed her up. His husky voice sent delicious shivers scurrying along her spine. She had an insane wish to ruffle his wavy hair.

What was she thinking? Later she'd ask a nurse if the painkillers they used in the IV affected patients' emotions. "I'm better, thank you, but some guy was standing at the doorway staring at me."

"Damn. I shouldn't have left you alone. What did he look like?"

"Average height and build with spiky blond hair. He's gone now, but I need to go to the TV station tonight. Would you take me?"

"Why there? I thought you worked at the newspaper, and your sister worked at the TV station."

"That's right, but the reason I was at the game was to write a piece about the female point of view at a football game. Jennifer was going to do it, but at the last minute she couldn't make the game so Lawton took me instead."

"Wait a minute. Showing up at the TV station might not be safe for you."

"But if you take me, I won't be in danger."

His lips clamped together. "I don't like it. I'm just one cop. I don't have eyes in the back of my head."

"But you have a gun, and you know how to watch for a tail."

"Hey, that's detective training 101. But I might miss it if there were two cars following and they traded off."

"Two cars?" A knot formed in her stomach. "Could there be more than one person after me?"

He shrugged. "I can't be sure."

She sat up in bed. "Then you'll take me to the TV station?"

He frowned. "You're determined to go. Might as well."

She stuck her legs out from under the covers. "If you'll step outside, I'll get dressed."

"Wait a minute. Will they let you out before you're discharged by the doctor?"

"Probably not. I'll have to sneak out." She grinned.

He scratched his head. "What am I getting myself into?" he muttered as he walked out.

As soon as he shut the door, Jessica called Miss Sharp to tell her about the TV stint she was going to do and remind her to watch it. Of course, she had to leave a message, but she hoped her boss would see it. Jessica struggled into the blouse Jen had dropped off earlier and pulled on the coordinating pants she'd left.

Once dressed, she opened the door to the hall. Michael was pacing the terrazzo floor.

At the nurses' station. Miss Prim had her back to them. "How will we get past her on the way to the elevator?"

Michael grasped her arm. Surprised she met his glance. "This way," he said, pointing in the opposite direction. "We'll take the stairs."

Forcing herself to walk at a normal pace, she looked up at him, noticing how tall and sturdy he was. When they reached the steps, she grasped the railing. Surprised at how weak she felt, she headed down the stairs.

Thankfully, she reached the lobby without feeling faint. Pretending to be a visitor, she walked through the revolving doors, glad they were moving slowly.

Once outside, she stopped to catch her breath.

"Wait here, I'll get my car," Michael said. Feeling shaky now, she backed up against a pillar, glad to have something to lean on.

Later, in his car on the way to the station, she asked, "Tell me about your family? Do you have brothers or another sister?"

He nodded. "One brother and a younger sister."

"Is your family close?"

His face clouded over. "Not exactly. My younger sister, Gina, tells me not to say anything about her boyfriends. She claims she's too smart to get caught in a situation like Sophia."

"What about your parents? Are they overprotective now?"

"Not really. Mom's too busy with all her activities, her bridge club, and the annual charity ball for the families of policemen killed on duty. She's sponsored that as long as I can remember."

"Sounds like my mother. How about your father?"

Michael looked down. "He was a cop. Got killed on duty when I was fourteen."

"Oh, I'm sorry to hear that. So, then your mom took care of you kids?"

He looked down. "Sort of. Enough talk about me. I guess you're close to your twin. What about the rest of your family?"

She smiled. "Whenever any of us were in a play or in a choir program, my parents would always be there. My siblings too. Seeing them right up front, helped calm any jitters I had. Afterward, they clapped louder than anyone else, making me smile."

His eyes looked sad. "Must be nice to have family support you like that."

She looked at him, his face stony, his eyes straight ahead. "Didn't yours?"

"I remember one play I was in. Mom claimed she took a nap after her bridge club luncheon and didn't wake up in time. Maybe she had too many glasses of wine with lunch, and that made her sleepy."

His strong jaw jutted out, and his lips were clamped together. Maybe she'd better drop the subject. "Michael—" she began.

He waved one hand in her direction. "Hold off. I need to concentrate." His gaze darted to the rearview mirror and then the side ones.

A tan van pulled beside them on the right. On the side someone had painted 'Joe's Flowers" in sloppy pink letters. Michael slowed his car. As the truck passed, the driver's eyes bored into hers, making her feel uneasy. She turned away.

That didn't seem to bother Michael. "Guess it's not surprising to see a florist truck near a hospital."

At the office building, Jessica told the receptionist Lawton Knight was expecting her. Of course, she had to wait while the station receptionist called to ask about Michael coming with her. By the time they'd got a visitor's badge for Michael, it was seven-thirty. No one asked her to wear a badge. They probably thought she was Jennifer. She didn't tell them anything different.

They rode the elevator to the TV station. Jessica's stomach gurgled. Now she was hungry. She turned to Michael. "I hope you're not starving. When I get out of the hospital for good, I'll buy you dinner."

"No need for that. I've had to skip meals or eat late before."

"Because of working on a case?"

"That too."

Wondering, she met his gaze, but he didn't say anything else. Maybe he grew up poor and didn't want to talk about it.

Lawton Knight finally emerged from a hallway on the left.

He looked at Michael. "Who are you, and what are you doing here?"

Michael reached out to shake Lawton's hand. "I'm Detective Steel. I drove her here."

"Wait out front until we're finished. We usually

don't allow non-station personnel in the studio. He nodded to Jessica. "Come this way." He stood at the doorway, waiting."

"After what happened at the game, I'm sticking with her, Michael said."

Lawton frowned. "Surely, she's not in any danger here. We've got security guards in the building. They check out everyone who enters."

Michael shook his head. "Maybe they're supposed to, but no one even asked her name when we entered the building."

"The guy at the desk must have thought she was Jennifer. Please hurry, Jessica. We need to get this done." He took her script and handed it to an assistant, then led the way to her sister's cubicle. "I'll call you when we're ready." Michael followed.

The small cubicle was crammed with make-up and wigs. Jessica found it hard to believe Jen managed to get ready in that small space.

Jessica had watched her sister apply make-up, then pick a wig style to flatter a woman's face. After Jen recommended a particular hairstyle, the station had a beautician fix her hair before they filmed the 'Afterwards' segment of the show.

Stuck amongst the triple row of various shades of lipsticks was a piece of paper. Jessica reached for it, but Michael grasped her arm. "Don't. Could be a threatening note."

She grabbed a pair of tweezers. "I'll use this to pull it out."

He shook his head. "Let me." He took the tweezers from her, sending a slight shock of awareness up her arm, then used the tweezers to pull the note up. "Okay, read it, but don't touch."

Dark lipstick letters scrawled in bold strokes stood out against the muted pastel background of pink roses and green leaves. She read it. "NOT ALL J'S ARE BITCHES."

She clenched her hands into fists. "Maybe someone wants my sister to think I'm behind these notes."

"Is there a bag around that I could put this in?"

"There may be one in the break room. I'll check."

He shook his head. "I'm coming with you."

She shot him a questioning look. "Do you really think I'm in danger here?"

"No sense taking chances." Glad she'd been here once before, she led the way. He followed her.

Once there, she opened a few drawers in the kitchen area, then handed him a Baggie. He shook his head. Paper's better. After rummaging around, she found an unused paper sack in a drawer and handed it to him. Touching his firm skin sent another spark of awareness through her fingertips. That and knowing she'd be on camera in a few minutes made her pulse race.

He slipped the note inside the bag. "Does this match the others she's received?"

"She only showed me one, but it looks similar."

Lawton Knight strode into the break room. "You look a bit pale. Put on more make-up. Then we'll shoot your part."

"Hold on a minute." Michael held up the note. "Someone left a note for Jennifer among her lipsticks."

Lawton squinted at it. "Don't know how that got here." He reached for it. "I'll have security check it against the signatures at the front desk downstairs."

Michael shook his head and pulled his hand back.

"I'm taking this and all the pages showing everyone who signed in downstairs for the last few days. Headquarters can check the prints."

Lawton scowled. "You can't just tear pages from the sign in book."

Michael shook his head. "I'll just make copies. If the guy at the desk doesn't release it, I'll get a search warrant."

Lawton rubbed the back of his neck. "Some creep must be after Jennifer. I hope you catch him."

Jessica's skin crawled at the thought of someone threatening her sister. She headed back to her sister's cubicle. Michael followed.

Inside, she made quick use of the foundation and blush. She was about to reach for a lipstick when Michael touched her arm. Surprised at the slight tingle she felt, she met his gaze.

He shook his head. "Don't touch any of the lipsticks near where we found the note. I need to have them dusted for prints too."

Jessica selected a creamy pink lipstick far from where the note had been. Had that creep who left the note touched this one too? Hurriedly, she ran it over her lips, then set it down. Michael raked all the lipsticks off the table with a fingernail file into the paper bag."

A moment later she stepped out and called to Lawton. "I'm ready." She followed the director down the hall. Was her sister in danger from whoever left the note? Surely, he wasn't hiding somewhere in the hallway outside the studio area to accost her. Her arms and shoulders felt a chill.

Lawton turned to look back at Michael. "Do you think that note's connected with whoever shot Jessica?"

Michael stuck the bag under his arm. "Could be. Does the station keep fingerprints of your employees?"

Lawton frowned. "Of course not. We do background checks before hiring anyone. We don't fingerprint them."

When they reached the studio, Jessica slid into the chair under the hot lights. Feeling a bit weak, she hoped the make-up wouldn't melt. Probably Jen had chosen some that would hold up under these lights.

She glanced at the camera equipment in front of her. Lawton pointed to the plain brown background behind her. "After we shoot you, we'll blend in a shot of crowds at the football stadium."

A camera zoomed closer, making her nervous. She'd never make a regular on TV with all those cameras aimed at her. Then she saw the teleprompter screen with her words and took a deep breath. She could do this.

"Smile," Lawton commanded. "And don't forget to look right at whichever camera is showing a red light."

Jessica crossed her legs, letting a little show and dangling one high heel like she'd seen her sister do. She smiled, then began speaking. Sooner than she'd expected, it was over. She stepped out of the studio.

As the cameras wheeled away, Michael rushed up and touched her arm. Again, a tingle caressed her skin and spread up her arm.

His eyes twinkled. "You did great." Bending close, he whispered, "If I didn't know better, I'd swear you were Jennifer. You even show the same dimples when you smile, but she doesn't have that cute, little tan mole. Now I'll take you back to the hospital so you can rest."

Downstairs, in the building lobby they passed the front desk, now manned by a slight young man with dirty blond hair and a well-trimmed mustache. He waved and smiled. "Bye Jennifer."

Jessica smiled and said, "See you later." She started to walk by, but Michael grasped her arm and faced the man behind the desk. "You part of the regular security personnel?"

The man nodded. "Name's Carl." He turned to face her. "Nice lipstick you're wearing, Jennie. Goes well with that outfit."

They walked past the desk toward the doorway. At the entrance Michael paused. "Wait here." He showed his badge to Carl and asked for the book for visitors to sign in. "I need to look at the pages for the last few days."

Carl stared but handed over the book. Michael tucked the book under his arm.

"What the hell are you doing? You can't take those." He reached for the phone. "I'm calling my supervisor."

Michael pointed to his badge on his belt. "It's police business. I'm just going to copy the last three pages. Then I'll bring the book back." He turned to Jessica. "Come on. We can use the copy machine upstairs at the station."

A few minutes later, after returning the book, Michael walked quickly with her to the car. "I have the names of visitors, but whoever wrote the note could work in the building. Might even be the person who shot you. I didn't want anyone looking at you long enough to figure out you aren't Jennifer."

After getting in his blue pick-up, Jessica leaned back against the passenger seat. "Coming here and doing that short segment took more out of me than I expected. I can hardly wait to get back in that hospital bed."

As they pulled into the hospital parking lot, the

florist van they'd seen earlier pulled up and parked close by.

Was that a coincidence?

Chapter Six

When Jessica awoke the next morning, Michael, wearing a tan sports coat over a yellow turtleneck shirt and jeans, sat in the chair across from her bed.

He smiled. "Good morning, sunshine. "When are they letting you out."

"Around eleven."

"I'll drive you home."

"Thanks, but you don't have to. Jen or Angela can pick me up."

"I want to be sure you get home safely."

"Don't you have to work today?"

"I'm off today. I'll take you to lunch and then home."

"You don't have to do that. I can fix something at home."

"That's okay. I want to do it."

She dialed her mother. She hadn't before because her mother worried so and would probably go on and on.

Before she could do so, the phone rang. "Hello," she said.

Jessica dear, whatever do you mean by not calling me sooner. For heaven's sake, I just found Tuesday's paper which your father hid. I don't know why no one told me you'd been shot. If I'd known, I'd have come to see you right away. All your father said was that you'd gotten hurt at the game."

"Hey, Mom, I'm okay. You have nothing to worry about. I'm leaving the hospital this morning. "

"I'm coming by your place this afternoon. I need to see for myself that you're all right."

"Never mind, Mom. I'll stop by later." As she hung up, Michael rose. "I'll step out so you can get dressed. I'll be just out in the hall." He walked out, closing the door behind him.

She quickly pulled on the clothes Jen had brought her. Jessica was signing the release papers when he knocked on the door. "You can come in now."

Opening the door, he gave her one of his wonderful smiles. She loved the way that lit up his face. She felt better now that he was here. He could protect her. Of course, the way he grinned when he winked at her helped too. As she picked up the release instructions, he held out his hand. "Let's go."

Feeling drawn to him like a child to cookies fresh from the oven, she stepped closer, then welcomed his warm fingers clasping her hand as he walked beside her.

"Wait," called a nurse. "You're supposed to leave in a wheelchair. I'll get one."

Jessica hesitated. "We'd better follow their rules. They're probably afraid of getting sued."

Michael tugged on her arm. "You look okay to me, and I don't have all day. Come on, the elevator door is open." He rushed her into it and pushed the button.

As the door closed, Jessica glimpsed the nurse pushing the wheelchair. "Wait," she called.

Grinning, Michael grasped her hand as the elevator descended. "Guess we showed her."

Jessica pulled her hand loose. "I hope she doesn't get in trouble for not following the rules."

"You have a right to walk out if you want."

The door opened to the lobby. Michael took her hand again and led her to the revolving door. "My chariot awaits. Why don't you stand here while I bring it around?"

Later, after he helped her into his car, he got behind the wheel. As they drove away, Michael kept looking in the rearview mirror.

"What are you looking for? They won't send anyone after us just because I refused to ride a wheelchair."

"It's not that. I'm looking to see if that florist van is following us."

"You're paranoid."

"No, I'm not. The sign painted on it didn't look professional."

"So, maybe the sign painter aspires to do flowers like the impressionists."

"The letters look more like some artist's signature than proper letters should."

"So, you can look the company up on the Internet later."

He didn't answer but kept checking the rearview mirror. "What's your address?"

She gave it to him, and he headed that way. Suddenly, he careened around a corner, then made several turns.

"Why go this way?"

"I saw that florist truck again."

"It's probably delivering flowers around here."

He made a few more turns. "No use taking any chances." He pulled into a driveway, leading to the back parking lot of a church. From there he exited onto the access road to Airport Freeway. At MacArthur Blvd. he made a U-turn under the freeway and headed down the access road on the other side.

As he crossed under the bridge at Story Road, she asked, "Are you satisfied we're not being followed?"

Leaning back, he nodded, seeming to relax as he left Irving and drove through Arlington toward her apartment.

"Stop, you passed it."

He drove to the next red light which had a no U-turn sign. When the light turned green, he made a U-Turn.

"Michael, the sign said no U-turns."

"I saw it."

"You should have gone around the block."

"Too much trouble."

He was pulling to the curb by her apartment building when a patrol car's flashing lights and a short siren blast alerted them.

As the officer walked up behind them, Michael held out his license and his badge.

The cop frowned. "Steel, you're supposed to be setting a good example, not flouting the law."

"So, write me a ticket."

"I have half a notion to do just that, but I'll yield to professional courtesy. Just don't do it again." He headed back to his car.

Michael pulled into the driveway of the apartment building and drove around back.

"Let me see you safely to your door." He opened his door, then slammed it shut. "Damn. Don't get out."

Puzzled, she looked at him. "Why not?"

Instead of answering her, he clamped his mouth shut. Gunning the motor, he shot away from the curb. Seconds later they were on the freeway again. "I caught a glimpse of that damn florist truck pulling up beside your building." He looked back. "And it's behind us now."

"She caught her breath. "Maybe it's not a coincidence."

"Now maybe you'll believe me. I'm not taking you home until we lose him."

"What if you're right, and he's already found out where I live?" Sharp shivers shimmied down her spine.

He stepped on the gas again, making the car shoot forward. Then he zig-zagged through several lanes, finally exiting at O'Connor.

Hunched over the wheel, his glance going to the rearview every few seconds, he made so many turns she lost track of direction. Finally, he pulled into a driveway of a small house. "Open the glove compartment and hand me the garage door opener."

A minute later they were inside the garage, and he pushed the button to close the door. He kept his eyes on the street outside until the door blocked the view.

She waited while he unlocked the back door. "Is this your place?"

"Mine and the bank's. Didn't want to wait 'till I got married to buy one."

Uh oh, here she was assuming he was unattached. He might already have a fiancée."

As soon as he opened the door, she heard the pounding of feet. Tail wagging, a large red Irish setter bounded up and licked Michael's hand.

Michael patted his head, then said, "Now, Dog, be nice to the lady."

She reached out her hand and let the animal sniff it before petting him. "Come on, you've got to call him something besides that."

"Why?"

"He needs a name."

"He followed me home from the park one day, but someone might claim him so I haven't given him a name. Besides, he comes when I call him Dog."

The animal left her side and went back to Michael.

He'd said earlier he didn't want to get attached to his dog. Did that go for women too? Had some woman broken his heart or was he still grieving for his sister and afraid to care for anyone else?

Michael slipped off his sports coat. "Let me fix you some lunch before I take you home."

She looked around the roomy kitchen in surprise. "You cook?"

"Is that so strange? Lots of men cook. They just don't let on. He grinned. Just like the next guy, I like having a woman fix me fancy dishes. He opened a cupboard and studied its contents. On the top shelf a few cookbooks stood, held upright by a pair of bookends with carved birds decorating them. He grabbed some garlic salt and shut the cupboard.

He took out some roast beef slices, poured some liquid into a pan, and heated the slices. He added melted butter, garlic salt, and some herbs, then spread the meat on French bread and put them under the broiler.

She offered to help, but he waved her off. After tasting the sandwich infused with some exotic flavor, she said, "This is delicious. Did your mother teach you to cook like this?"

He shook his head. "She wasn't much of a cook. My sisters, my brother, and I had to fend for ourselves."

"You mean she wouldn't feed you?"

"She'd rather drink than eat. By supper time she was usually so sloshed, she couldn't manage to cook anything without burning it."

"That's awful."

"While I was going to school, I stopped bringing friends home." He ran his fingers through his hair. "I was afraid I'd find her in her nightgown passed out on the couch."

Jessica asked, "How come you were the one to cook? What about your sisters?"

"They were pretty young." He dished out some ice cream. She was about to take a bite when he said, "Wait. I've got something to add."

He spooned out something thick and brown into a little pitcher and set it in the microwave. A minute later, the aroma of chocolate filled the air as he handed her the pitcher.

"Oooh, hot fudge sauce, yum."

She enjoyed it to the last bite. "Do you feed all your lady friends this well?" Then she wondered if she really wanted to hear about the others.

He cleared the dishes and leaned over a chair, resting his arms on it. "Believe it or not, you're the first I've cooked for."

"But you're so good at it. Bet women would fall all over you, wanting to marry someone who can cook like this."

"I don't think I'm the marrying kind."

"Lots of men say that until they fall in love."

"I try not to get attached to anyone. People can be cruel, even sometimes to a friend."

Was he talking about a personal experience or had he just watched others act that way? From the creases in his forehead, she sensed he was remembering something in the past. Best not to ask. "Don't you have to get back to work? Surely, it's safe to drop me off at home now. I can't wait to take a shower."

He grabbed his sports coat. "Okay. Let's go."

On the way to her place, she noticed he paid the same attention to the rearview mirror. When he parked behind her apartment building, she also looked around for suspicious vehicles, but didn't see any.

He insisted on walking her to her door and entering first. Snowball came running but stopped and stared at Michael.

"He's okay," she told the cat and reached down to pet him. Snowball rubbed up against her leg, then looked at Michael who held out his hand for him to sniff. The cat let Michael stroke his head. Jessica glanced at her computer in the spare bedroom she used as an office. She'd forgotten to turn it off before she left. She'd check her e-mail before turning it off.

She sat down, and Snowball jumped up into her lap. Jessica stroked the white cat, then glanced at the new messages.

Seeing an e-mail address she didn't recognize, she was about to delete it when she read the subject line. It said, "Jennifer, you bitch." She gasped.

From the scent of his aftershave wafting her way, she sensed Michael was standing behind her. He leaned over her shoulder. "Nice e-mail buddies you and your sister have."

She clicked on 'properties' to see the full e-mail address, but didn't recognize it. Click. She deleted the message.

"You shouldn't have done that. A computer guru

could gain some information about the sender."

"There's only one thing I want to know. How did that person get my e-mail address?"

Chapter Seven

At work on Friday, Jessica asked her boss what she thought about Jessica's TV performance.

"Oh, yes, I watched it," Miss Sharp said. "What you did was good, but it was too short. Television news reporters don't do justice to news stories the way newspapers do."

Jessica gritted her teeth. So much for impressing her boss. Damn. She'd left her hospital bed for nothing. She'd have to do something else to really impress her boss.

After work the next day, she walked into her apartment and dropped her purse on the kitchen counter. In her bedroom, she booted up her computer and glanced off to one side.

She stared at the gray cardboard rectangle on the floor. Large bold letters shouted the word "BITCH." Light from the window shimmered on the knife blade sticking the cardboard sheet to the floor. Her underwear drawer was sticking out, and it looked like someone had been pawing through her bras and panties. A shiver ran down her spine.

What if whoever did this was still in her apartment? Her pulse raced. Where was her cat? Had some perverted soul hurt him?

"Snowball," she called. A slight breeze from the window ruffling papers on a table made the only sounds.

Then it struck her. The intruder might have killed her cat. Worse yet, he could still be here, waiting for her.

The hairs rose on the back of her neck, and knots twisted inside. She glanced toward the kitchen at the knife holder hanging on the wall. Two knives were gone, the one stabbing the cardboard on the floor and the butcher knife. Was someone in her apartment waiting to attack her? Should she call 9-1-1? If no one were here, she'd sure feel foolish having cops come rushing in.

She held her breath. Looked around. Listened. Heard nothing but branches outside creaking in the wind.

She grabbed her purse, ready to run, and checked her apartment for intruders. Thank goodness, no one was lurking in the bathroom or the bedroom closet.

Only one possible hiding place was left.

She went to the coat closet door and listened. Surely, she could hear someone breathing in there.

But if someone were inside, he could hear her footsteps. She walked away, being sure to make a lot of noise, then opened the front door, ready to make a run for it if necessary.

She shut the door with a bang and listened. Nothing happened.

The apartment was quiet. She tiptoed to the closet door and pressed her ear to it. She heard a faint meow.

She wrenched the door open. At least no one was hiding there. But Snowball lay there, curled up in a ball and making pitiful moaning sounds. She clenched her hands into fists. If some man had hurt her cat, she wanted to wring his neck.

Get a grip, she reminded herself. A guy who'd hurt animals wouldn't hesitate to kill her too. Was he even now waiting on her balcony?

She bent down, stroked the cat's fur, and checked it for injuries. She couldn't see any, but Snowball lay there, licking his belly and whimpering piteously. Had the burglar kicked him?

She picked him up and murmured to him. There might still be someone lurking to attack her. She grabbed her purse and ran out her front door into the hall.

After locking the door, she ran down to the lobby, then called Michael. "Someone broke into my apartment, hurt my cat, and stuck a knife into a piece of cardboard on my bedroom floor. He could still be there, hiding out of sight on my balcony."

Michael's deep voice seemed calm and matter of fact. "Where are you now?"

"I'm in the lobby of my apartment building. I locked my door, but if someone's hanging around the area, he could follow me. Except the manager's on duty so I don't think someone would try anything here."

"Did you see or hear anything that would make you think someone's still there?"

"No, but I'd feel stupid if I called 9-1-1, and they didn't find anyone."

"That's what the police are for. Now, think. Someone might have hurt your cat to get you out of the place so he could follow you?"

"I'll take my chances. I've got to get Snowball to a vet right away." She stroked his long white fur and was rewarded by a look that at least seemed to register that she was holding him.

"Call the police, tell them what you suspect, and wait in the lobby until they get there. Tell them you think the intruder may still be there. They'll come quickly."

Where did he get off telling her what to do? She was

going to the vet's office immediately, regardless of what he said. "I'm not going to wait. Snowball might be seriously injured. I need to take him to the vet right now."

"Okay, take the damn cat to the vet, but call the police and leave the key with the manager. Where's the vet's office? I'll get there as soon as I can. Stay there until I come."

She didn't like the way he ordered her around, but she had to admit his directions made sense. She gave him the vet's address. "I'll tell the manager to let the police in."

She called 9-1-1 and gave them the address and instructions about entering her place. Then she explained everything to the manager and told him to let the cops in. She also left him her cell phone number.

On the way to the vet's office, she checked her rearview mirror. There was a black pick-up behind her. It had no license plate in the front. As she made a right turn, she was glad to see the truck stop for a red light. She circled the block. Surely, that pick-up would be gone by the time she returned to the intersection.

Back at the same light, she pulled up behind a line of cars, now moving slowly toward a green light. She looked for that black truck. A red SUV blocked her view. When it moved, she switched to the right lane. Still no black pick-up. Had it gone on ahead or backtracked and stayed behind her? She checked her rearview mirror. Nothing.

Snowball moaned. Stepping on the gas, she headed for the vet's office and hoped she'd lost the black pick-up.

At Dr. Davies' office, she told the receptionist she

feared Snowball had been injured by a burglar. She was informed her cat would be the next patient he saw.

By the time the vet asked her to bring her cat in, Snowball was snuggled in her lap and snoozing.

After she repeated what she suspected to Dr. Davies, he examined the cat. "His belly is bruised, and I don't like the way his eyes look. He's not very alert. I can't tell if something might have been given to him or if he ate something he shouldn't. We'd better see if we can make him expel it. Hold him still while I take some blood."

Jessica could smell the tang of alcohol as the vet rubbed some on the cat's skin. After the vet got a needle ready, Snowball barely flinched when the needle went in. Then the doctor squeezed something into the cat's mouth with something looking like an eye-drop applicator.

After waiting a few minutes, Jessica cringed when her cat spit out sour smelling liquid and a small hairball. She wrinkled her nose at the smell.

The vet assisted the animal to stand, supporting it with his hands. "See that small dish on the counter. Put some water in it and set it where he can reach it."

She did that and watched anxiously. Snowball just stood there, his legs shaking. Finally, he bent his head and took a sip.

"Come on, now," the doctor urged. "Drink some more." He pushed the cat's head down toward the dish. Snowball drank some more.

Satisfied the cat had drunk enough, he said, "Sit out in the waiting room with him. I want to check on him in half an hour."

Seated in the waiting room with Snowball snoozing in her lap, she kept listening to his breathing. She didn't relax until it settled into a steady rhythm.

The door burst open, and Michael breezed in. "You okay?"

She nodded. "The intruder must have kicked snowball. He's bruised, and he vomited a little while ago."

Michael eyed the animal. "He looks okay to me, but what do I know. Did you call the police?"

She nodded. They should be checking my place now. She stroked Snowball's fur, encouraged by his steady purring.

Michael put a hand on her shoulder. It felt reassuring to know that he cared enough to come by, even though there was nothing he could do except offer moral support.

"I brought some bread for him. That's what my vet suggested when my dog ate something that disagreed with him. It should dilute any harmful substance that might be in his stomach."

"Thanks. I'll ask the vet if that would be okay to give him."

Just then, the vet stepped out, looked the cat over, and lifted a paw. The cat pulled it back and meowed.

Dr. Davies patted its head. "I believe he'll be all right now."

"Should I feed him bread to dilute anything he might have eaten?" Jessica asked.

Dr. Davies nodded. "Good idea. If he acts strangely in the next few hours, call me at my emergency number and tell me how he's acting." The vet took a card from the receptionist and gave it to Jessica.

She rose. "Thanks for coming, Michael. I feel better now that you're here."

As they walked of the vet's office into the parking lot, Michael said, "Wait until I call the officer who's checking on your place."

He pulled out his cell phone and dialed, then listened. "She found what? A picture of who?" He listened a moment longer, then hung up and turned to Jessica. "A knife was stuck into a picture lying on the floor."

"Whose picture?" she asked. It had to be hers or someone she knew.

"A female cop claimed it was a picture of Jennifer. She recognized it from watching TV."

Chapter Eight

Michael walked with Jessica toward her car. She looked shaken. Her hands didn't seem very steady as she unlocked her car.

Her face turned pale. "That damn stalker knows where I live, and he thinks I'm Jennifer."

She petted the cat. "Snowball, it's you and me against the bad guy. We have to protect my sister." Then her face clouded over. She scowled. "I'm through being a victim. I'm not taking this lying down. There must be something I can do to stop him."

Michael patted her shoulder. "Let the police handle this. That's their job, and they're trained for it."

She stiffened. One hand clenched into a fist. "I wish I could stand face to face with that coward, look him in the eye, and tell him what a bastard he is to break into my place and hurt my cat."

She stroked Snowball again. "Anyone who would treat a pet this way is sick." She shuddered. "Isn't that how serial killers start - by tormenting or killing animals?" Now she was gripping the cat so tightly that it squirmed. She relaxed her grip.

Michael wanted to hold her in his arms and kiss her until her worries evaporated, but that wouldn't make the trouble go away. He needed to stay with her to keep her safe. However, he wasn't sure he could persuade her to let him. Jessica's stance and the fire blazing in her eyes reminded him how independent she was.

He put his arm around her shoulder. "I'll call the chief and see what I can talk him into as far as protection for your sister. But I'm staying with you tonight."

She straightened her back and shook her head. "It might take a while for the police to catch him. I can't expect you to stay with me until that pervert is stopped." She looked at her watch. "I'll lock the windows tighter than a drum. There must be a twenty-four-hour locksmith. If I can get a locksmith to come out tonight and put in a bolt for my door, you won't need to stay."

"You'll probably have to wait until tomorrow for that."

He brushed a tear from her soft cheek, one no doubt she hadn't realized had escaped. "You need me. I'm staying. At least until tomorrow."

"But that doesn't mean—"

"Of course not." He frowned. What must she be thinking? "I'm a gentleman. I won't be there to seduce you." Not that he wouldn't enjoy that, but that wouldn't be ethical or honorable. "I just want to protect you."

He took her hand, the one that wasn't clasped about her cat. "Trust me. No one's going to harm you as long as I'm with you."

"But don't you have to work tomorrow?"

He frowned. "I'm on administrative leave?"

"Is that the euphemism they use for suspension now?"

He swallowed. "Yeah, but they won't tell me how long it will be."

"But they won't fire…I mean they won't let you go, will they?"

He ran his fingers through his hair. "I don't know. I

hope not, but I can't be sure."

He'd been in the police force ever since he got out of college. Who was he if he wasn't a cop? "I don't know what else I'd do."

"You're a caring person and one who wants to protect others. Someone who goes beyond the call of duty. I admire that. Some employer who wants a good man helping him should be glad to have you work for him."

Her words warmed him like summer's heat on a sunlit beach. It felt good, made him want more. But caring for another woman and getting involved right after Melody dumped him was not a good idea. No words hurt more than "I don't ever want to see you again." He tried to swallow the lump in his throat.

True, he'd been relieved not to have her clinging to him at every chance. She'd pouted when he hadn't taken her out to dinner on Valentine's Day. Hell, he'd bought her a dozen roses. Should have been enough, but she'd lambasted him about having to work that night. She must think he could take off whenever he wanted to.

Jessica seemed independent now, but if they started going together, she'd want more, just like Melody. No. He wouldn't fall for Jessica, but he'd make damn sure she was safe. He couldn't bear having to identify another beautiful woman's body like his sister's, a woman he knew, one who had a promising future, who might have married an adoring husband and have cute kids.

Strange how appealing having a family sounded, but he wouldn't think about that. He was a loner, not clever at conversation. Besides, what woman would want to hear about dead bodies and interviews with dangerous criminals? He'd make a lousy husband. Besides, after that last drug bust where another cop was killed, he could never be sure he'd come back from some of the riskier situations he might have to deal with.

Jessica pulled her hand from his. Now she was staring at him. How long had he been lost in thought?

Her lips were pursed, and that tiny tan mole beside her lip quivered. She was scared all right but bound and determined to stand on her own two feet. He met her gaze. "I'm staying whether you like it or not."

He tried not to think about holding her close, smelling her perfume and brushing the hair from her face. He caught himself wondering what her lips would taste like. He couldn't stop thinking about that, couldn't help wondering how she'd react to his kiss.

Would she kiss him back with all that breathless energy or shove him away? He let his gaze rove over her. He hoped she'd like his company and feel safer, but taking advantage of her because she was scared wouldn't be fair or gentlemanlike.

As tall as she was, she probably could push him back. "By the way, have you ever taken karate lessons?"

She shook her head and smoothed her hand over the cat's back. "No, but I'm going to as soon as I finish the police citizen's academy class."

"I didn't know you were going to do that. Maybe then you'll understand some of the things I'm up against. By the way, do you have a carrier for Snowball in your car?"

She nodded. "Why?"

"Let me take you out to dinner. It will be a while before the burglary section cops are done with your place, and you must be hungry."

"I hadn't thought about food until you mentioned it.

Guess I could use some supper."

"Put Snowball in his carrier and follow me. I know a good place where both the food and the atmosphere are good."

"That sounds great."

"Follow me," he said and unlocked his truck.

****

After Jessica parked beside the restaurant he took her, she glanced at the passenger seat. Snowball purred softly as he slept. She got out of the car and locked it. Michael joined her and they headed toward the place. Half timbers decorated the outside of the building.

Inside, old-fashioned coach lamps with the lights slightly dimmed hung on the walls, and a candle burned in a hurricane lamp set on a table in the entryway.

A hostess led them past a pewter tea service gracing an antique table. English ivy hung from baskets and filled pots on the tables. She led them to a table. Nearby a brass, bed-warming pan hung on the paneled wall. Its long handle gleamed in the light from a crackling fire.

When a waitress arrived, Michael insisted on ordering steak and lobster for both of them.

Later, savoring the taste of lemon juice and melted butter on a forkful of lobster, she leaned back. Basking in his admiring smiles, she wondered what he'd expect if he stayed with her more than tonight? Things had changed since she'd been a teen. Sooner or later in a relationship—after three dates you couldn't even call it a relationship—but men expected a woman to put out. And when you didn't, well, that was often the end of the so-called relationship.

She'd be better off without such guys, but she couldn't help wondering if some guys she'd dated just found her too boring. Of course, none of them would tell her why they didn't call again, but it would be nice if a guy found something else about her to like besides sex.

She looked up at Michael, wondering what he was thinking behind that guarded expression of his. She leaned forward. "When will they know if the fingerprints and handwriting on that note in my apartment match those found on the note in my sister's desk at the TV station?"

"Arlington doesn't have the facilities to determine that immediately. They'll have to send it to AFIS."

"AFIS?"

"FBI's fingerprint data analysis program."

"So does that identify the burglar?"

"Sometimes. It depends on whether the person's fingerprints are already on file."

She bit into warm, dark bread, appreciating its rich taste. Flirting was something she'd never been good at. Now if she had a terrific figure and a beautiful face, she might have tried it. Her sister Jennifer seemed to do all right for herself, and she was a great flirt. Somehow, all she had to do was smile a certain way, and guys fell all over her. That had been true even in high school when Jennifer made the cheer-leading squad. Mom had been so proud of her.

Okay, Mom had also beamed all over when Jessica's debate team went to the state finals, and her dad had clapped louder than anyone and even whistled at the end. Too bad, they'd lost to another team, but her father's words had thrilled her. He'd said, "You did great. I'm so proud of you. Maybe you can run for president someday."

She looked up at Michael. He was smiling at her as

if he found her fascinating. Too bad he didn't really know her. Well, if she let him stay and talk with her, he'd find out. She didn't even have a decent nightgown to tempt him. She'd be wearing her pale-blue satin PJs. However, he was right. She'd feel much safer with him there.

Michael looked at his watch. "Time we called to see if our burglary team is done with your place."

He pulled out his phone. "How soon can you be finished?" He listened a moment. "You're almost done? Great. We'll be there soon." He closed his phone. "Want some dessert? They have great carrot cake."

She licked her lips. "I shouldn't, but I'll share a piece with you." He grinned and waved to the waiter. "I like a woman who knows how to enjoy her food."

Moments later they took turns forking pieces of the moist rich cake. Jessica remembered watching her older sister and her husband Bill at their wedding feeding each other cake. Would she ever find someone she wanted to do that with?

Too soon the table was cleared, and she'd swallowed the last of her coffee. Michael paid the bill and walked out with her, his hand extending gentle pressure on her back. His gaze met hers, his eyes darker now. She could tell he was interested in her. He'd said he'd act like a gentleman, but could she take him at his word?

He opened the door for her. "I'll follow you to your place. I'm staying the night to be sure you're safe." He headed for his truck, and she got into her car and started the engine.

Why hadn't he mentioned stopping at his house to pick up some pajamas? Maybe he slept in the nude. Or maybe he was afraid she'd change her mind if they didn't go right to her place. Now she felt awkward. She was glad her place was neat—or at least it was when she'd left it, except for that knife stuck in a picture of her sister.

After parking in her space at her apartment complex, she lifted out the carrier with Snowball inside. Michael offered to carry it for her, but she shook her head. "He'll feel more comfortable with someone familiar toting it."

Inside her apartment building, the manager's office door was closed, and the lobby was dimly lit. That was just as well. She didn't want the manager to look at Michael and think they were sleeping together. Sleeping, now that was a euphemism. Those who did probably didn't get much rest.

Holding her cat carrier, she fumbled with the key. Nerves, just nerves she told herself. And for what? She knew how to say no. And Michael, as sexy as his looks were, really did seem like someone who'd take it like a man, without any snarky comments. Wracking her brain to come up with some clever phrase, she kicked herself for not being able to do it. Hell, she worked with words every day. Why couldn't she think of some?

"Let me," Michael said and took the key from her hands, his touch sending an electric charge through her. He opened the door and nodded to the two officers inside.

"We're through now," one officer said, "but we have a few questions for you."

After she answered their questions and thanked them for coming, they waved and left.

She looked around and sighed. Her light walnut tables were coated with black dust. So was her glass table in the entryway. She picked up a small vase encrusted with tiny pieces of colorful tile and blew the dust away.

Michael took hold of her hand again. The warm tingle returned. "Don't breathe in that fingerprint dust. It's not good for you. "Do you have a feather duster?"

She set the vase down and looked at him. "Uh, no, but I have something similar that should do." She opened the coat closet, remembering when she'd found Snowball huddled there. It seemed like ages ago, but it had only been a few hours.

She pulled out the duster with its long handle and green feathery fronds that somehow resembled cotton candy. Visions of riding the Ferris Wheel and eating cotton candy with Michael holding his arm around her shoulders filled her mind before she shook them away. Time to clean up, not fantasize.

"Here, give me that," he said and held out his hand. "You need to settle your cat down. He probably needs a little attention from you after his ordeal."

She opened her eyes wider. "You're offering to dust? I thought guys were allergic to housecleaning."

"Not my favorite task, but I've done it once or twice. Mom wasn't much of a housekeeper, so when we had company coming, I'd lend a hand. Didn't want anyone to see how bad things usually looked."

He seemed embarrassed to admit that, and she didn't press him to say more. She held out the duster. He smiled as he took it, apparently pleased to help.

That was amazing. The few men she'd invited to her place for a home-cooked meal had never even offered to help with the dishes. Michael made her wish for a protector, a friendly companion, and Prince Charming all rolled up into one. That person probably didn't exist, but Michael came close. Some lucky woman should win him for a husband.

She opened Snowball's carrier. He stepped out and wandered around like he was checking that familiar things were still there. As he looked up, Michael bent to pet him, then scratched behind his ears. The cat began to purr, then rubbed itself against Michael's legs. Michael grinned. "I think he likes me."

"I appreciate your help. I hope you had a chance to feed your pet before you took off to help me."

"Don't worry. I did."

"Won't he find it strange when you don't come home tonight?"

"I doubt it. When I worked on patrol, my hours varied. Guess he got used to it, but he's always glad to see me when I get home. And he won't let any burglars inside."

"Snowball's just a cat. All he can do is growl and not very loudly at that." She looked at her watch. Nine o'clock. Too early for bed. "Would you like a glass of wine?"

He nodded, and she got out two wine glasses and a bottle of Asti Spumonte she had been saving for a special occasion. Seeing his darkened eyes and interested grin, she decided he was definitely special. Even if he were not Prince Charming, she could live with his type of charm for as long as it lasted.

But sex with him? She wasn't ready for that. After all, she didn't know him very well, but she liked what she'd seen so far.

****

Michael leaned back in an easy chair, glad to relax at last. She handed him a glass and poured the sparkling amber liquid. "I hope it's not too sweet for you."

Glancing at her luscious curves barely visible in her knit top beneath her suit jacket, he said, "I like sweet," but he was really wondering if he might soon be able to talk her into letting him touch those sweet curves. He'd take her on a few dates first. He bet her skin would be smooth as satin and warm to the touch if he kissed it. Already, his pants felt too tight.

Jessica didn't sit down. She straightened the couch cushions, which hadn't seemed to need it. With one hand, she pulled back one of the drapery panels just enough to see out, then closed it again. She checked her watch, then took off her suit jacket. The nice view of her soft breasts pushing against that form-fitting sweater spurred a hard on.

She laid the jacket on the couch beside her. Apparently unsatisfied with the way it lay, she refolded it and laid it down.

She seemed nervous. He'd promised to be a gentleman, and that meant no sex. Somehow, he'd gotten the feeling she didn't do casual sex. Maybe after she got to know him a little better. If he were lucky, he'd catch a glimpse of her in a close-fitting nightgown after she got ready for bed. Oh well, one step at a time, but he wasn't ready to get deeply involved.

She got out sheets and a blanket. Watching her cute behind as she bent to spread them, he almost forgot to offer to help. Reluctant to give up that delightful view, he rose and helped her spread them.

When they finished, she said, "This couch is kind of short. Maybe you could sleep in my bed, and I'd—"

"Yes, that would be wonderful." He grinned to let her know he was kidding but hoped one night soon she'd offer an invitation.

She looked flustered. "I mean I'd sleep in here."

He took her hand, raised it to his lips and smiled. "I know what you meant. I won't hear of it." He suppressed a sigh. The couch was short, and sleeping in her bed with his arms wrapped around her would be heavenly, but damn it, he'd promised he'd be a gentleman.

She gave him a surprised look and pulled her hand away. "You can take the first shower. I put out an extra towel and washcloth. There should be plenty of hot water."

Hot water? He needed a cold blast to cool him down. He hurried inside the tiny bathroom, hoping she wouldn't notice how aroused he was. Her shower was big enough for two. He wished she'd want to share it with him. Even though the water was barely tepid, his hard on got harder. Damn.

When he finished, he put his clothes back on. He'd wait until she went to bed before stripping to his silk boxers. Retreating to the living room to wait, he flicked on the TV as she headed for the bathroom. Even late-night TV host's jokes couldn't stop him from thinking about Jessica, naked in the shower, rubbing soap over her breasts and thighs—like he wanted to.

Then he heard her singing. A little off key, but charming. It sounded like "Someday my prince will come." He recognized the tune from watching the DVD of Cinderella with his niece. If she were looking for a prince, he needn't consider applying.

He'd mentioned the rough informers he interviewed. He could just imagine what she'd think of them. Damn, he hoped one of them wasn't Jennifer's stalker. Or Jessica's stalker.

Then Jessica emerged wearing pale-blue silk

pajamas that clung in all the right places. His pants became very tight. He wanted to rush over and grasp her in his arms. She looked at him with a tremulous expression, her lips parted. Her hands rested on her hips, making the fabric cling even more. How he'd like to pull her close and run his hands over her sweet butt. Then she'd know how she affected him. Man, would she know.

He stepped closer and took her hand. He'd have to play this carefully. "Good night," he whispered and pulled her close enough to kiss. Tentatively, he brushed his mouth over hers.

Her lips were soft and wonder of wonders she didn't pull away. In fact, she seemed to nestle against him like a soft kitten. And she was soft, except for the firm tips of her breasts pushing against his chest. It was all he could do to not run his hands over her lush curves.

But she was kissing him back with fervor. He'd take as much of that as she was willing to give. And much as he wanted to, he wouldn't mention anything more. Not tonight anyway.

Damn, with any other woman, he'd be edging her toward the bedroom before she even knew what he was about. But not with Jessica.

She broke off the kiss, disappointing him until he looked at her. The bemused look on her face encouraged him. He moved closer, and she let him kiss her again. He kept it light and soft, but it was over too soon. "Good night," she whispered and hurried to her bedroom as if afraid she'd revealed too much of her feelings.

He smiled. She'd let him know she liked it, and that was almost enough, well, it would have to do for now. Damn it, he might not touch more of her unless they became more deeply involved. But then again, did he want to? He'd seen his sister's boyfriend get so besotted with Gina that he agreed to everything she wanted in a big fancy wedding. Even with the small part Michael had played as a groomsman, the wedding had been a big hassle. He'd never let a woman talk him into such an affair.

And then the big house, which Gina had insisted they had to have, took a lot out of his brother-in-law's paycheck. Michael remembered all the times after the wedding they'd eaten at his mother's house, not just on Sunday but on weeknights. He'd even bought a fancy stroller for his nephew when Gina had said they couldn't afford to get one. Well, he wasn't going to get into that trap.

****

In her bedroom, Jessica snuggled beneath the sheets. Man, could that guy kiss. Her lips still tingled. The way his lips moved over her mouth was like no other man she'd kissed. She found herself wanting more. More of those wonderful kisses. More satisfying hugs with someone she felt connected to, at least for the moment. She'd never felt like that before, not even with Harry, who'd left her for a topless dancer, the creep. Michael seemed to understand her. But sex with him, she wasn't ready for that.

However, she had to admit he'd been wonderful at keeping her safe and helping with Snowball. Her cat seemed to like him. That was a good sign.

Maybe tomorrow she'd try to get him to pick a name for his dog. Idly, she wondered if the animal would get used to being called by a new name. She recalled the dog her family had gotten from the pet shelter. They'd given him a new name, and he'd seemed to adjust to it pretty well.

She also remembered how sad she'd felt when her parents said they were too busy to take it for walks every day and took it back to the shelter. Knowing if the shelter got too crowded before someone else adopted it and they put it to sleep, she'd cried herself to sleep worrying that's what happened. She didn't ask her mother to call and find out. She didn't want to know.

Just then Snowball jumped up on the bed and looked at her, his golden eyes glinting in the moonlight from the window. The cat knew he wasn't allowed to lie on her bed, but tonight Jessica didn't have the heart to chase him away. He settled at the foot of the bed.

Pulling the cover over her more tightly, she almost wished she'd answered Michael's unspoken invitation to share her bed. No, she wouldn't go there. That would be asking for trouble.

She closed her eyes and dreamed he was tickling her naked body and looking at her with appreciation.

And then she woke. What was that noise? Curtains were blowing wildly at the window, and rain was spattering the roof. Lightning flashed and thunder rumbled ominously. Someone was pounding on her bedroom door.

"Jessica, wake up," Michael said. "I just heard a tornado warning on the TV."

Now she could hear sirens wailing. She rose up in bed.

He switched on the light. "Get up. I'll shut the window. We need to go where it's safe."

As he slammed the window down, she reached for her robe. It wasn't on the bedside table. "I need to get my robe."

"No time for that." His voice filled with urgency, he grabbed her hand. "Come on. We'll be safer in the bathroom."

She let him pull her into the bathroom. It seemed very close in there. He still held her hand as he shut the door behind them and flicked on the light.

"The tub. We need to climb in the tub. Get in." He held her hand as she stepped over. Then he climbed in. She sat at one end. He folded his large frame into the other. A trace of moisture, from their showers seeped through her pajama bottoms.

"Turn around," Michael said in a commanding voice, one he probably used on criminals he apprehended.

She looked at him knowing he could see her unspoken question in her face. He'd promised he wouldn't try anything, and she wanted to hold him to that, didn't she? "Why?"

"I want you close to me where I can protect you." He frowned. "I'm not trying to make a move on you." The suggestion of a smile said he wouldn't mind doing that."

Seeing the look in his darkened eyes, she could tell he meant it. He seemed tense, as if he were restraining himself from doing exactly what he said he wouldn't.

"I want you next to me so I can lean over you and protect you in case the ceiling falls in."

"Oh." She scooted closer and realized she'd have to stand to turn around. She did and was about to squat with her back to him when the lights went out.

She screamed and fell backwards, right into his arms.

Chapter Nine

"It's all right. I've got you," Michael said as the wind howled outside. He settled her against his firm chest. His legs surrounding hers felt firm and sturdy as the tub they sat in. Her pulse raced, but she couldn't help noticing his desire.

His arms cradled her waist. Leaning against his bare chest, she felt safe and secure. Bright lightning flashed through the small bathroom window. Immediately after, a horrendous thunderclap sounded. Jessica hunched her neck into her shoulders and leaned against Michael. He clasped her tightly against him.

Her breath came in short gasps. Her heart beat frantically against her ribs. "Do you—do you think it hit the building?"

His arms tightened about her. "I don't know." His warm, bristly cheek against her forehead made her feel safe.

However, she couldn't stop worrying. "What if the roof catches on fire?"

"We'll smell smoke. Don't borrow trouble. Just hold tight and see what happens." Then his fingers grasped her shoulders. He turned her head to face him. For a breathless second, she waited.

His kiss felt hungry and reassuring at the same time. She gave herself up to it, opening her mouth to his tongue, letting it dance with hers.

She turned and sat on her knees facing him. She grasped his shoulders and kissed him back, reveling in the wonderful taste and feel of his mouth. She enjoyed all the sensations he caused…the tingling of her lips…the comfort of his embrace…and exhilaration from knowing he felt the same attraction she did.

His hands slid beneath her pajama top and grasped her waist. He held her firmly, banishing her fears. He was here, protecting her. Nothing she couldn't endure as long as he held her close. Then he relaxed his grip and let his fingers slide upwards, warming her midriff, moving ever closer to her breasts.

And she let him, her heartbeat growing stronger, and her breaths coming faster in anticipation.

His warm hands like fine sandpaper, slid over the undersides of her breasts and set her nipples tingling. She leaned into his caress, savoring every second. His hands against her flesh felt so good, so right, and so damn enticing. The way he squeezed and teased her made her feel treasured, adored…and hot.

Closer, she craved being closer. Craved feeling skin against skin. Craved feeling his chest against hers. To hell with caution. To hell with holding back until she knew him better. She wanted him now. Balancing on her knees, she faced him, barely noticing the hardness of the tub as he caressed her shoulders.

Her fingers fumbled with her buttons until the sides of her pajama top fell apart. Lightning flashed through the small window, followed by a thunderclap. His hands on her shoulders, he looked into her eyes, then at her bare breasts and smiled.

She leaned against him, her breasts pressed against his muscled chest. She grasped his arms. Felt his warm skin and corded muscles. Felt his heartbeat against her breasts, steady, throbbing, like hers.

Now his hands caressed her bare breasts as if he couldn't get enough. "Jessie, you feel so soft, so wonderful. I don't want to stop touching you." His whispers, the way he said her name, so musical, flowed over her.

She heard his quick intake of breath, then felt his mouth on her breast, suckling greedily, rocking her senses. She couldn't help herself. She leaned toward him, pushed her breast even further into his mouth. His fingers, squeezing and kneading her other breast, set her senses on fire.

He switched his mouth to her other breast. A delicious ache developed between her legs, and he hadn't even touched her there. His little nibbles and kisses worshiped her from her neck to her navel. No other man had made her feel so sexy, so desired. Being adored like this —there could be nothing better.

Still suckling her breast, he slid his hand between her legs. His touch so electrified her she felt an orgasm building. She was ready to pull down her pajama bottoms and give herself to him when he pulled back.

"What–?"

"Someone's pounding on the door."

She listened. Someone was knocking. "Huh? What could anyone want now that they were under a tornado warning?"

"Hey in there. Are you hurt? Do I need to kick in the door?"

"Damn, it's Lewis, my next-door neighbor."

She couldn't let him see her like this. The sounds of the rain, the wind, and thunder lessened. "Lewis," she yelled. "I'm okay. Don't break the door down."

"What? I can't understand you."

"Wait. I'm coming." She struggled to get out of the tub.

The lights came on again. Michael helped her step out. "Better button your top."

She glanced down at her rosy skin showing between the gaping sides of her pajama top. Buttoning the top, she hurried to the door, but didn't open it. "I'm okay. I was hiding in the bathroom after the tornado warning on TV."

"Then you're all right?"

"Yes."

"Thank God. Open the door. I brought some glasses and a bottle of wine." During a momentary lull in the storm, glasses clinked. "It will help settle your nerves," he said.

She didn't want him to see her looking like she'd been ravished. "Uh, thanks, that's awfully sweet of you, but I'll be okay. My nerves are fine now."

"You sure? Let me step in for a moment to see for myself that you're all right."

"I'm sure." She glanced down. She'd gotten her buttons all mismatched. "I'm ready for bed, and my hair is a mess."

"I've seen you with your hair mussed before. That won't bother me."

"It was really nice of you to come check on me, but I'm fine. I'll see you in the morning." Being with Michael, she was more than fine. She couldn't wait to get back to him.

"Okay." Lewis sounded disappointed. She felt bad for refusing his thoughtful offer, but there was no way she was going to let him see her like this or see Michael here.

She listened carefully until she heard his footsteps and the closing of his door. That was close.

Still tingling from Michael's sexy caresses, she stepped back toward the bathroom. But the door was shut. "Michael, let me in."

"Not now."

Had she imagined it or was his voice a bit husky. When he came out, she'd tell him she was ready to share her bed. Her heart beat faster in anticipation. She bet he'd thrust hard and fast. And she'd meet him halfway each time. Her breasts, still moist and tingly, ached for his touch again. She couldn't wait to be close to him. He'd be a fabulous lover she was sure. Her heart beat faster.

She heard the shower running. Why? Hadn't he already taken a shower? Or was he taking a cold one to tamp down his desire because he didn't want to become involved? They called a woman who backed off like that a tease. Was there such a thing as a male tease?

Disappointed, she waited. Could she get him in the mood again?

Finally, he opened the door, wearing only red silk boxers. Shiny droplets glistened on his broad hairy chest. His wet hair stuck out every which way, like a little boy after swimming. She felt an absurd urge to smooth it down. She wanted to touch him, run her hands over that marvelous chest and nibble at his male nipples. She stepped closer and reached toward him.

His hand stuck out like a quarterback fending off a tackler. "Don't."

"But–but?"

"I'm sleeping on the couch, where I can stay alert. It's better that way. Now step aside." His determined tones put her off. How could he be so cold after what they'd shared? Could men turn it on and off just like that? Or maybe it was just sex to them, another tumble in the hay. Did it even matter with whom?

She felt cheap. And used. She frowned. And stood there, not knowing what to say.

"You're in my way." He spoke as if she were an animal, too dumb to move out of his way. She hadn't felt this insignificant since she was a little girl.

She clamped her lips together to keep from saying something she'd regret–like calling him a bastard. After stepping aside, he stalked through the bathroom doorway without meeting her gaze. He strode toward the couch in those damn red, silk boxers. Climbed onto it as if nothing had happened between them. Snuggling under the sheet, he met her gaze. "The storm's over. Good night," he said, his voice cold and harsh as the north wind.

Then he turned his face away, the bastard.

"Well, if that's what you want, good night yourself. Sleep tight." *And I hope the bed bugs bite.*

She walked into her bedroom and slammed the door. Waves of heat spread from her chest to her neck and then her face. What had she done? Thrown herself at him like a common tramp. He'd taken what she'd given and thrown it back in her face like a basin full of cold water.

Angry tears dripped down her cheeks, then became a torrent. She couldn't decide which was worse, his taking advantage of her, or the humiliation of being cast aside like a shirt he was tired of. Well, if that stalker broke in and started a fight, she hoped Michael would get a taste of what he deserved.

Cold, she grabbed her robe and wrapped it around her. If only she'd worn it going into the bathroom, this fiasco might never have happened. Would she ever feel warm again? Would she be able to enjoy a man's embrace without wondering if his attentions were real?

Would she always feel that a man's caresses were just a ruse to get her into bed? As long as *he* was in the mood——like Michael wasn't anymore. She rubbed tears from her cheeks with the sleeve of her robe. Might as well try to get some sleep, so she could go to work in the morning like nothing had happened. As if she could relax enough to sleep now.

Thunder rumbled in the distance. Was another storm coming? Right now, she'd rather face that alone than face Michael.

****

In the living room, lying on that ridiculously short couch, Michael squirmed and shifted. The cold shower didn't help. No matter what he did, he couldn't get comfortable. Thunder rumbled again, reminding him how aroused he'd been earlier. What had he been thinking? He was staying here to protect her, not ravish her.

She deserved better than that. Besides, she was part of a case he was investigating. He almost hadn't heard that meddlesome neighbor knocking at the door. Except the guy hadn't really intended to meddle. He'd been looking out for Jessica.

Unlike her caring neighbor, Michael had been so overwhelmed with her softness, her willing lips, the feel of her breasts crushed against his chest, those tight little nubs pressing against him, he'd gone way past protecting her from the storm.

Touching between her legs, even through her pajama bottoms, he'd known she was wet and ready.

And he'd been ready to take her in that hard cold tub. She should have been loved on silken sheets on a bed of rose petals. With romantic music murmuring in the background.

And by a man who could offer her a future and treat her right. He'd only wanted to keep her safe–safe like he hadn't kept his sister. He should have been there that night. Hell, he knew his sister just wanted to go out and have some fun. Why hadn't he offered to take her to that damn club? He could have watched over her and taken her home when she was ready.

Jessie deserved the protection he hadn't given Sophia. If he was acting on his attraction instead of watching out for her, how could he protect her? Tonight had been a big mistake. Yeah, he had to face it. He'd taken advantage of her fear. That was unforgivable.

Hell, he was only human, and she'd felt so good in his arms. Maybe by morning she'd realize what they'd done was a mistake. Maybe they could pretend that never happened–and go on with their lives. Except, he'd never forget how she'd snuggled against him, how she'd returned his kiss so eagerly, how soft her breasts were, and how much he wanted to plunge into her. He needed to stay as aloof from her as possible.

He'd stay as many nights as she'd let him. Hopefully, he'd get enough leads to nail the bastard stalking her. But how could he go back to work next week, knowing she was in danger, knowing he wanted to be with her every chance he got? Wishing he could spend his nights in her bed and wake up next to her when the sun rose.

He wanted to take her swimming and dance the Texas Two Step to country western music. Wanted to walk through the woods at the Fort Worth Nature Center and shuffle through fallen leaves. Wanted to show her an Indigo Bunting or a wild turkey strutting through the woods. There was a lot he wanted but couldn't have.

Granted, he might be able to do some of that by himself in his spare time. But it wouldn't be the same. And he wasn't supposed to get involved with a victim in a case he was investigating. If he did before they caught that perp, his boss would have his head.

His critical boss always acted as if Michael couldn't do anything right. Okay, so he bent a few rules, but he usually managed to get to the bottom of whatever case he was investigating. Results were what counted, weren't they?

Well, next time the exams were held, he'd be there. If he got promoted enough times, someday he might be in line for police chief. By then his cantankerous boss surely should be ready to retire.

And even though Michael loved the thrill of chasing bad guys and catching them, that was no life for a woman like Jessie to share. No, he couldn't be the right man for her. Not now. And by the time he could get promoted to a safer position, some other man, a better man than he, would probably win her. He clenched his fingers into a fist. That man, whoever he was, had better treat her right or he'd have to answer to Michael.

Knots twisted in his gut at the thought of some other man making love to her—Jessica leaning into his arms, Jessica pushing her lovely breast into another man's mouth—Jessica making those endearing cooing sounds as he teased her into readiness.

He shut his eyes tightly, tried to banish the images from his mind. He had to get some sleep or he wouldn't be able to resist the urge to walk into her bedroom, sweep her off her feet, and take her. He needed to keep acting like he didn't want her.

She deserved better. After all, he was only an investigator. Why should she feel more than a passing attraction to him?

****

Jessica awoke to bright sunlight. Outside, a few leafy twigs lay on the ground, evidence of last night's storm. But restless feelings kept reminding her of that wondrous time in Michael's arms. Feelings she should ignore because nothing could come of it. Best to send him off with breakfast and a cup of hot coffee.

Damn, she was out of cereal and eggs. And all that was left of the last loaf of bread she'd bought was a heel.

She had nothing to offer him except her body, but no way was she going to put herself out there like some sex object. For all she knew, he'd found her breasts too small and her hips too curvy. No wonder he'd stopped when he did.

She dressed quickly. In a blouse that didn't fit too close. No use emphasizing her less than perfect figure. In the kitchen she busied herself making coffee. Wait a minute. She had everything she needed to make biscuits. That was the least she could do. After setting out some food for Snowball, she got busy.

Soon the air was filled with the aroma of baking biscuits and perking coffee. Then she heard his footsteps. She waited expectantly. However, he only gave her a half-hearted wave, strode to the bathroom, and shut the door. Minutes later, she heard the sound of running water.

After setting her mixing bowl in the sink, she put

plates and utensils on the table. Outside a mourning dove cooed. She looked up and held her breath. It was standing on the window sill pecking at some breadcrumbs she'd spread there. She hadn't expected to actually see a bird eating there, but she'd hoped.

She felt a hand on her shoulder. "Shhh," Michael said. "Look at that bird. They usually don't get that close. That's something you don't see often."

Her pulse stepped up its pace. At least he still wanted to talk to her. She swallowed. "I know." Damn. Why couldn't she come up with something clever to say?

He sniffed. "What's that I smell? Coffee and biscuits too?" He grinned. "Now that's a treat."

She stepped aside. "I need to check on them. Watch the bird and tell me when he flies away." She turned toward the oven.

He grabbed her wrist and pulled her back against his firm chest. "They don't smell like they're burning yet. Stay and watch. That bird won't sit there long."

His grasp was strong. She snuggled against him. He could hold his own against a strong pull in the opposite direction. She caught herself remembering how tender and sexy his fingers had been last night. That was then. Things were different now. His manner and his voice seemed matter of fact. His eyes were on the bird.

"I remember you said you had to learn how to cook," Jessica said. "I'll have you know those aren't canned biscuits. I made them from scratch. Sorry, but I don't have any eggs or bacon to go with them."

He smiled, setting hope stirring inside. "Actually, homemade ones will be a treat. Since I live alone, I depend on canned ones."

After the mourning dove flew away, she pulled the

biscuits out, put them on a plate, and set it on the table. He sipped the coffee and took a bite of one. "Everything's good."

If he wasn't going to mention last night, she certainly wouldn't. A few minutes later he pushed back his plate with nothing but crumbs and drained his coffee cup. "I have to go. We're shorthanded, so the chief relented. Today, I'll work on a homicide case the mayor wants solved yesterday."

His intent look caught her attention. If she didn't know better, she'd think he wanted to walk her into her bedroom and finish what they'd started last night. If that were true, what would she do?

His expression turned serious. "If you don't go to a hotel tonight, I'll be here and …." He bent to tie his shoe. Then his words came out in a rush. "And I'll sleep on your couch to keep you safe. That's what's important."

Then he left. Without a kiss or even a smile. His last words resonated in her head. At least he cared enough to make an effort to keep her safe. But was that all?

Her phone rang. She grabbed it.

"Hi, sis," Angela said. "How about meeting me for lunch?"

"Sure. Where do you want to go?"

"I can't get away for long. Can you meet me in the company cafeteria? If you have time, you can say, 'Hello,' to Dad."

After Jessica hung up, she got in her car and headed for the newspaper office. Once there, she collected her assignments and started working on them. She tried not to think about the way Michael's hands felt on her shoulders, on her breasts and more. Tried not to remember how he'd kissed her—as if he couldn't get enough. And most of all, she tried not to recall how impersonal he'd been at breakfast. How he'd said he'd protect her–as if she were a wounded bird incapable of defending herself–as he would protect anyone who needed it.

Stop it, she told herself. You need to concentrate on work like she was sure he was doing. She looked at her assignment. Well, that was a switch. She'd been asked to interview the CEO of an up-and-coming company. Amazing. Her boss had given her someone important to interview.

After making the call, she wrote down a list of questions to ask, then headed out to interview the head of a restaurant chain with headquarters in Dallas.

The man was surprisingly easy to talk to. His name was Michael too. She tried not to think of that other Michael as she asked if he'd started the company or been hired to run it. Turned out he'd been picked out because he'd been assistant manager of the Mansion on Turtle Creek, a prestigious Dallas gathering spot for the well to do.

He smiled, putting her at ease. "They want me to combine a friendly relaxed atmosphere with elegance. It's the decor and the little touches that matter. I've hired the best decorator in the area. Now it's up to me to develop the little touches that will make our metroplex establishment famous and hopefully spawn many more to come."

Jessica filled pages and pages of notes and kept her tape recorder running to pick up any interesting quotes. "I'll call you and read it over the phone to be sure I don't have any inaccuracies. Thank you for seeing me."

Back at the office she wrote up the article and was

pleased with how it turned out. After reading it over the phone to the CEO and putting it on her boss's desk, she headed for her car and lunch with Angela.

****

He sat in a coffee shop in the warehouse district of Dallas, yawning. Tonight, he'd tell his supervisor he hoped someone else could take the night shift tomorrow. Covering it for a few days was one thing, but he couldn't wait until the regular guy was back.

He rubbed his eyes. He supposed he should go home and sleep, but he couldn't lose this opportunity to watch her. Maybe she'd go home for lunch. What if he surprised her in her apartment? He'd been working out. Would she be impressed with his muscular abs?

He smoothed back his dark blond hair. Picturing her face with all that long hair next to his in the mirror—now that would be a sight to see. He'd only caught a glimpse of her cleavage the last time he'd watched her show. She was a classy dresser, but he'd like to see her cleavage all the way down. And touch her. He bet she'd be velvety soft and smell like heaven.

Good thing he'd ducked in the restroom to shave and pat cologne on his face before his shift was up in case she walked by in the morning on her way to the TV station. He looked good. Better than that asshole director he'd seen her with at a nightclub.

He'd waited too long to connect with her again. Thank goodness, he'd had the smarts to place a tracker on her car a week ago. Strange he hadn't seen her car at the building parking lot lately. Maybe she'd put it in the shop to get fixed. He'd cruise by and see if it were back. Then if she went out for lunch, he'd follow, maybe even sit at a table near her.

He checked his watch. Eleven-forty-five. Time to cruise by the station. He hurried to his car. It didn't take long to get downtown. There was the TV station office building, but he didn't see her car. Damn, was he too late? Had she already left for lunch? He drove around the block and activated the tracker apparatus in his Jeep.

She was close. Then he saw her car and followed it. After ten minutes she finally parked in front of a pharmaceutical company. What was she doing there? Then he caught the name of the company. Ballard. So, she must be related. Probably didn't have to work, just did that TV show for a lark.

He watched her walk inside. What great legs she had. He'd wait. When she came out, he'd speak to her, get her to notice him at last.

****

Walking down the tiled floor of their father's company, Jessica strode past laboratories with stainless steel counters and equipment. The company lunchroom seemed more comfortable with green granite tables and salmon-colored walls. The aroma of beef soup mingled with that of apple pie. They had apple and cherry turnovers too. Jessica carried her tray to the table where her sister sat with nothing but a small salad in front of her.

Angela was munching on a celery stick. "Hi. I've been waiting. Since you work on assignments, couldn't you leave in time to get here by twelve. I mean, I have lots of work to do and can't just sit here doing nothing."

That was Angela all right. She couldn't stand to be idle. Maybe that's why she stayed so thin. "Hi, yourself. I'd have gotten here sooner, but I had a deadline to meet for Sunday's edition, and I stopped to see Jen for a moment."

"Sunday's three days away. Doesn't your boss trust you to do it right?"

"It's not that. We have to have most of the articles for Sunday in by Thursday at noon. That's so the editor can be sure everything fits. If it doesn't, they omit articles or cut them."

Angela leaned forward, her blue eyes meeting Jessica's. "You mean after you slave over an article, your editor has the nerve to cut it? What if she takes out your best paragraph?"

Jessica leaned back in her chair. "I learned long ago to write articles so they'd read okay if the last paragraph were dropped. If my boss wants more cut, she usually asks me to shorten it myself."

As they ate, Angela talked about a new formula the company was working on that would really aid weight loss. "I tried it myself," she said, "and look at me."

Jessica looked. "You do look thinner. In your face and everywhere else." Angela had always been able to lose weight when she put her mind to it. Jessica envied that.

Angela took another bite of her salad, then nibbled on the celery. "Mom says I look too thin. What do you think?"

"Stand up."

Angela did. Unlike Jessica, her hips were only a gentle curve, and her waist was slim enough to wear a size six. Okay, so her sister had a smaller bone frame. Neither Jessica nor her twin would ever be a size six without almost starving for a few weeks. "You look great."

Jessica leaned forward. "Mom keeps giving me that

old song and dance about getting married and giving her some grandchildren. I know it's none of my business, but do you and Bill plan to have a baby any time soon? Sure would take the pressure off Jennifer and me."

Angela shook her head. "Bill thinks we need to save a lot more money and buy a house before we do that. However, he says with the new business he's starting on the side we might be able to in a couple of years."

Jessica took a bite of her sandwich. A dollop of mayonnaise dropped on her suit jacket. She dabbed at it. "Damn, it still shows. I'll have to go home and change."

Loud voices arguing drew Jessica's attention to a booth in the corner. The man facing in her direction looked average with dark wavy hair and a pronounced aquiline nose. He leaned forward. "Are you sure? If what you say is true, that formula will make us rich. We need to move fast and set up distribution centers in other states.

The other man whose face Jessica couldn't see, was leaner with a rangy build. Wearing a brown suit, he stuck his legs out in the aisle. "Don't get ahead of yourself. We haven't tested it sufficiently to put it on the market yet."

Angela turned to look and frowned. "That's my husband with his back to us," she whispered. "The other man doesn't work for the company any more, but he's Bill's new partner in the little business he's starting."

"What's this new drug they're talking about?"

"It's something new Bill and he are developing for Ballard Pharmaceuticals. Hopefully, it will make money for the company and the stockholders." She looked at Jessica. "By the way, what percentage of the company will you and Jennifer hold when Dad dies?"

Puzzled, Jessica stared at Angela. "Why are you

asking?"

Angela leaned forward. "Bill thought maybe, like he did for me, you and Jenny brought extra shares."

Jessica shook her head. "I have enough. As I understand it, when Dad dies, one-fourth of Dad's shares will go to Mom, and we three will inherit nearly three-fourths of the company." Hoping that wouldn't happen for a long time, she watched the two men. "Sounds like Bill is talking to that man about a new drug? Isn't that confidential information?"

"I don't know, but I'm sure going to ask Bill when we get home."

Chapter Ten

Jessica glanced at her watch, then at Angela's husband and the mysterious lean stranger with the bushy mustache wearing a charcoal pinstripe suit. Could he be the guy who'd tried to mess with her IV the second time? As he rose, she stood. "Excuse me, but I've got to go."

After pulling out her compact, she freshened her lipstick and followed the men out of the cafeteria. They didn't seem to notice her.

"We'll make a killing if this drug does all it promises to," Angela's husband said.

"I'll make sure the tests come out okay," said the other man.

That was strange. Was he planning to manipulate the tests, or was she jumping to conclusions?

"I'm counting on it," Bill said.

The two men shook hands. Bill said, "Bye, Kelvin. I'm looking forward to doing business with you. If this works out okay, we should both make a killing."

The stranger handed Bill a business card but kept standing there talking. She'd have to pass them or risk attracting their attention. She wanted to hear more. Could she fake a sneeze and make it sound authentic?

Better not try. But she could blow her nose. And she did. Except she didn't get the name of the other man's company. Drat. If she wanted to learn more, she'd have to follow him.

The two men walked down the hall, heading for the back door instead. Bill punched in a code and held the door open for the man. She hurried up, hoping Bill would continue to hold the door.

He faced her. His eyes had a cold angry look which vanished so quickly she wasn't sure what she'd seen. In college she'd dated him briefly before he fell for Angela. They'd broken up because he'd been miffed because she spent so much time with her heavy course load. Surely, he wasn't still resenting her for that.

After all, since she'd been one of Angela's bridesmaids at their wedding, they'd partied well into the night after the rehearsal dinner. He'd gotten so drunk, he'd kissed Jessica, then said, "Oh, thought you were my bride to be," and promptly kissed her sister."

Now he was all smiles. "Hey, good to see you. What brings you here during the day? Thought you had a slave driver for a boss."

"I was having lunch with Angie, but now I have to get back to the office. My boss expects us to be prompt."

"I see," he said and looked at his watch. "I'd better hurry back to my office too." But he didn't seem to be in a hurry.

Through the glass door, she could see the man in the pinstripe suit get into his car. She needed to find out where his company was. "She looked at her watch. "Oh, dear. I'm going to be late."

Practically running through the door and down the steps, she pulled out her keys, hurried to the car next to Kelvin's shiny black one. A Viper she thought. She made a show of pretending to unlock the car next to it.

Kelvin sat behind the wheel, writing down some notes. He turned on the radio. Stepping to the rear of the car, she acted as if she were checking out her rear tire and memorized his license plate number.

He gunned the engine. She backed away, barely missing being knocked down. She ran toward her car. Jumped in and backed it out. At the entrance to the street, she nosed her car out, hoping to see which way he went.

There he was. She followed. Not too close. She didn't want to raise his suspicions, but he'd raised hers.

Damn, there was a yellow light. He didn't slow down. She followed. Ran the red light. Uh, oh. There was a police car behind her. The flashing lights came on, but no siren. Maybe it was tailing someone else. But no. It continued right behind her. Damn.

She pulled to a stop. Pulled out her driver's license.

The cop strolled up to her window. He brushed his mustache. A breeze lifted strands of his dark hair ringing his balding head. "Good afternoon, ma'am. Can you tell me why you were in such a hurry?"

No, she couldn't. "Sorry, officer, I thought I could make that light. My lunch hour is over, and I'm late returning to work."

He started writing. "Better be safe and not endanger anyone else. Listening to your boss complain about your tardiness is better than explaining to someone in the hospital why you crashed into him or her."

He handed her the ticket. "Sign here, and don't forget to take care of your fine or show up in court." He frowned. "You're lucky you don't have to explain to some grieving parent why you hit their little darling."

She swallowed. She hadn't thought of that. What if he'd been right, and she killed someone? That was too horrible to think about. She'd been hot on what was probably a wild goose chase. No doubt Bill and Kelvin

Carolyn Rae

were only intent on making money for Ballard Pharmaceuticals, unless of course, they were working on something else.

She met the cop's gaze. "I promise I'll drive more carefully in the future."

His steely dark eyes stared into hers. "That's a good start. I don't want to have to stop you again." He tore off a copy of the citation and handed it to her. "You have until the date on the ticket to take care of it. Better handle that soon so you won't forget."

His look and manner annoyed her. He was treating her like a ditzy blonde. She wanted to tell him not to be so patronizing to citizens but pay more attention to catching crooks. One look at his face told her it was better to keep her mouth shut. But she did make a note of the officer's name.

When she got to work, she wrote down Kelvin's name as well as the license number of his car. Maybe she could ask Michael to check him out, but for now she needed to get started on her assignments.

Much later, after turning in her assignments, leaving work, and fighting traffic for half an hour just to get out of Dallas city limits, Jessica glanced in her rearview mirror. That black Jeep Wrangler had been behind her all the way. Even when she changed lanes. She told herself that he was just trying to pick a faster moving lane as she often did.

A baseball cap shadowed the driver's face, and sunglasses masked his eyes. From what she could see, he appeared to be well tanned, lean, and wearing some kind of print shirt. Not bright colored, but the pattern was reminiscent of Hawaii. Maybe he'd just returned from vacation and wasn't ready to face returning to work.

Michael had been only too anxious to leave for work this morning. Did he want to forget last night? He'd acted as if nothing had happened. Maybe he could put it aside and forget it, but she couldn't. What was it with this man? He blew hot and cold.

On the other hand, Lewis next door was steady and friendly. Why couldn't she fall for him? He'd been helpful when her TV went out, always gave her a cheerful "hello" when they left their apartments at the same time, and accepted packages for her when she wasn't home. Unlike her, he didn't need to rush to get to the office on time after oversleeping as she did sometimes.

Now if she had Michael in her bed every night, she wouldn't be tempted to stay up late and read. Thinking about that made her feel warm and cozy. They'd probably stay up late and cut short their sleep too. But what a way to spend the nights.

However, after what he said, that wasn't likely to happen. Frowning, she wrenched her wheel to the right, barely making it to the exit ramp where she turned off each day.

Wheels squealed behind her. That Jeep Wrangler was turning also. Probably lived nearby. No wonder he was following her.

Keeping her eye on the rearview mirror, she drove past her street for two blocks and turned at the next street. The other car pulled to a stop in front of a house near the corner.

She let out a sigh of relief. She was being paranoid. Heading to her apartment, she drove around in back and parked under the carport assigned to her. As she entered the back entrance to the building, she looked back. There was that Wrangler cruising down the alley. Had he seen her walking to the building? She couldn't be sure.

She climbed the stairs to the second floor. Maybe Michael was right. Maybe she did need protection. And she enjoyed having him close by.

She unlocked her door, feeling the hairs on her neck tingle. She looked over the railing to the lobby below.

There stood that guy, his wrinkled shirt emblazoned with palm trees and ocean. He was studying the mailboxes. Hers was labeled J. Ballard. He pulled at the knob, but without a key he couldn't open it.

He looked up and removed his sunglasses. Their glances met, his cold and menacing, as if he wanted to put his hands around her neck and squeeze until he choked her. Something about him looked familiar, but before she could figure out what it was, he put the sunglasses back on.

Still, he kept looking at her. She tensed, hoping he couldn't tell which apartment was hers, but of course he could. She was standing right there with the door open.

She hurried inside and locked the door. Her breaths came in short pants. What should she do? Call the police? They'd say she was imagining a threat without any solid proof. At least the apartment was quiet with only the faint hum of the heater.

She wondered when Michael would come. She grabbed a note pad and tried to write down as much of a description as she could remember. Tan skin, black eyes, spiky dirty blond hair sticking out from that cap of his. Wouldn't someone who planned to harm her be calm enough to comb it and walk more casually? But he hadn't done that—just strode right in as if he had a right to be there. But she knew in her gut he didn't belong here.

Her door was locked, but she still felt uneasy. After pulling out her cell phone, she pushed Michael's cell number, the one he'd given her to use in case of emergency.

"Michael, there's a strange guy in my apartment building, and he followed me most of the way home."

"Stay there. Keep the door locked and bolted. I'll be there as soon as I can."

"Don't you want a description?"

"Sure, give it to me."

She did. "Have they found any fingerprints on the knife that was stuck in Jennifer's picture?"

"They're checking it against AFIS." He seemed preoccupied, so she hung up. Then she called Lewis next door. "Hi, there's a guy I think followed me home. He's in the lobby. He's got on a Hawaiian shirt. Would you look and see if he's still there?"

"Sure, neighbor. Be glad to. I'll call you right back."

When the phone rang, she grabbed it. "Hello."

"Hi, Jennie baby. How are you?" The voice was deep and low and sounded menacing."

She gripped the phone to keep her hand from shaking. "You must have the wrong number. My name is not Jennie." She slammed the phone down and sank into a chair.

When the phone rang again, she hesitated, then answered.

"Hi, it's Lewis. That guy is still in the lobby, but he's heading for the back door."

Jessica let out a sigh of relief. "Thanks for letting me know." She disconnected.

She wanted to fix a nice dinner for Michael, but she didn't dare go out to buy groceries. She looked in the refrigerator and saw only a pound of ground beef. She'd make spaghetti, except she didn't have any tomato sauce. Maybe she could use cream of mushroom soup. She pulled out some noodles and set a pan of water to boil.

*Too nervous to read–she didn't want t*o be drawn into a thriller and feel even more anxious, she dialed her mother.

"I'm so glad you called," her mother said in dulcet tones. "I was just about to call you."

Uh, oh. That meant her mom wanted her to do something, but listening to her mother's chatter might take her mind off the nosy stranger down in the lobby. She frowned. She had to get a hold of herself.

"Jessie, baby, I need your help," her mother said.

"What is it, Mother?"

"I just got back from the doctor's office. I had a little accident and broke my right arm. It's in a cast now. I need you to address my Christmas cards."

"But it's not even Thanksgiving yet. Why so early?"

"The doctor said I had to wear this cast until after Thanksgiving. I don't want to be late getting my cards out. If you write the addresses on them, maybe by the time I get the cast off, I will be able to write a short message on each one. Perhaps by then I'll have some good news to share like an engagement to announce or a baby on the way."

"Mother, you can't rush those things. They'll happen one of these days." Jessica wasn't about to tell her what Angie said.

"But Jessie, I keep hoping for you or Jennifer to become engaged. I'd love to plan a nice wedding for you or your sister."

"Mother, you need to be patient. Jennifer is dating

her boss. Maybe that will develop into something more serious."

"But I worry about you. You're not seeing anyone now."

"Hey, I'm a career woman, but who knows, maybe I'll meet someone who sweeps me off my feet." Like Michael she thought, but she couldn't see him as someone interested in settling down. Except right now, he dominated her thoughts. She definitely didn't see anyone else as a prospect. Not even steady and reliable Lewis, who seemed to like her.

"Can you come by and pick up the cards and my address book tonight?"

"But, Mother, your it's your arm that's broken, not your hand."

"It's so awkward trying to write with it. Be a dear and do that for me. I'll give you a batch of cookie dough."

"Oh, okay," she said and hung up, hating herself for giving in.

Someone was knocking on her door. Her heart jumped into her throat. She gripped the edge of the table holding the phone so hard she could see the color disappearing from her hands. "Who—who's there?"

"It's me," said Michael. Sighing in relief, she rushed to open the door.

"Did they get a match on the fingerprints from the knife yet?"

He shook his head. "Those things take time. And when they do, we'll get twenty-five near matches to check manually. Our fingerprint expert has more urgent cases to work on. Recent murders for example."

"I could have been a murder victim."

"But you weren't, thank goodness." He held up a large shopping bag. "I've brought dinner."

Now she could smell it. Definitely Chinese. And the bag had Chinese symbols on it. "Oh, that smells wonderful." She turned off the heat under the pan of water and put away the box of spaghetti noodles.

He set the bag on the table. "Can you give me a spare key, so I can have one made for me?"

"Sure, but please come with me to get it."

"Why? Did you give one to your neighbor, Lewis?"

Looking at his frown, she wondered if he were just a little bit jealous. That made her feel good. She shook her head. "I keep one in the back of my mailbox. No one but me and the mailman can open it. That's in case I get locked out."

Michael frowned. "That's stupid. What if the mailman finds it and decides to ransack your apartment? I guess you'd be better off giving it to Lewis. He likes you."

"Dick the mailman's a nice friendly guy. He wouldn't do that."

"You can't be too sure now a days."

"Okay, I'll give it to Lewis instead."

"Let me have it to get a copy made. Then if you get locked out, you can call me."

"I'm not going to bother you at work to get a key."

He grinned. "Might be nice to have my fellow officers see I have a woman begging me for help."

"Hey, I don't beg things from anyone."

"Sorry, I forget. You women like to be independent."

"All right, you can have it, but I want you to come with me while I get it from the mailbox. Just in case that jerk in the Hawaiian shirt is still hanging around."

They were about to go downstairs when her phone rang. Michael answered it and pushed the button to put it on speaker mode.

"Oh," said the caller. "I must have the wrong number."

"No, you don't," said Jessica, reaching for the phone. "It's my sister. Hi, Jen."

"Who's the guy with the nice voice?"

Jessica switched off the speaker button. "Just a friendly cop who's checking to see if I'm all right."

"He has a great voice. You sure he's only there to protect you?"

"Yes, but he brought me dinner. Can I call you back later?"

"I'll only be a minute. I have a favor to ask of you. My apartment is being painted tomorrow. Can you take care of Charlie?"

"Who's Charlie?"

"My puppy."

"I do have to work you know. Do you have a crate for him?"

"Not a crate. Those are so small. No, I bought a playpen for him. It's too big for that narrow kitchen of yours, but you can fit it in your living room. It will only be for a day or two. Please?"

"Well, okay, but bring a leash so I can take him for a walk."

"Don't worry. I've almost got him trained to whine at the door when he needs to go out. I'll bring him over first thing in the morning."

"Uh, what time?"

"Better make it eight-thirty," said Michael in a low

voice.

"Oh, I heard that," her sister said. "Bet he looks as good as he sounds."

Jessica stole a glance at Michael who stood looking out the window. She bet he was picking up everything she said. "You're right, but he's just here to be sure I'm safe."

Jennifer's laugh tinkled over the phone. "And who's going to keep you safe from him?"

"Don't worry. I've got things well in hand, including my protector. I'll see you in the morning." She stuck out a finger to close the connection but pushed the speaker button by mistake.

Jennifer laughed again. "Enjoy him then. Bye."

Michael's glance met hers. He had a knowing smile. Jessica could feel her face getting hot as she disconnected the phone call.

He put his hands on her shoulders. "So, you think you have me well in hand. I know where I'd like your hands."

Her face got hot. She'd never forget last night. She couldn't forget the way he'd set her senses on overdrive, even though they didn't finish what they'd started. She'd been ready to let him go all the way. If only Lewis hadn't been at the door.

Making love with Michael would be earthshaking she was sure, but she couldn't let it happen. She'd die if she let him make love to her, and then he stalked off like he'd done last night. She couldn't live with someone who was off and on again. Mr. Hot and Cold might be a fantastic lover, but he'd never be there for her all the time.

She swallowed, then met his gaze. "Last night was

a mistake. Best we pretend it never happened."

Okay…if that's the way you want it. Besides, I'm still investigating your case. But something in his eyes called to her. His hands on her shoulder moved ever so slightly, almost like a caress. She willed herself not to let him get to her, but he was doing a good job of exactly that. Her heart beat faster, and she couldn't help smiling at him.

After they ate, Jessica led him downstairs to get the door key from the mailbox. With the mailbox key in hand, she was about to insert it when he held out his hand. "Let me do it. If there are any fingerprints, I don't want to mess them up." From his pocket he pulled out some plastic gloves and slid them on. Without touching the door, he inserted the key, pulled out her mail and handed it to her. The apartment key he slid in his pocket. "Go back upstairs and lock the door. I have to get a finger print kit from headquarters." Then he was gone.

Jessica had no sooner locked her door when she heard footsteps outside, someone knocking, and a dog barking.

"Jessie, open up, it's me," her sister called.

Jessica sighed in relief and pulled the door back. "Thought you were coming in the morning."

Jennifer edged in, dragging a playpen while her puppy kept running away as far as the leash let it. "Changed my mind."

By the time Jessica had the door shut, the dog had pulled the leash from her sister's hand and was racing through the apartment.

Snowball ran yowling through the living room and jumped up on Jessica with a force that shook her. At her feet, Jen's puppy was barking and jumping up and down with excitement.

Jennifer caught his leash. "Here, Sis, hold onto this while I set up his playpen."

Holding Snowball with one hand, Jessica tightened her hold on the leash. He was still barking, but now he pulled at the leash, trying to get to the end table where the slashed picture of Jennifer used to be. She hadn't told her sister about that yet. Didn't want to, but she had to. One or maybe both of them were in danger, and Jen needed to know.

After setting up the playpen in the middle of the living room, Jennifer picked up the rambunctious puppy and set him in it. The room looked crowded, but at least Jessica's furniture and knick-knacks were safe.

Jennifer flashed that bright smile she sported on TV. "Bye now. Got to run." She took hold of the door knob.

"Wait. There's something you need to know."

"Okay, what?"

"Someone's been stalking me and somehow thinks I'm you."

"How can that be? We don't look identical. Your hair isn't as long as mine, and you don't keep it curled like I do. "Concern shone in her green eyes, her carefully plucked and brushed eyebrows coming together in a puzzled frown.

"It's a long story."

Jennifer plopped down on the couch. "Make it short. I need to get home to get ready for the painters."

"First I got shot at the football stadium during a game."

"You mean that wasn't a random shot by some crazy?"

"I don't think so. Then I got a threatening e-mail.

Since my e-mail address is jballard@thenews.com. It's possible someone mistook that for your address."

"So. That doesn't mean he knows where you live." She leaned over and picked up a piece of glass. "What's this from? Did you break something?"

"My apartment was broken into. Your picture, the one I kept on the end table there—" she pointed.

Jennifer looked. "It's not there. Was it stolen?"

Jessica shook her head. "My apartment was broken into. Your picture has a knife stuck through it and the word 'BITCH' written on it."

Jennifer gasped. Her mouth dropped open. "Omigosh. That guy is sick." She looked shaken. "Do you still have it. I want to see it."

Jessie shook her head. "The police took the picture, the frame and broken glass to check for fingerprints."

"You mean that cop who came to see you in the hospital?"

Jessica shook her head. "He's investigating the shooting. Other officers came to check out the break-in."

Jennifer grinned. "I'd keep him around if I were you. He sounds yummy."

Jessica nodded. She remembered how his hands felt on her body, how he'd suckled her breasts, how she yearned to let him do more not too long ago.

Jennifer touched Jessie's arm. "You can't stay here. It's too dangerous. Come home with me."

Jessica shook her head. "That may not be any safer. Michael has been staying with me so I should be okay. But maybe the guy that's stalking me is after you and thinks this is where you live. I worry about you. If he follows you home and finds out where you live, he might transfer his sick obsession to you and your place."

Jennifer gasped. "And maybe he hates both of us. What are we going to do?"

Chapter Eleven

Still smarting from the argument with Sergeant Dexter at headquarters who'd demanded to know why he had to have a fingerprint kit right now, Michael had to admit he hadn't much to go on except that a suspicious man had fingered her mailbox.

Dexter had made a snide comment about not spending too much time with someone whose case he was investigating. Damn. Apparently, Michael hadn't kept as low a profile about being with Jessica as he'd thought.

Except after what Jessica had said, they weren't a couple. Still, he'd do all he could to keep her safe.

When his co-worker handed over a kit, Michael thanked him and drove to Jessica's apartment building where he dusted the mailbox. He used sticky tape to transfer the prints to cards, then headed to the station to compare them with fingerprints taken after the break in. They matched. He checked to see if there was a report back on the fingerprints on the picture of Jennifer they already had from Jessica's place, but AFIS didn't have a match.

He was glad he didn't work in CSI anymore. He'd seen enough slashed bodies, smelled enough blood, and picked through enough trashed living quarters to last a lifetime.

He'd hated speaking to the sorrowful family

members, wishing he could give them comfort or at least answers to their anguished 'whys' in some cases.

He liked investigating better. Each crime was a puzzle to solve, a chance to catch the perpetrator, and get him behind bars. He usually managed to zero in on the evidence, keep it in a tight chain of custody—no OJ Simpson mistakes for their department—and present it well enough in court to nail ninety percent of the perps.

The next morning his boss called him in and went over the new rules he'd explained at the last staff meeting that Michael had missed. "And," his supervisor continued, "I expect a sizable number of speeding tickets on Monday, Wednesday and Friday. Maybe then you'll think twice about breaking the rules."

"You can't do that. I'm a detective, not a patrol officer."

His boss towered over him. "One word to anyone here about that and I'll refer you to Internal Affairs. After your unlawful search and seizure of marijuana last month, there could be some question about keeping some of that pot for yourself."

"I didn't," Michael said and stalked out of the office. How could he get anything done if he had to camp beside Highway 30 to nab speeders?

Sleeping on the couch at Jessica's place at night would be cold, lonely, and frustrating. She might not say much except 'hello' and 'good-bye.' Now the weirdo knew where she lived, so Michael wasn't leaving her unprotected. Later that afternoon, Jessica called. "I won't be back at my apartment until late tonight. Mom and Dad invited me for dinner."

"What if that guy follows you there?"

"I don't want to miss seeing my family and eating a

good home-cooked dinner."

"What if I take you there in a police car?"

"He wouldn't follow me then, but why don't you come with me?"

"Wouldn't your mother mind an uninvited guest?"

"She'd be delighted to see me bring a…male friend home."

"But we're not exactly going together." He wished they were. He'd want to take Jessica out as often as he could. Maybe it was just as well. His mother always worried about him setting up drug busts or going undercover. A girlfriend would worry too. He didn't want to think about when her stalker was caught, and he had no reason to stay with her. He'd like to get closer to her before then.

Jessica's voice broke into his thoughts. "You're welcome to come, but you'll probably have to put up with questions about your intentions. You can say we're just friends."

"When shall I pick you up?"

"Five-thirty."

Later, wearing a tan blazer and khaki pants, he was looking forward to an evening with Jessica. However, meeting her parents and wondering if she'd still be cool toward him—that made him nervous.

After she buzzed him up, he took the stairs two at a time, then rapped on her door. She was a knockout in yellow slacks and a form-fitting yellow top that matched her golden blonde hair.

Would they ever return to the intensity of the other night during the tornado watch? Remembering that made his pulse race. He'd better cool it, except he wished he could become more than a friend.

Seeing her smile gave him hope. "You look great in those clothes. Are you ready?"

She nodded and pulled out her key.

He held out his hand. "Let me do it. I want to be sure it's locked securely."

As she gave him the key, her soft hand brushed against his, sending a frisson of electricity up his arm. Was she feeling those sparks too? Judging from the intent look in those green eyes, she was. Great—except after what she'd said earlier, was there a snowball's chance in a hot oven, things could return to the way they were before?

After they caught her stalker, would the connection between them evaporate? Not if he could help it. Then he'd be free to see her as much as she'd let him and go as far as she'd let him. He got hot just thinking about it. But it wasn't just that she turned him on. He loved being with her.

Outside, he held the truck door open for her, then got behind the wheel. Visions of Jessie, naked—on her bed, on her couch, on her rug or in his bed, filled his mind. Just thinking about sinking into her softness made him hard as steel. Trying to keep his mind on what she said, he asked about her latest assignment at the paper, then listened.

When she asked him about his work, he let slip he'd been assigned to write speeding tickets as punishment for missing a staff meeting. "But you're an investigator. You don't even wear a uniform."

"I'm tired of following all the chief's damn rules, but he's making an issue of it."

"But isn't it important to make sure everyone follows procedure. I mean, don't you have to handle evidence properly so it can be used in court?"

He nodded. "We have to keep exact records of who handled it so we can swear no one tampered with it."

"Do you do that?"

"You bet. And most of the murderers I arrest get convicted."

She looked at him. "You wouldn't manufacture evidence to do that, would you?"

He slapped the dashboard. "Hell, woman, what rotten kind of cop do you think I am?"

"One who doesn't always follow the rules."

"I follow the important ones. I don't torture suspects. I mirandize them before questioning when it's called for."

"You mean you can ask them questions without doing that first?"

"If it's minor stuff, like name, address, where they were at the time of the crime—if they're not under arrest, I don't have to mirandize them."

"But doesn't ignoring the rules get you in trouble?"

"Yeah, but no innocent man ever got convicted because of me." He clamped his lips together. Was she going to keep on criticizing him?

He frowned. "Haven't you ever broken any silly rules?"

"Only once, and I got caught."

"What happened?"

"At college I tried to sneak into the dorm after hours by climbing in someone's basement window. She was a friend of mine who unlocked it for me."

"So, what did they do?"

"I got campussed. That meant I had to stay in my room all weekend. After that, they watched me like I was a criminal for a month. From then on, I followed the rules. You should, too. I know you love your job. I'd hate to see you lose it."

He shot her a dirty look, but kept his lips buttoned. Where did she get off, second guessing his situation at work?

****

Back at Jessica's apartment building, a man pulled the brim of his baseball cap lower and grasped the handle of the lobby's rear glass door. Couldn't knock on her door with that damn cop hanging round, but when she left, he'd get into her apartment again. Leave her a message she couldn't miss. She hadn't even noticed him waiting outside Ballard Pharmaceuticals that day at lunch time. Later, at her apartment he'd thought when their gazes met over the railing, they'd finally made a connection. Maybe now she'd remember him and their date so long ago.

Why'd she have to go and call the damn pig? He hadn't threatened her, just fingered the keyhole on her mailbox. He wanted to send her a note, remind her how much he'd liked touching her, how much he wanted to touch her again.

He'd waited outside, hoping the pig would leave, but not only did the bastard hang around the lobby, but then the cop glanced toward the glass door where he stood. He'd had to duck out of sight.

He'd waited till the man left, but then someone wearing a scarf had come in the front entrance with a dog. She had her head down so he couldn't see her face. Her shape was something like his Jennifer's. Maybe she was a sister. Jeesh, his sweetheart's apartment building was like Grand Central Station with people coming and going.

Finally, after the other woman left, he'd sneaked upstairs and listened outside her door. He heard his sweetheart talking on the phone, but the damn dog barked up a storm so he left. He'd get something to quiet that animal. Couldn't have that dog alerting the whole building.

****

At Jessica's folks' house Mr. Ballard, wearing a pinstripe suit and red tie, smoothed back graying hair. He greeted Michael and invited him to sit. Michael perched on the cream-colored couch, feeling a bit nervous. Unlike his place, everything matched, but the room looked comfortable and lived in. He settled back, feeling a bit more at ease.

Her father sat in a recliner, then set his glasses on an end table. "So, what do you do?" he asked.

"I'm a detective for the Arlington Police Department."

Jessica's mom, dressed in a frilly white blouse and a black skirt and looking a bit harried, entered with a plate of pastries.

Jessie introduced her mother, who said, "So nice to meet you." She set the plate on the coffee table. "Help yourself to appetizers. Angela and Bill are on their way, but Jennifer's running late as usual."

Michael savored the spicy taste of sausage tempered by the roll of bread surrounding it. "It's delicious, Mrs. Ballard."

She smiled. "Thanks but call me Sophia."

Michael swallowed. "I think I'll stick with Mrs. Ballard if you don't mind. I had a sister named Sophia…." He swallowed. What a chilling coincidence.

If only he'd been watching out for his sister, she'd be safely married by now. Maybe even have a couple of toddlers he could play with. He tried to ignore the emptiness inside. "My sister was killed before she reached twenty."

"I'm sorry to hear that," Mrs. Ballard said. She vanished into the kitchen.

The doorbell rang. Mr. Ballard opened the door and shook hands with a short stocky man. "Hello, Bill, long time no see." Both men laughed. Mr. Ballard turned toward Michael. "Meet my oldest daughter, Angela, and her husband, Bill Dunstan. He's my senior financial officer at Ballard Pharmaceutical. She works there too."

Michael shook hands with Bill and nodded to Angela. She had hazel eyes, more brown than green, and hair a darker blonde than Jessie's, but the resemblance was plain.

The phone rang. Jessica's dad answered it, then said, "Jennifer isn't going to make it."

At the table, while they ate fried chicken and mashed potatoes, Angela mentioned a long-ago fire at their house. "Mom had already left the house with Jessie, but Jennifer was being ornery and kept saying she didn't want to walk to Grandma's house. Finally, I picked her up—she was kicking and struggling—and carried her out the door. We had just left when I heard a terrible explosion inside. Then I saw smoke. I ran around the corner to Grandma's house. Jennifer stopped fussing. Guess she was scared. After Mom called the fire department, we watched the firemen put out the fire."

"So, what caused the explosion?" asked Michael.

"The refrigerator blew up. It had been making funny noises, but we never dreamed it would explode."

Jessica set down her fork. "That was close. If you hadn't carried her outside, she'd be dead."

"Hey, she was just a little kid," Angela said. "She didn't know any better. By the way, have you gotten any other assignments at the News besides obituaries? Don't know why they keep you if they think you aren't good enough to write better articles."

Jessica swallowed a lump in her throat. "I just interviewed the CEO of Chicken and Eggs chain."

"I never heard of them. They must be small potatoes."

Jessica leaned forward. "Breakfast is big business in the Dallas area. They have one restaurant in the area, and plan to open a second in Grand Prairie soon."

"Well, I hope after you write the article, they let you do more. You should be an experienced writer by now."

"She is a good writer," Michael said. "Her article about being shot was great."

Angela leaned forward. "Anyone can write a great article about something traumatic that happened to her. Now if I'd been older, I could have written a great article about the fire and saving Jennifer. The reporter did a pretty good job of it. He said I was the heroine of the day and only nine years old." Angela leaned back and looked around the table.

Michael added, "That was a brave thing for you to do."

She beamed and nodded. "That's what everyone said at the time."

Jessica's mom rose. "I was very proud of you that day." She picked up their dinner plates. "We're having strawberry shortcake. I need to whip the cream." She walked into the kitchen.

As the sound of beaters filtered into the dining room, Angela's husband Bill stroked his mustache. "I recall another time when your mom wasn't so proud. Remember the night of the senior prom?"

Angela frowned. "For heaven's sake, don't bring that up."

"What happened?" asked Jessica. "That was the week I went to Houston for the state debate team championship. I remember you and Jen were grounded for a month, and she wasn't allowed to date again until our next birthday. Mom wouldn't say what you did, said it was too shameful. I couldn't get Jen to tell me either."

Angela laughed. "It wasn't that big a deal. Not like we went skinny dipping naked."

Jessica's mouth dropped open. "You went swimming after the prom?"

"All of us, Bill and I and Jennifer and her date, Jason, Jared or Jeremy something, stripped to our underwear and played around in the lake. I don't know where Bill picked him up, but Jen needed a date, and Bill said he knew a guy who was a security guard at some office building."

Bill laughed. "Afterward, we sat around shivering and telling dirty jokes until our underwear dried enough to get dressed and go home. Your mother met us at the door. Guess she saw our wet hair, because she made us tell her what we'd done."

Jessica looked at Angela, wondering why Jen never told her about that. "Y'all must have been quite a sight."

Bill had the grace to look sheepish. "Guess that was a dumb thing to do, but you know how hot it gets in May. Must have been at least eight-five degrees even though it was after midnight."

Later, as Jessica and Michael walked out to his car, he said, "I'm not sure what to make of Angela."

Jessica met his gaze. "I've always looked up to her after the fire. Whenever Mom left Jen and me with her while she and Dad went out, I felt safe."

Michael reached over and put his hand over hers. "She can't keep you safe now. But I can if you'll let me. Your sister is milking that occasion for all it's worth. I didn't like the way she talked about your writing."

"She always has to one up someone."

He squeezed Jessica's hand. "She works for her daddy and didn't have to go out and convince someone she could do a good job, but you did. That takes guts and persistence."

After they climbed into Michael's car, she called Jen. "Hey, Sis, you always share everything with me. How come you never told me about going swimming in your underwear after the prom? I had to find out from Angela."

Jen laughed. "I was too embarrassed to tell you. At first it was exciting. That guy looked at me like he wanted to eat me up or give me a hickey and kiss me all over. When he kissed the tops of my boobs with wet sloppy lips, I felt dirty and ashamed."

"So that's when you told him to stop?"

"Uh huh. He looked kind of shocked but finally pulled away. That wasn't the worst part. I nearly died when I got home, and Mom said, 'Jennifer Ann Ballard, I'm so ashamed of you I could cry.'"

"Bet you felt small. I always do when Mom does that to me."

Jennifer nodded. "After she got through telling me I'd shamed the Ballard name and disgraced the whole family, she made me and Angela promise never to tell anyone, not even you about it."

"I'm surprised Angela even brought it up at the dinner table with Michael there."

"Guess she figured he might become part of the family soon. You really like him, don't you?"

Jessica stole a glance at Michael. "Yes, I do. A lot."

"Have you slept with him?"

"Well, uh...not yet."

"But you will, won't you?"

Jessica sighed. He'd be wonderful she was sure, but was she ready for that? "Look, I've got to hang up now. He's just driven me to my place. I'll call you later."

Michael pulled into a parking space at her apartment building. "I need to pick up some stuff at my house and feed Dog, but I'll be back. You're not spending the night alone."

"I hate it that you feel you have to do that, but I do feel safer with you there. I wish my couch were a hide-a-bed. It must be uncomfortable."

****

Michael let out his breath. "It's okay." The couch wasn't really long enough for his six feet plus, but he'd manage. Sure would be nice to share her bed, run his hands over that lush body of hers. That night of the storm he hadn't been able to get enough of touching her. She'd been ready to melt in his arms. Damn that nosy neighbor for coming to the door when he did.

He drew a deep breath, felt himself harden. He wouldn't go there. Jessica deserved a forever kind of guy, not one like him. He might not have dangerous assignments now, but he could be shot next week or the week after that.

Okay, so even a nine-to-five sit-at-the-desk guy could get killed in a car accident. However, he didn't feel he had much to offer. But he could keep her safe. He walked her to her door and watched her unlock it.

Jennifer pushed it open and gasped. "Omigosh. Not again."

He and Jessica looked at her living room. Books littered the floor. Stuffing stuck out from slashed couch cushions. A lamp lay on its side.

"By the way, didn't you lock the place before we left?" he asked.

She frowned. "Of course, I'm sure I did. I even pulled at the knob to be sure it was locked."

"You should have called a locksmith the same day you were broken into before. Not having a bolt lock put in was just asking for trouble."

"I was going to, but I didn't think the same guy would come back and do it again so soon. Wouldn't he think the cops were watching the place?"

Michael shook his head. "He probably knows we don't have the manpower to run by burglarized houses constantly. Call a locksmith. I'll see if a window has been broken." He walked around. "I don't see any signs. The perp must have picked your lock. You need a bolt lock you can secure with a key when you leave."

The empty playpen sat in the middle of the floor.

"Oh my gosh, Jen's puppy's gone. Where is it? Charlie, come, Charlie."

A whimper came from the coat closet. She ran to it and opened the door. Bending over, she picked up the dog. A rag was tied over its mouth, keeping it from barking.

She untied the gag, and he let out a whelp, then

147

snuggled in her arms. "I can feel his heart pounding frantically against his ribs. He's scared. Goodness knows what someone did to him." She put him in the playpen and petted his head. "You're okay now, puppy."

She looked around. "Snowball. I've got to find him. I can't bear it if he's been hurt again. Snowball, where are you?"

She rushed through the place. "He's not in my closet or under the bed. Please, help me find him."

Michael came in the kitchen with her. Together, they pulled the lower cupboards open. As she opened the last cabinet, he stepped into the walk-in pantry. "Jessica, I found him. He's wedged in the corner between a bag of charcoal and one of kitty litter. "Snowball, come here." He held out his hand. "Come on, I won't hurt you."

"Back out of there. Let me get him." She hurried into the pantry and snatched up Snowball. He clung to her. "He seems scared, but I don't think he's been drugged.

"Don't touch anything else. I'm calling this in." He pulled out his cell phone and punched some buttons. After speaking to headquarters, he glanced at Jessica. She looked frazzled.

"I'll get a locksmith out tomorrow. Is it okay to use the bathroom?"

"I'd wait until the crime scene folks are through. We can go out for coffee while they work. They'd let us stay here, but we'd be in the way."

"I need to put some lip gloss on." She walked into the bedroom, took one look at her mirror and screamed. "Michael, come look."

Michael rushed in from her living room, saw a message scrawled on the mirror in lipstick, and put his arms around her.

****

Jessica glanced at the mirror again. It said, "Look pretty for me. I'll be back to claim your body." Her heart pounded, and she could hardly breathe.

She gripped the edge of the dresser so hard her knuckles turned white. He'd hurt her sister's dog and it was just a matter of time before he found her alone—and did who knew what to her. Her pulse raced.

Michael held her close. Little by little her trembling eased. She snuggled into his arms, glad for the warmth of his body and the woodsy smell of his aftershave. That guy had no right to hurt Charlie or terrorize her like this. But she wouldn't become imprisoned by fear. With Michael by her side, she'd fight back.

She clenched her hands into fists. "I want to beat that guy to a bloody pulp."

****

Michael smoothed a lock of hair from her face and tightened his arms around her shoulders. If she needed strength, he was more than willing to give it to her—to protect her as he hadn't been able to protect his sister.

But when this was over, and they caught the guy—not seeing her every day, not talking with her about things that mattered, and not hearing her laugh—would leave an emptiness inside—one he didn't want to face.

Chapter Twelve

Still shaken, Jessica sat with Michael in a coffee shop. She didn't want to stay in her apartment while the police were working. She sipped her coffee. "I can't believe I've done anything to deserve this–this obsessed pervert."

Michael patted her hand. "It's not your fault."

She sighed. "His look while I watched from the balcony lining the fronts of the second- floor apartments was so intense. I felt as if I'd been scorched." She frowned. "It makes me mad that he terrorized Snowball and Charlie. They're innocent victims. I'm taking them to the vet tomorrow for a checkup."

Michael called the crime scene investigators, who said it was safe to return. He drove her back, unlocked the door, and insisted on entering first. As Jessica answered the investigators' questions, she noted the black fingerprint dust littering the end tables. She'd clean up after checking the animals. Finally, the police officers left.

Charlie was in the playpen, but she had to coax Snowball out from the pantry again. She picked up pillows and books and straightened things, dreading going in her bedroom.

Charlie, usually very frisky, just lay there in the corner of the playpen. He vomited, filling the air with a sour smell.

She patted him on the head and wiped it up. He lay there, with his big brown eyes focused on her. "He looks pitiful," she told Michael. "I'd better call a vet tomorrow."

Another smell tainted the air. Diarrhea this time. Weakly, Charlie crawled away from the messes. Then she saw a dab of raw hamburger in the corner of the playpen she hadn't noticed before.

"That bastard tried to poison him." She ran to her desk, rummaged for her vet's number, and dialed it. She listened, then hung up. "Damn. All I got was a recording. He's out of town. He'll be back Monday, but he left an emergency number." She dialed it but when she did, a recording told her to leave a message. She explained what happened, left her number, then hung up. "I'll just have to wait until someone calls back."

She reached down to pick up the meat.

"Stop," Michael said. "Don't touch it. That could be evidence the police missed."

She scooped it up with a paper towel and set it in the kitchen. "I have to clean him up."

After dampening a paper towel, she wiped Charlie's mouth. Using a couple moistened towels, she gently sponged off his rear end. He just lay there and moaned. "You poor thing." After she scooped up the mess, she sprayed the bottom of the playpen with Lysol and wiped it with another damp paper towel.

Michael spoke to someone at headquarters. After hanging up, he said, "Put that clump of meat in a Baggie. I'll take it for testing."

"I hope that emergency vet calls back soon. I feel awful that someone might have tried to poison him while he was in my care. I've let Jen down."

Michael touched her arm. His touch felt comforting. "It wasn't your fault. It could have happened if Charlie were at Jennifer's place and someone broke in. You even said the stalker could be after her instead of you."

She walked over to the window and looked out. "Surely, he's figured out by now that there are two of us." She swallowed. "I'm not sure who he wants."

Michael stepped up behind her and put his arms around her. "If he wants you, that's not surprising. Except you're my woman."

Jessica smiled. He was being possessive, but she liked it.

He turned her in his arms and kissed her.

His lips were warm and demanding. Voracious and nibbling. Tender and hot. She couldn't resist. Her arms crept around his neck. She kissed him back. Kissed his mouth, his cheeks, and his forehead. She couldn't seem to stop.

His tongue slid between her lips, exploring, tasting, then pulsing with a determined rhythm. He was squeezing her breasts, setting them tingling with desire. She leaned into him and grasped his powerful arms, felt his muscles, his strength.

He could protect her. He was tender. And he wanted her. That was enough for now. Except he pulled his mouth away and gazed into her eyes.

She met his gaze. "I-I want…

Grinning, he met her gaze. "You want what? Me I hope."

Charlie let loose with vomit, much more this time. The odor made her gag.

Reluctantly, Jessica pulled away and walked to the playpen. "But I need to take care of the animals. I'd never forgive myself if one of them died because I was too busy to take care of them."

She cleaned up the mess and wiped his mouth again. Charlie lay down and closed his eyes. Since he seemed to be resting peacefully, she stood. "I'll just check to see if the cops cleaned the mirror in the bedroom."

"The police came to look for evidence, not clean up. Where's your cleaning stuff? I'll take care of it."

"Thanks. Look under the sink." She walked into the bedroom. Sure enough, those hateful red words, superimposed over the reflection of the bedroom, taunted her from the mirror.

The tube of lipstick he'd used to write the words was gone. She slapped her palm to her forehead. Duh. The police must have taken it for evidence.

Or maybe—or maybe the stalker had. Would he break in again and leave more messages? She read it again, cringing at the words, "I'll be back to claim your body."

Goose bumps formed on her arm. Shivers ran down her body like rivulets in a rain shower. Was the bastard planning to rape or kill her? Aftershocks pummeled through her, chilling her to the bone.

She turned and bumped into Michael. "Thanks for offering to clean up, but I can't stand to look at that bastard's words a minute longer. I need to clean him out of my place and take control of my apartment." She grabbed the Windex from his hands and scrubbed until her arms ached.

She rubbed the mirror with a vengeance, wishing she could rub her enemy's skin with sandpaper. Forget his skin. She wanted to pummel him for scaring her and hurting the animals.

She rubbed her hand across her forehead. "What kind of monster is stalking me?"

"A twisted one. Occasionally we see one who gets off on terrifying women. With luck we apprehend them and put them in jail. We'll get him, I promise. And I'll be here to see that he doesn't get to you." He took her in his arms again.

She buried her face against Michael's cheek, felt the prickles of his five o'clock shadow and the firmness of his chin. A pleasing, spicy aftershave teased her nose. Almost covered up the stinky smells from the dog.

He held her tightly. That felt good. He'd protect her—as long as he was with her.

She snuggled closer. "You make me feel safe."

"I'm glad I can be here for you."

"But you can't stay with me all the time. I have to go to work—at least I'll be safe there."

"Until you leave work. Call me every day before you do. I'll meet you there and follow you home. Then I'll spend the nights here—until we catch him—as long as it takes."

After the way he'd kissed her and with all the sparks flying between them, she knew what could happen. It was inevitable. She wouldn't be able to hold out. Just thinking of having his hard firm body against hers, his hands on her breasts and touching her everywhere sent delicious sparks all through her. Maybe he could lessen the fear that dogged her, make her feel a little bit safer. Having him in her bed would be wonderful and banish her worries for a while.

He obviously liked her and cared what happened to her. He could be gentle as well as ravishing. His kisses and the way he'd fondled her breasts proved that.

The phone rang. It was the vet on call. "I'm not in the office. If you feel your pet has been poisoned—"

"I'm pretty sure he has. He's real lethargic, and I found some tainted meat nearby. He's vomited twice, and he's got diarrhea too." She put the phone on speaker so Michael could hear.

"I hope he's expelling most of it. My office isn't open now, but I'll call in a prescription to your local drugstore. Which one do you use?"

She told him.

"Now tell me his breed, his size, and his weight. Watch him for a few hours after you give him the medicine. If he doesn't seem better after a couple of hours, call me again."

After she hung up, Michael asked, "Where's the nearest drug store? I'll go pick up the stuff."

"On the corner, two blocks down."

"I'll be back as soon as I can." He took her hand, his firm grip reassuring. "Lock the door and brace a chair under the knob."

"I will."

He let go of her hand and cradled her chin in his hands. A quick kiss, and he was gone.

After he returned, he held Charlie while she force-fed him the medicine. She laid him on a thick plastic sheet Jennifer had brought with the playpen. Charlie upchucked two more times. After each time, Jessica washed his face and talked gently to him.

While not as energetic as usual, he seemed more alert. His tail even wagged a few times. Jessica rose and picked up the phone.

"You calling Jennifer?"

She shook her head. "It's late, and I don't want to

wake her. Worrying about a stalker will keep her awake all night. I'll tell her tomorrow. I'm calling the apartment manager now. They need a better security system here."

After she finished telling the manager what happened, Michael looked at his watch. "I've got to go and feed Dog." He took her in his arms again and kissed her. His lips, warm and wonderful, filled her with comfort and something more.

She responded to him almost without thinking. "Thanks so much for being here when I needed you."

He squeezed her hands, then headed for the door. "I hate like hell we spent most of the evening dealing with your apartment being broken into again. Dog is probably ready to chew on the woodwork. I'd better go, but I'll be back soon." He gave her a long, sweet kiss that made her want to hold onto him and not let him go. Finally, he pulled away, still looking as if he didn't want to leave. Wind chimes warbled in her heart, hinting maybe this relationship might last after all.

Not ready to let him go, she touched his lips again and clasped her hands around his neck. She liked kissing him, more than she should.

Except he seemed to like it too. Hallelujah. She'd hoped he was not only attracted to her, but that he liked her. His lips said that when he kissed her. And his hands caressed her shoulders like he treasured her.

She could get used to having this all the time—but she'd better not. This closeness might not last. She should pull back, but she couldn't—she wanted to savor just a few seconds more of comfort in his arms.

She snuggled closer. "I hate to take up all your time, just to protect me. You need to have a life of your own. Staying with me during all your free time--that's too

156

much to ask."

"I don't mind doing it—at least until the perp is caught. That's what I do, remember. I wish I could spend all my time on that until he's caught, but I have to work on any other assignments I get."

He pulled away, his gaze full of longing. "Lock up after me." He clenched one hand into a fist. "I'll get that guy put away, no matter what it takes."

"You must be tired. You need to sleep in your own bed tonight. Don't bother coming back tonight. I'll lock the doors, and Charlie will bark if someone tries to break in. I can't believe that weirdo would be stupid enough to try again tonight."

He frowned. "You're crazy not to have me stay here. If that guy knows you're alone, he just might come back. You're asking for trouble."

"Just leave. I'll be okay."

He strode toward the door. "Fasten the chain after I leave. If you don't have those locks changed immediately, you're just asking for it." He stormed out, slamming the door behind him.

He must think she was a lost cause. Maybe he wouldn't want to spend any more nights with her. She tried not to think about how empty her apartment would seem. She'd miss all those sparks flying. He seemed upset with her now, but she hoped that wouldn't last long—but if he got over his mad and made a play for her, how long could she hold out?

Except they'd never make it as a couple. All her life she'd followed the rules, all of them. And he thumbed his nose at every one he could.

She shouldn't be wallowing in that dilemma. She should be keeping an eye on Snowball and Charlie. They were sleeping peacefully now. She crossed her fingers, hoping they'd be okay.

She worried about Jen, too. Her sister had gotten threatening notes also, but it was Jessica's apartment the bastard had broken into. Was he so fixated on getting control that he couldn't tell them apart? Was she his real target or was Jen? If her sister was, who would protect her? Jennifer worked in a large building. She could be attacked in a deserted corner. Fear for her sister made Jessica tremble. She'd have to warn Jen this guy was even more demented than she'd thought.

She locked the front door and attached the chain. If he tried to get in again, would that stop him? What if he got her alone, here or somewhere else? Would he rape her and torture her before he killed her?

He'd stuck a knife in Jen's picture with such force it tore a big hole in the picture. If he got in again, would he slash her and curse her while she bled to death? Cringing, she shut her eyes. Couldn't think about that anymore. She'd have nightmares.

Glancing at the mirror, now shining clean and spotless, she could still see those hateful words. She could pretend she wasn't scared. But she was. Mad too, that someone had violated her home.

But she wouldn't give in to fear. That was what the bastard wanted. Just in case he was watching her, she'd stride proudly and hold her head high wherever she went as if he didn't bother her. But he couldn't see the ever-tightening knot in her gut. And she'd be careful. Damn careful.

Then she realized she hadn't called a locksmith yet. She flipped through the yellow pages for a locksmith, wondering if forgetting to get the locksmith out here sooner had been a Freudian slip. She had to admit she wasn't looking forward to not having Michael stay with her.

She picked up the phone and dialed. After calling three places and getting a phone message—it was after business hours—she found one that sounded reliable and made an appointment for someone to come out tomorrow morning. She hoped her stalker wouldn't try anything before then.

Charlie was whining. No doubt he wasn't feeling too chipper yet. She scratched him under his ear. Then she noticed dried blood flaking off onto her hand.

She clenched her fists. Damn bastard had cut the pup's ear. She wanted to shove the man down on a bed of nails or some other medieval torture device. Even that would be too good for him.

She took Charlie into the bathroom, washed his cut and dabbed alcohol on it. He yelped and squirmed, but she held him tightly. A few drops of fresh blood oozed from the cut, darkening the fur. Gently, she washed the cut again and put on more alcohol. The bleeding seemed to have stopped. She drew a sigh of relief and set him back in the playpen.

She debated about calling her sister. She didn't want to make Jennie nervous for her screen test. Maybe she should let her know about Charlie.

She picked up the phone, her finger poised to dial. The phone rang. She snatched it up.

"Hello, sweet thing. You weren't home today, but one of these days .... I can't wait to show you what a great lover I can be." His voice, syrupy sweet, had a gravelly undertone. Like blood tainting clear water, a trace of steel permeated his low tones. "Bye for now. Sweet dreams."

Chapter Thirteen

Jessica gasped. Still trembling, she stared at the phone. She wanted to reach through the wire and strangle him. She felt cold all over, cold, and so damn vulnerable. She checked the chain on her front door. It still held. Michael was gone. What if her stalker broke in before Michael came back? What if the pervert raped and tortured her? Maybe killed her. Her heart raced and her breaths came in short gasps.

If she called the police, it was probably too late to trace the call. They wouldn't send someone just to talk to her about a phone call. Michael might come back soon, probably tired and ready for bed. If she called him now, he'd think she was a nervous Nelly. He'd done enough, spending practically every night here. She could tell him when he returned.

Maybe next Monday night when she showed up for the Citizen's Police Academy class she'd enrolled in earlier, she'd ask if they could have her phone bugged. She'd have to get a new unlisted number for her land line and her cell phone.

She tried to punch in her sister's number but got it wrong. She tried again. No one answered. Jennifer was probably asleep.

She tried once more. This time Jen answered. Jessica told her what happened.

"That's terrible," her sister said. "What is the world

coming to when burglars try to poison innocent pets?"

"Charlie's all right now, and I'll take him and Snowball to the vet tomorrow to get checked out, but I've got enough to deal with. You need to come get him in the morning."

"I don't do mornings, remember. Can't I get him after you get home from work?"

"Listen, I have as much trouble getting up as you do, but I have to be at work by nine. You'll have to take him before then."

Jennifer groaned. "All right. I'll be there as soon as I can. I'll call first in case you and Michael are...you know."

Jessica frowned. "We aren't sleeping together. He's just staying here a few nights to protect me until I get my locks changed, which I'll do tomorrow."

As she hung up, she stood straighter. She'd been firm with her sister. A favor now and then was okay, but she wasn't letting her family take advantage of her any more.

Thankfully, before too long, Michael came back. She told him about the phone call. He hugged her and suggested she get the guy's number next time and block it. "Even after you get your lock changed, "I was thinking of staying with you for several more nights. Hopefully, by then we will have apprehended him."

"A locksmith is coming tomorrow."

"It's about time. I'm surprised you didn't have him come sooner."

"Once he gets the locks taken care of, you don't need to stay. I'll be all right."

Good night, now." He kissed her sweetly, as if afraid to press for anything more. He dropped his arms and lay down on the couch.

That made her feel relieved enough to fall asleep almost immediately.

The next morning, the doorbell and Charlie's barking startled her. Checking her watch, she realized it was five to eight. Damn, I should be dressed by now. "Just a minute," she called and raced to get her robe and then the door.

Michael, already dressed, beat her to it. "Who is it?"

"Aaron, AAA locksmiths."

He undid the bolt and let him in. ""I'll call you at work later." Michael said and walked out the door.

She told the locksmith she also had a door that opened onto a balcony. While he worked on the front door, she called the paper to say why she'd be late and dressed quickly. The way things were with her boss, she didn't dare show up any later than she had to. She pulled out the cookie dough her mother had given her. She bet Michael would like fresh cookies if he stopped by after work tonight.

After she'd told him he didn't need to stay with her anymore, he might not. But she'd be ready if he did. She turned the oven on, scooped cookie dough onto baking pans and shoved them in the oven. When the cookies had cooled, she piled them in her cookie jar. It had sat empty since her mother gave it to her. She put some cookies on a plate for Michael, hoping he'd spend the night or at least stop by to see how she was. By then, the locksmith had installed the bolts on the front door and the balcony window door. She wrote him a check, tucked the two keys in her purse and left for the newspaper office.

Michael followed her home from work but didn't come in. She ate a microwave dinner and wondered if he had taken her at her word. Finally, at midnight when he hadn't called, she yawned and decided he wasn't coming. Just in case, she wrapped the plate of cookies and set it on the coffee table with his name written in big letters on a Post-it note on top.

Things just weren't the same. Now she wished she hadn't sounded so independent or gotten the locks changed so quickly.

The apartment seemed awful quiet without him. She started a CD of soft music, glad her player would shut off by itself if she fell asleep before the album was finished. Michael had sounded so disgusted with her for not calling a locksmith sooner. Maybe he wouldn't come back. Or maybe he figured she'd be okay without him.

Come morning, she dragged herself out of bed and anxiously inspected the couch. With a sheet and blanket still piled neatly on one side and the plate of cookies untouched on the coffee table, everything was just as she'd left it. Served him right for not coming. Maybe she'd bake more cookies and take them with her to her Citizen's Police Academy class Monday night. If she went early to the class, maybe Michael would be there. Then she could give him some of the cookies. At least that would give her an excuse to talk to him.

Monday morning, she dressed and got ready for work. Tapping her fingers on the kitchen counter, she waited for her sister to pick up Charlie. Where was Jennifer? Late as usual. She dialed her sister's cell phone.

"I'm on my way. Got in late last night, so I overslept, but I'll be there in a few minutes."

Finally, her sister picked up Charlie. Jessica followed, carrying the collapsed playpen to her sister's car. Then Jessica drove to work.

That evening she dressed carefully in a green blouse with a green and black plaid skirt, hoping she might see Michael. On the way to the Citizen's Police Academy class, she wondered if he'd stop checking on her now that her apartment was more secure, and the burglary department was checking fingerprints from the break-in.

She arrived half an hour early for class and asked at the desk if Michael was in the station or out interviewing someone.

The man at the desk pushed some buttons. "Hey, Steel, there's a babe here to see you." He grinned. "Steel's all about work. I've never heard a woman asking about him before."

Michael strode into the lobby, looking harried.

She fumbled in her bag for the Baggie of cookies she'd set aside for him. "I brought some cookies. Thought you might have time to share them over coffee before my class starts."

"Sorry, but I'm on my way to check out a shooting in the mall parking lot. Can't stop to talk."

"Well, I just wanted to tell you no one's broken in since I got the locks changed."

"That's good." He glanced at his watch and shook his head. "I've got to go now."

She held out the bag of cookies. "Here, take these."

He reached for them. Even with his off-putting attitude, the touch of his fingers as he took them sent a tingle up her arm. His no-nonsense-I'm-busy expression didn't change. Apparently, he didn't feel the same about her as she did about him. Bummer.

He pulled the bag open, took out a cookie and bit into it. "Hey, these are great. Thanks." He turned and strode down the hall without another look.

Remembering his sister who'd been murdered, she wondered if staying to protect her had been his only interest. He hadn't called. Maybe he'd decided she didn't need him anymore. Or perhaps he'd written her off as a woman who wasn't careful enough to ensure her own safety.

She wanted to stand on her own two feet, but she wanted to keep on seeing him, too. She wished he enjoyed her company as much as she did his. Did she even stand a chance compared to women who made the most of their looks like Jennifer? He'd said he preferred the natural look to Jennifer's highly made up one, but surely, her sister could improve Jessica's looks in an understated way.

That decided, she took a seat in the front row for the Citizen's Police Academy Class. When she got home tonight, she'd call Jennifer. Michael might not come back, but she'd feel more confident with a make-over. And maybe after a while, she'd find another man she liked almost as much as Michael. Not likely—no one else could stir her half as much as Michael.

The instructor, a wiry, but muscular man, varied the lecture about the departments and what each one handled with humorous tales of things that happened to him when he worked in the different areas. During the break, she handed out cookies to the other students.

Munching on one of the last three cookies, she debated whether to save one in case Michael showed up afterwards. She might as well face it. He probably wouldn't. Maybe her comments about rules had turned him off.

Why did she have to fall for someone who didn't

bother with rules? She wondered what so-called rules of society he didn't bother with either. If she let him sleep with her, would he kiss and tell at the police station? Somehow, she didn't think he'd be that crass.

However, he'd probably consider it just sex, rather than something meaningful. She didn't need that. Not with Michael.

Her heart ached, more than she'd ever thought possible for someone she'd met only a little over a week ago. Why him? Just because he'd protected her when she needed it wasn't enough reason to be so drawn to him.

He was one incredibly sexy guy. That night of the storm he'd almost convinced her to let him make love to her. Except he wouldn't call it making love. He'd call it making out—or something cruder. She clamped her lips together. She needed to forget about him.

Class was about to start up again. She needed to concentrate, needed to find out what made cops different from other men. Maybe she could get a handle on what made Michael tick.

In class the instructor handed out a clipboard with slots for eight-hour ride-alongs with a cop on duty. By the time the assignment sheet reached her, there was only one slot left. And it was only two nights away. Writing her name, she felt flutters in her stomach. She didn't know whether it was due to excitement or anxiety. What if the cop got her into a dangerous situation?

After class she walked to the parking lot with another woman, who headed in the other direction because her car was at the opposite end of the lot. Feeling alone and cold in the dreary misty rain, Jessica trudged toward hers.

"Jessie," Michael called.

She turned. His voice sure lightened her spirits. "Did you like the cookies?"

He nodded. "I had to eat them fast because other guys would want me to share."

"But you didn't?"

He laughed. "What do you think? I'm glad you gave me big ones. They were good." He moved closer and crooked his arm in hers. "Why are you walking to your car alone?"

Surprised, she faced him. "Surely a police station parking lot should be safe enough."

"I'd hope so, but you can't be too careful. I'll follow you home."

"You don't need to do that. A security guard patrols the parking area at my apartment building." She watched his face, hoping he'd insist.

"And where was he when that perp broke into your place?"

"I don't know. Maybe he had the night off, and his replacement didn't show."

"Don't make excuses for the piss-poor security at your apartment building. I'm following you whether you like it or not."

Being gracious couldn't hurt. "Thanks." She almost added 'I'll wave to you after I'm safely at the door,' but thought better of it. Maybe he'd offer to stay. Why was she kidding herself? Their attachment was only tenuous—and not destined to last.

He not only followed her inside the building but insisted on checking her apartment. She told him about her class. "Seems there are a lot more break-ins than I realized. Would you like some coffee?" Holding her breath, she waited for his answer.

"That would be great. Got any more cookies?"

She shook her head. She'd have to get another batch of dough from her mother or the store.

Later, after pouring him a second cup of coffee, she glanced at his face. Now came the awkward part. Should she ask if he were staying or wait until he got up to leave?

She wouldn't beg him to stay. If he left, she'd know he wasn't interested in her. But if he stayed, she wouldn't know if he liked her or was only worried about keeping her safe.

She washed and dried the cups, but he didn't say anything about leaving. Her pulse sped up. Maybe he'd stay.

Then he stood and walked to the door. Her heart plummeted to the bottom of her stomach. He was leaving.

She swallowed her disappointment. "Have-have a good evening."

He checked the lock on the door and fiddled with the bolt lock she'd had installed. "Seems sturdy enough. I'll feel better about leaving you here alone."

Damn, he was leaving. Dare she come right out and ask him to stay? Somehow, that seemed too forward.

He faced her, a hesitant look on his face. "Do you want me to stay?"

What was he asking? She wished she knew how to take his offer. "I'd feel safer if you did."

Now why had she said it like that? It was true, but didn't she want him to know how much she wanted him here. Would that ruin her image as an independent woman? Make her sound needy. She didn't want that. Especially since she wasn't sure how he felt about her.

He grinned, lighting up his whole face. "I could

sleep on the couch unless ....." A question lingered in his eyes.

Now she felt awkward. Did she want him in her bed? Want him caressing her all over the way he had the night of the storm? Her blood heated as she remembered that night. Hell yes, she wanted him to stay. He'd be a fantastic lover, she was sure.

Her blood stirred, but she had an ache that was almost painful. Should she risk the heartache if he made love to her and then never came back?

They were like oil and water. She followed rules religiously, and he didn't. He didn't seem to mind breaking them as long as he caught the bad guy.

She met his glance. Studied his eyes. She couldn't tell if that was a seductive look or a pleading one. Her pulse raced as she imagined what could happen.

His expression turned glum. "Guess that's a no. Don't bother to let me out but lock the door. I'm going home. Guess I'll go to bed early."

He looked disappointed, but he'd acted like a gentleman by graciously accepting her non answer.

What the hell—did she want to miss the chance to be in his arms, taste those fabulous kisses and more?

"I don't want you to leave." She stepped closer and put her arms around his waist. "My couch is too small for you to rest peacefully. I want you to sleep in my bed." She smiled.

"Only if that's where you'll be."

She leaned up to kiss him. "You bet," she whispered. She hesitated. Had she made the right choice? Would heartache follow ecstasy if great sex was all he wanted?

She looked at his face and then took a deep breath.

It was worth taking a chance. Taking his hand, she led him to the bedroom.

Chapter Fourteen

Michael followed her into the bedroom, holding onto her hand as if he feared she'd change her mind.

She wouldn't. Making love with Michael would be exciting and wonderful. Right or wrong, she'd enjoy his loving to the fullest. For just an instant she wondered if she'd be disappointed like she'd been with Harry.

No, that wouldn't happen with Michael. She was sure. She'd loved the way Michael touched and caressed her in the tub on the night of the storm, and she couldn't wait to be in his arms again. And share his kisses—wow. Those were almost enough to live on for a long while. Except she kept hungering for more. And tonight, she'd get her fill.

He paused in the doorway. "You sure?"

"As sure as the sun comes up in the morning and the stars shine at night." She pulled him into her arms. "Now kiss me."

He grinned, gave her an enthusiastic kiss, then picked her up and carried her to her bed. She could have lit some candles or set some incense burning for atmosphere but, somehow, she knew he wouldn't miss that nor would she.

He laid her down on the bed gently and leaned over her. She lay there, her pulse racing and her lips waiting.

His kiss was gentle and fleeting. She grabbed his neck and pulled him down for another. He undid the top two buttons on her blouse, then cupped her breast. "Why do you women have to bundle yourselves up so tight?"

"To keep warm, I guess."

His lips came down on hers, warm and seductive. He raised up just enough to meet her gaze. "But it makes so much work for us guys. Besides, I'm going to keep you warm, very warm." By now, he had the third button of her blouse undone.

He slid his finger under the top of her bra and ran it in half-circles from one strap to the other. Her skin tingled at his touch. Then he pressed a ring of kisses on her throbbing flesh, setting little sparks everywhere his lips touched.

Her heart beat so fast she could hardly stand it. It was like riding a Roman chariot, hurtling forward with his arms around her as he gripped the reins and guided a mighty stallion.

He released the front clasp of her bra. "Beautiful," he said, setting her aglow inside. Then he planted tender kisses on her breasts and neck until she was hot and quivering all over. Wow. What a man.

When he came up for air, he was grinning.

She rose up, met his mouth with hers. Excited by the feel of his hands, caressing and squeezing her breasts, she let the kiss go on and on until she wasn't sure who was kissing whom.

One thing she was sure of. She'd never get enough. She kissed him again. He clasped her waist and raised her up. He kissed her nose, then laid her down and suckled her breasts.

They swelled and firmed as she arched toward him, loving every minute. He twisted a lock of her hair with one finger, then moved up to kiss her lips. His searching mouth seemed even sweeter and more possessive than the last time. She felt treasured and desired beyond her wildest dreams.

She unbuttoned his shirt and ran her hands over his firm chest. Wrapping her arms around his neck, she pressed her cheek against his warm flesh. "I like touching you."

He smiled. "You're so sweet. I could kiss you all day, but I want more."

She grinned. "I bet you do. And…and I want it too."

Even as she spoke, his fingers moved between her thighs, exploring and caressing. She ached to feel him inside, to feel him strain against her, and yes, she ached to push back, to show how much she wanted him, not just now but for the rest of her life. Except she dared not bring that up. Not now. He might say no, and she couldn't bear to hear it.

She looked into his eyes. "Please."

He grinned. "Please what?"

"You know what I want."

He was grinning. "What do you want?" His fingers touching her down there were driving her to distraction. How could he speak so calmly?

"You. I want all of you," she whispered.

"Well, then we need to get rid of these clothes." Moving quickly, he pulled her up and slipped off her blouse and bra.

Quickly, he ripped off his shirt and pants, kicked off his shoes, and peeled off his socks. He bent over. She heard a crinkle of foil. Glad he'd come prepared, she toed off her shoes, and shoved off her skirt, panties, and pantyhose all in one motion. For an instant she felt a chill. But then he settled on top of her, warming her all over. This was what she'd been waiting for.

He kissed her again, caressing her shoulders as he ravished her mouth. She watched him lay a trail of kisses down to her nest of curls. Then his fingers took over, setting little flames between her thighs until she thought she'd go mad if he didn't hurry.

He met her gaze. "I can't wait any longer. I'll try to go easy." He raised up just a bit. "I don't want to crush you. You're too sweet and wonderful."

She smiled. It felt wonderful to be cherished like this. If only it would last. She wouldn't think of that now. She strained forward to meet him. He filled her more than she'd ever imagined possible. She met his thrusts, feeling full of life and thrilled to be one with him.

He kissed her over and over. "Jessie, you're wonderful. I can't get enough of you." The glow in his eyes said he meant every word.

No one ever told her that. Wrapped in his arms, she felt so close to him, so enthralled in his presence. Thrilled beyond measure Was this love?

Michael set her to tingling inside, swelling deep within until everything inside burst like a field of dandelions caught in a puff of wind, then like a windmill gone crazy. She grasped his shoulders, feeling as if she had to hold tight to keep from flying into outer space.

He gripped her tighter. His release sent everything inside tingling again and again. "Oh, Michael," she said. He kissed her and rolled them both to their sides. Lying there, he met her gaze with a bemused look, as if he, too, couldn't believe what had just happened.

She lay wrapped in his embrace, wishing they could be together for always. No wonder people rushed to get married. But could he and she make a success of it? She shouldn't try to change him—to pester him to see the importance of following rules the way she did. Could she live with that? Maybe she could suggest reasons why it would be a good idea...occasionally.

Could he even fit in with her family? They were all like her, upstanding citizens who did what they were supposed to, no matter what they felt like doing. Truth be told, they never yearned to do anything that wasn't proper or against the rules of society. She'd worry about that later. Right now, snuggling in his arms felt so warm and wonderful, she didn't care. She fell asleep in his arms.

Come morning, it was nice to wake up beside him when the alarm rang. She shut it off and snuggled next to him, wanting to lie there just a little bit longer. Then she realized he had to get ready for work, too and jumped out of bed.

He looked at her with one eye open. "Is it morning already?"

She nodded. "Last one in the shower has to wash the other's back."

"No fair. You're already out of bed."

"I'll count to three. One, two. three."

On the count of two, he had thrown off the covers and was running around the bed. She still beat him to the shower. "Now you have to wash my back."

He grinned. "I get dibs on washing your front too."

That made her breasts swell. She turned on the water and stepped inside.

She was adjusting the spray when she felt his hands on her breasts, soaping and rubbing. He stood behind her, caressing more than washing. She let go of the water controls and leaned back. At this rate, she'd be late for work, but she'd sure enjoy getting clean.

He rubbed her back vigorously, then spun her around to face him. He was aroused and ready. He pulled her toward him. "Yes?"

She let out a happy sigh and nodded.

This time he was fast and furious. He nibbled on her shoulder, worried her nipples with his lips and covered her with wet kisses. She leaned against him, thrilling in the feel of his hard chest pressing against her soft breasts.

He slid his hands between them enough to squeeze her breasts, then kissed them all over before entering with a mighty thrust.

Grasping his tight buttocks, she pulled him even closer. He thrust faster and faster until they both climaxed in glorious bursts of energy that shook her all over.

He kissed her. "Might be nice to spend all my free mornings wrapped around you like this." He grinned. "Now I'd better leave for work or I'll be tempted to spend all day with you."

She smiled. "I can't think of anything nicer."

"I can't afford another bad mark against me," he said, but insisted on toweling her dry. She kept grabbing at the towel, but he wouldn't release it until he was through.

"Let me dry you now," she insisted.

He shook his head. "Guess I'll drip dry. I have to get dressed, and we both need to get to work."

He threw on his clothes. And then he was gone without a "See you tonight," or even a "See you later."

Had all those wonderful feelings had only been on her side?

After dressing and eating a bowl of cereal, she

wondered what he was doing now. Was he sipping coffee and munching doughnuts with other cops—maybe some female ones?

She didn't think he had another girlfriend, but she didn't know. She looked at her watch. Time to leave for work.

During the next week Michael followed her home and called every night around ten to be sure she'd locked the door and was safe. But all he talked about was the weather and a few tidbits about amusing incidents at work. Sunday night he chatted about visiting his married sister and her kids. He hadn't offered to take her to meet his mother or his married sister. Was he afraid his sister would blab about another girlfriend?

On Monday evening when it was time for another session of the Citizens Police Academy Class she'd signed up for, she managed to run into him at the police station. "Michael," she said. "There's a picnic at River Legacy Park after the last class. Would you like to go with me? Each teacher from the class will demonstrate their specialty or put on a skit showing how they do it. Class members can bring a spouse or a date. And the K-9 division is going to give a demonstration with the dogs."

His smile warmed her all over, making her hope it had only been work that kept him away. "I might. When is it?"

"Three o'clock Saturday afternoon."

His face fell. "Don't know if I can spare the time. We've been shorthanded all week, and I've worked late until I was bushed several times. Besides that, I've got another case I have to check out, something that can only be done on Saturday."

That might explain why he hadn't come to see her. At least he had called to be sure she was safe. But his excuse sounded a bit lame.

Michael put a hand on her shoulder. Footsteps sounded in the hall. Michael glanced back and let his hand drop. Leaning closer, he whispered. "There's my boss. I'm still on his blacklist."

A burly man paused and looked quizzically at Michael.

"Jessica, this is Detective Sergeant Black. Sir, this is Jessica Ballard, the woman who was shot and whose apartment was broken into not long ago. She's taking our Citizen's Police Academy class."

"Nice to meet you, ma'am," he said. "Detective Steel's one of our most dogged investigators." His stern expression left no doubt how he felt about Michael.

She stole a glance at Michael, wondering if he were nervous or at least unsettled to be seen with her. Except she figured he was too macho to let it show.

Detective Sergeant Black nodded toward Michael. "Few perps get by once he catches their scent." The man resumed his march down the hall, his heavy footsteps consistent with his sturdy body.

Michael's eyes opened wide. "That's the first time he ever said anything good about me," he said in low tones.

"You didn't ask if you could get off to go to the picnic. It won't be the same without you."

"Later. I don't want him to think I'm involved with you. After all, I am working on your case. Maybe I can say it's good public relations or something like that."

Uh, oh. She didn't want Michael to get in trouble at work because of her. Maybe he wouldn't go, but she found herself wishing he would.

Two days later Jessica showed up at the police station ready for her ride-along on a 3-11 shift. She'd gotten off work at 2:00 by promising to write an article about it.

When Jessica inquired at the desk, the clerk pointed to a good-looking Hispanic man with curly hair and a ready grin. He approached her. "I'm Pedro Sanchez. You'll be riding with me. He winked at the female clerk behind the desk. "I'll take good care of her." He put a hand on her forearm. "Come on. I'll take you out in the country and show you how fast my Crown Vic can go. We can turn on the sirens. Won't bother anyone but the cows."

"Jessica," called Michael from the doorway to the hall. "What are you doing here?" He had a sour look on his face.

"I'm taking my ride-along with Pedro. He promised to show me how you cops work."

Michael frowned. "I could do that."

"This is part of the Citizens' Police Academy Class I'm taking."

As Jessica and Pedro walked through the door, she turned to see if Michael was watching. His back was turned as he stalked down the hall.

Pedro did indeed take her out along a country road and push the speedometer to 100. Then he turned on the sirens. Up ahead a cow started across the road. Pedro jammed on the brakes and swerved, barely missing the animal. "Damn farmers can't keep their pastures fenced."

The rest of the shift was uneventful. He wrote a few tickets, then checked out a report of a woman being beaten by her boyfriend who'd threatened to take her Ford Focus.

When they got to the woman's second-floor apartment, Pedro told Jessica to stand down the stairs away from the door. "Don't know what might happen."

She caught a glimpse of the woman. Heard anguish in her voice as she said, "I don't know what got into him."

"Do you need to see a doctor?"

The woman shook her head.

"Okay, call him and tell him you want to meet him for supper at — let's see, there's a Jack-in-the Box at the corner. Wait a minute before you call." He pulled out a phone, spoke into it, then hung up. "Now make that call."

Pedro hurried down the steps to Jessica. "Get in the car. I've called for back-up."

As he drove toward the Jack-in-the-Box, she heard him talking to other cops. He jerked to a stop in a parking lot of a building next door to the fast-food place. "Stay here. I'll leave my mike on so you can hear what's happening. Do not get out, I repeat, do not leave the squad car." He ran to the next parking lot. Two other police cars pulled up.

Soon a man walked slowly to a green Ford Focus. The cops stood talking and pretending to ignore him. The minute he pulled at the door handle, they rushed over.

After she saw them handcuff the man, Pedro returned to her. "They're taking him to the station. Now do you have any other questions about police work?"

"Do cops in one division get along with those in another?"

"We have some good-natured rivalry when one group challenges the other to a baseball game, but we get along pretty well."

At eleven at night when Pedro's shift was over, he drove back to the station. "I'll walk you to your car. It's dark, and I want to be sure you get home safely."

Beside her car Michael was waiting. "So, you're back," he said. His tone didn't seem very friendly. "I'll follow you home. At this hour you don't know who's about."

Jessica turned to Pedro. "Thanks for a very interesting ride."

He grinned and winked. "Glad to be of service ma'am." He headed to the station.

Michael was frowning. "Why the hell did you have to pick him to ride with. He's a terrible flirt. It's a wonder he didn't ask for a date or try to seduce you."

"Michael, how could you say such things about a fellow officer?"

He flirts with all the female clerks."

"Maybe he's just being friendly."

"Friendly, my eye. Who knows how many he's seduced?"

"For your information, he's married and has two sons. Any flirting he does is probably just that—flirting and nothing more."

Michael looked surprised. "I didn't know."

"Well, if you weren't so much of a loner, you'd know that. All I had to do was ask."

"I see. Well, we'd better get going. You have to work tomorrow, don't you?"

She nodded and slid behind the wheel. Torn by mixed feelings, she both wished he'd spend the night and was glad he hadn't offered. She didn't care for his mood.

At her door, he watched while she unlocked it, then

he did a walk-through.

"It's safe. Good night."

"Thanks for seeing me home. Are you going to be able to go to the picnic with me?"

"Not sure. I may have to work." After a long, powerful kiss, he was gone. But he didn't hug her. Was the other night just about sex? Had she made a fool out of herself? Or was he jealous of Pedro?

****

Thursday, after a long, trying day spent getting her articles written and rewriting an article to meet Ms. Sharp's satisfaction, Jessica trudged up the steps to her apartment. Glad to get home, she walked along the landing, glancing over the railing at the mailboxes on the main floor. She'd forgotten to pick up her mail but she'd get it later.

As she turned the key in the lock, she heard Snowball whine, then stop abruptly. Something inside fell with a resounding thump. Had he fallen? Dropping her purse, she wrenched the door open.

"Snowball, where are you?" she called.

"I've been waiting for you, sweetheart," answered a man. His raspy voice sent shivers down her spine.

Her stalker. He was here—in her apartment!

Her heart in her throat, she gasped. She snatched her purse and ran out onto the landing. If she could only run downstairs, she could get help. Pounding footsteps caught up with her. He grabbed her around the middle. Her heart lurched.

She started to scream, but his hand clapped over her mouth. Clutching the railing, she tried to kick him. He yanked her loose and dragged her back to her apartment. He shoved her inside, then slammed the door. "You scream, and you'll wish you hadn't," he growled.

She caught her breath but didn't dare scream. "Let go of me or I'll call the police." She stared at his spiked dishwater-blond hair and mustache. What would he do next?

He clutched her arm and rasped in her ear. "I'm not letting you call that asshole detective." He turned her to face him and gazed into her eyes as if mesmerized. Except he was drumming his fingers on the wall. "That prick doesn't deserve you. He doesn't love you like I do and can't give you what I can. He hasn't longed to be with you every day all these years. He can't know how glad I am to find you home at last."

She tried to pull loose, but he was too strong. She dropped her purse and slapped his face. "Let go of me or I'll scratch your eyes out." She kicked toward his groin but couldn't connect. His growl frightened her. Had she gone too far?

He raised his hand to slap her, then let it fall. He turned her to face him. "Is that any way to treat me after that wonderful time we shared at your senior prom?" A lurid grin lightened his face. He took hold of her hands and clasped them to his chest. What was with this creep?

She tried to tug her hands loose, but he wouldn't let go. "What do you mean? I never went to a prom or anywhere with you." He was delusional.

He frowned. "You're lying. I remember every minute we were together, how you felt in my arms on the dance floor—how you nearly matched my outstanding talent as a dancer. We were such a charming couple. Everyone watched us.

"Shall we dance now?" He smiled, but it didn't reach his eyes. "I bet you have some music we can dance to."

She looked him in the eye. "What? I don't think so. Why should I dance with you?"

He ran his hand along her arm. "Because I want to. I won't hurt you. Don't scream. I just don't want anyone interrupting us. This will be our special time."

Her mouth was dry. It was all she could do to keep from shaking. Her heart beat so loud, she marveled that he didn't hear it. She couldn't let him see how scared she was. She'd thought she'd be safe with the new locks. Now she wished she'd asked Michael to stay tonight. "How did you get in this time?

He grinned. "I can pick any lock. I've got talents you haven't dreamed of."

"But the bolt? How did you get past that?"

"There's a slight space between the door and the door jamb. Took a little work, but I pulled it loose. I brought a pair of tweezers."

"You're too darn handy. Look, I need to go to the bathroom."

"Only if I go with you." He grinned. "I want to watch you pull down those lacy white bikini panties and see you plant your bare butt on the pot."

She scowled. She'd been revolted that he'd pawed through her underwear with his grimy hands. She wasn't about to let him see her bare bottom. She needed to get her phone in her purse. "I'd rather not. I mean, a girl needs her privacy, especially at this time of the month. Let me get a clean pad from my purse to take into the bathroom cause I'm having my period. You don't want to see all that blood, do you? I mean, it's nasty and smelly."

"I don't believe you. You and that damn cop were

doing it last week. I bet you're taking those pills that keep you from having periods. Damn it all to hell. You couldn't even wait until I had a chance to be with you. Well, I can have you under me now or any time I want you."

Jessica nearly gagged. "This isn't the stone age. You're supposed to ask a woman if she wants to be with you—and I'm not doing that with you."

"You were ready to do it that night after we danced and went swimming in our underwear. I wanted to tear off your strapless bra and suck your boobs, but you had to complain about being cold and start swimming back to shore."

"Omigosh." Jessica remembered Jen refusing to talk about that night. "You were the blind date for the senior prom."

He grinned. "That's right, Jennifer. Now do you remember me?" He grinned. Holding both her arms, he pulled her so close the mix of musky body odor and cigarette smoke nearly choked her.

"I'm not Jennifer, and I never went out with you." With all her strength she struggled to pull away from his iron grip but couldn't.

"You can't fool me. I watch your show every night it's on."

"I'm not Jennifer. I'm Jessica, her twin sister, and I don't have a TV show."

"You're lying. If you're her twin, why didn't I see you at the prom?"

"I was out of town for a debate. Our school was a finalist in the state competition. It's Jen you want. Now let me go."

"You're just trying to get rid of me. I'm not leaving

unless you can prove you're not Jennifer." He studied her. "And if you're not, you're almost as pretty, so maybe I'll fuck you instead. You should be so lucky. I get really big, and I can last. All the women I've been with say that.

A nervous laugh bubbled up inside. She clamped her lips together, afraid to let it out. She needed a thirty-second crash course in deviant psychology. She tried to yank her arms loose. "Let go of me."

"Why?"

"I need to get closer to the light to show you my mole. Jennifer doesn't have one."

"Where is it? On your breast I hope." He stared at her chest so hard she felt as if he were stripping her. She fought off the urge to cringe.

"It's on my face. I need to point to it."

"Where?"

"Let go of my arms."

"He released her left arm.

She pointed to the mole near her mouth. "Jen doesn't have a mole on her face. I do."

"You're lying, Jennifer. You could hide it with make-up. You're good with that."

"She is. I'm not."

"But I saw you Thursday night, talking about women and football. Think I saw a mole that night."

Uh oh, she'd have to explain. "Well-uh, that was me. No one but Jennifer and the news director knows that. I did the shoot because Jen couldn't make the game. But Jen will be in all the other shows you'll see. It was you who shot me at the game, wasn't it?"

Oops, shouldn't have said that. She held her breath. Tensed for his reaction.

What would he do next? Her pulse raced, and her heart beat like a metronome set for andante. She had to keep calm enough to figure a way out of this.

He glanced out the window and then back at her. "What makes you think it was me that shot you."

"I don't know anyone who'd want to shoot me. And if you thought I was Jennifer, well, you might have wanted to get her attention."

He shoved her down on the sofa. "Why the hell would I shoot someone I'm crazy about?"

"To get Jen's attention. Only you hit me, not Jennifer." She frowned. "It hurt—a lot. That's the worst way in the world to get anyone to notice you."

He pointed to her. "What if whoever shot you was aiming for that guy from the TV station, the one you were with?"

That would make some kind of crazy sense. She tried to pull loose again, but he didn't let go. "Then you did shoot me."

"I'm not admitting anything."

"Never mind that. I'm not Jen. I must have a picture of us together. If I show it to you, will you let me go?"

"Maybe. First, you have to find one."

She looked around. Where did she have a photo of the two of them? "Let go of me so I can look for one."

"Where are you going to look?"

"There might be one in my desk." Finding it hard to breathe with him so close, she turned her head toward it. Was there anything in her desk she could use as a weapon? Jab him in the eye with a pencil? As frightened as she was, she'd probably miss. And he was muscular enough to overpower her.

Since he wouldn't let go of her arm, she dragged him

toward her desk and pointed to a two-inch filigree frame. "There, see the two of us together?"

He grabbed it and squinted. "it's so tiny I can hardly tell."

"Look. You can tell there are two of us, and that we look alike."

He sighed. "Okay, I believe you. You do look alike." He stuffed the picture in his pocket.

If that were all he took, she wouldn't complain. "Now, let me go, please."

"Give me your cell phone?"

"It's in my purse, but the battery's dead." She grabbed her purse, stuck her hand inside, found her phone and pushed the speed dial for Michael.

He knocked the purse away. Her wallet slid across the floor. He grabbed the phone and wrenched it from her.

She winced but suppressed a groan. Showing weakness wasn't good.

He stomped on the phone and glared at her.

She drew in a deep breath. Would he let her go now? If only he would leave, she could call the cops from Lewis's place if he were home.

Her attacker snatched up her wallet.

"You can have the money. Just leave my pictures." She hoped he wouldn't take her credit cards. But hey, she was unhurt and maybe he'd go now.

He yanked out the cash, then pulled out a picture of Jen. After stuffing both in his pocket, he tossed her wallet down. "Now give me Jennifer's address. I have to find her."

"No."

He glared at her. "Give it to me or you'll be sorry."

Her heart pounded so hard she thought he might hear it. She hadn't seen a gun, but he could have one hidden. "I'm not giving you her address."

He wrapped his arm around her neck, held it in the crook of his arm and squeezed. Gasping, she grabbed his arm and pulled with all her might. She couldn't break his iron grip. Was he going to choke her because she wouldn't give him her sister's address? "Let go. I…I can't breathe."

He let up on the pressure on her neck—just a little. She gulped in air.

His voice was harsh. "If I let you go, I'm going to have to tie and gag you, so I can leave."

It was all she could do to keep from shaking. It wouldn't do to let him see how scared she was. "Please don't do that. I promise I won't scream." She hoped he believed her.

Still, he didn't let go. She took in air in short gasps—all she could manage. She raked her nails down his arms.

"Hey, stop that,"

She had to get him to let go or she'd die. "Not until you let me loose." She tried to jab him in the eye and missed.

The door burst open. Michael stood there with a fierce scowl on his face and a gun. "Let her go or I'll shoot."

Chapter Fifteen

Michael stood in the doorway of Jessie's apartment. Damn intruder had Jessie in a choke hold. The bastard spun her around. He'd crooked his arm around her neck. If he held that steady pressure on her neck much longer, she could pass out and die. Michael glared at the stalker. "Let go or I'll shoot." Except he couldn't. He might hit her.

She pulled at the guy's arm, trying to free herself. White-faced and gasping for breath, she looked as if she might collapse any second.

The stalker glared at Michael, his eyes radiating hate. "Go ahead. I'll make sure she gets the bullet instead of me." He seemed to revel in his power. The glee in his voice sent chills down Michael's spine. The scum would do it too.

Michael aimed but couldn't find a safe spot to shoot. What if she moved? He felt torn. He wanted to knock the bastard down and pound his head into the floor. His finger on the trigger, his feet braced, he waited, frustrated, and so scared he could hardly breathe.

Jessie's eyes drifted shut. She dropped her hands. Was she giving in? Not his Jessie. Why wasn't she fighting back?

Jessie slumped, and her attacker shoved her at him. As Michael ran to grab her, he stumbled over the coffee table. Her attacker ran past him. Michael laid her still form on the couch and ran to the door.

Her attacker was at the bottom of the steps. Michael got off one shot. The guy swore but kept running. Michael charged down the steps. The lobby door clanged shut behind the perp. By the time Michael yanked the door open, the guy had disappeared. Michael grabbed his phone and called headquarters. Taking the steps two at a time, he rushed back to Jessie.

Back in her apartment, he knelt beside her. She didn't move.

His heart jolted. She couldn't be dead. She'd become the sunshine in his life. Had the sorry SOB choked her to death under his very eyes?

How could he go on without her? Why hadn't he stopped the bastard before it was too late?

Panic stricken, he felt her neck. Couldn't feel a pulse. "You've killed her, you pervert." He pressed his ear to her chest. Felt the faint rise and fall. He let out the breath he'd been holding. "Thank you, Lord."

Her eyes fluttered open. "What happened? Where'd he go?"

"You fainted. He's gone, sweetheart. Damn, I should never have left you alone." He wanted to kick himself to the ends of the earth.

"But you got here in time to save me."

Michael swallowed. "I couldn't shoot. I was afraid I'd hit you."

He cradled her in his arms. Felt her tremble.

****

Jessica leaned against his welcome strength and let out a long sigh. She felt numb. She couldn't believe she'd almost been choked to death. Would he have really done it, or was he just trying to scare her? She couldn't stop shaking. Would he try again?

Gently Michael moved her hair aside and pressed a soft kiss on the side of her neck. "Hold on a minute. I have to report this." He yanked out his phone, called headquarters, described her attacker, then hung up. "I'm so sorry. I should have insisted on staying with you until we caught him."

She took in a quick breath. "Please stay with me every night until they catch him."

"Maybe we'll get a fingerprint match soon. I'll check on it."

"Wait a minute. Jen will know his name. She had a blind date with him once—to the senior prom. I'm sure she wouldn't forget him. That was the night she and Angela went skinny dipping."

"Skinny dipping on prom night?" He grinned.

"Well, it wasn't exactly skinny dipping. They had underwear on."

"Never mind that. Call Jennifer." He held out his phone. "Get his name."

****

Jessica dialed her sister. Relieved to hear her 'hello,' Jessica told her what had happened.

"Oh, Jessie, that's awful. Are you okay?"

Jessica took a deep breath, glad she finally could. "I am now. Just tell me the name of the guy you were with the night of the prom."

"I'll never forget that night or being grounded for a month afterward, but why do you want to know that creep's name?"

"That's who the stalker is. He broke into my apartment. Thank goodness, Michael got here and chased him away."

"Omigosh. I don't remember much about what he looks like, and he's older now. He may not look the same."

"Does he have spiky dirty blond hair?"

"He didn't that night. He had it greased and slicked back neatly. He was a creep, but I never thought he'd go this far."

"What's his name?" Jessica asked.

"Jamison or Jared something. I don't remember his last name."

"I called the police and will give them a description. They may not catch him right away, but there's something you should know."

"What?"

"I finally convinced him we were twins. It's not me he's after; it's you."

"Me?" Her gasp reverberated through the phone. It zinged on Jessica's ears like a plucked guitar wire and rasped on her heart until it quivered.

"Remember those notes you've been getting. He's obsessed with you, so please be careful. Don't go out to your car at night without an escort."

Jessica could imagine her sister's face, see the pinched ridge above her nose and the furrow above her brows. Jessica gripped the phone, pressing it against her ear. "I only hope the cops get him before he gets to you. Just be careful, especially leaving work, okay?"

"I will."

Her sister's determined tones should have reassured her, but Jessica couldn't help worrying. She handed the phone back to Michael.

He dialed headquarters and spoke with them about protection for Jennifer. "You mean all you can spare is a patrol officer to cruise by regularly?"

His forceful tones carried roughness, but the fingers of one hand clenched and unclenched. The scowl on his face showed his frustration.

At least she had Michael to stay with her, but she worried about Jen. "Michael, maybe you should stay with her. Jen's the one he's obsessed with." She didn't want to give Michael up, but Jen was in danger. She hoped he'd refuse. Did that make her a heartless sister?

He took her hand and kissed it. "If he's obsessed with her, he won't kill her, but you're the one I want to protect. I'm staying here." He put his arms around her and held her close.

She sighed in relief. "I'm glad."

He rubbed his forehead. "Do you suppose that director might stay with her to keep her safe? Aren't they hanging out together?"

"He probably wouldn't mind staying with her. For all I know, they're sleeping together."

A knock on the door startled her. "Who's there?"

"Police. We got a call about an intruder. Are you all right?"

She opened the door. "Yes, come in."

Two officers came in. One asked questions. The other dusted for fingerprints and lifted what he found onto white cards with clear tape. He also took hers and Michael's. By the time they left it was after midnight. Michael locked the door and slid the bolt. "I'll sleep on the couch."

Jessica shook her head. "Make love to me, please? I just want to forget what happened for a little while."

"You sure you aren't too upset and tired for—"

She smiled. "No way. Make me forget Jen's stalker.

I don't want to have nightmares."

Michael kissed her, a long lingering kiss. He grinned. "Twill be my pleasure." His warm fingers clasped hers as he led her to the bedroom. Once there, he unbuttoned her white silk blouse and pushed it from her shoulders. After unfastening her bra, he slid that off too. He looked long as if he enjoyed the view. Then he kissed her breasts all over, making her feel treasured.

She felt warm and adored, loving the feel of his lips on her skin, loving the way he caressed her shoulders, and loving the way he kissed her once more. He pushed her slacks off and squeezed her buttocks. As he pulled her close, she worked on his pants and undid his zipper. His black silk boxers were already tented with his arousal. She could hardly wait.

He slid off his knit shirt and stepped out of his pants. "Don't go away," he said as he shucked his shoes and socks.

She laughed. "As if I would."

Then he laid her on the bed, looking at her with such longing, she couldn't help smiling.

His hands on her breasts made them swell in response. He suckled first one and then the other, lighting a flame inside, heating her whole body. He sure knew how to pleasure her.

"Jessie, you are so sweet. I could stay like this with you forever." Then he laughed. "Well, until one of us gets hungry. Except all I want to do now is to love you, to comfort you, to satisfy you and—" His smile broadened. "Make you forget everything and everybody but me." He nuzzled her neck.

She ruffled his hair. His hands slid to her thighs, and his fingers teased her tender folds as he kissed his way up. Then his fingers worked magic between her legs until she was so aroused she could hardly stop writhing. The pleasure was intense. And he hadn't even entered her.

After a crinkle of foil, he did, filling her to perfection. His lips came down on hers, nibbling and tasting. He whispered, "You're beautiful. You're wonderful. You make me feel like a king, like I'm the luckiest man on earth just to be here with you."

She clung to him. Who could resist a man like Michael? His kisses covered her face. His hands caressed her breasts, and her heart beat in rhythm with his loving thrusts. Now she wished it could go on forever except as late as it was, he must be tired. He was so caring to do everything he could to make her forget the horror of what happened earlier.

She hugged him tighter and kissed him again and again. If only she could have him beside her always, she wouldn't care if he didn't follow any rules. Somehow, she'd learn to live with that.

He pushed harder and harder. She rose to meet his every thrust, thrilled to be his partner in this dance of love. With a sudden burst of pleasure, she rose with him to meet the stars and soar over the milky way. Holding him tight, she hurtled through space, leaving the earth behind. As they floated back to earth, she wished they could stay together always.

He kissed her gently. "Good night my love."

She snuggled in his arms and slept, warm, toasty, and safe as a kitten nestled against its mother's fur.

On Saturday, the day of the class picnic, Michael called at 1:00 o'clock. "Hey, I got the day off. I'll pick you up."

"So, your boss was understanding?"

"Not exactly. I told him I needed some down time, and I'd work an extra day next week to catch up. And besides I promised Scotty I'd help with the grilling."

After trying on several outfits, Jessica finally picked some pink shorts with a matching knit top. She snatched a sweater in case she got cold. Michael's whistle when she opened the door made her smile. She still wasn't sure how he felt about her. She'd wait for him to say anything about sharing a future. He pointed to her purse sitting on the couch. "You ready? Let's go."

Inside his blue pick-up, he pushed a button. Dolly Parton sang the song from "Nine to Five." Michael sighed. "Wish I only worked from nine to five. It often takes weird hours to find some of the perps I hunt down."

Jessica looked at him. "Michael, am I going to get you in trouble by coming to the picnic with you?"

"I doubt it, since I'm helping Scotty cook hot dogs."

"He's one of the teachers for the class. But doesn't the force have a rule about getting involved with people in cases you're investigating?"

"Yes, but they don't have the manpower to spare to protect you like I can. And if I want to do it—so what?"

"I'll save a seat at a table near the barbecue grill. Then it won't be so obvious that I'm with you."

"I won't avoid you if that's what you're expecting. I don't care what others think."

"Will your boss be here?"

"He usually doesn't come to these things."

After they got there, Michael helped Scotty, a lean, lanky cop, lay wieners on the grill and cook. As he rolled the hot dogs over, brown stripes appeared on their surface. Their aroma filled the air, and Jessica's mouth watered. A cool breeze caused goose bumps on her arm.

She put her sweater on.

Soon Michael filled paper plates for both of them and climbed onto the bench. He inched close until the heat of his body warmed her.

A cop from the K-9 division led his black Labrador through his paces, sniffing out hidden drugs. When he asked for a volunteer to hide. Jessica raised her hand.

The cop had the dog sniff her hand, then he blindfolded the dog, whose name was Inky. Following his directions, Jessica walked to the grill, then the table he pointed to.

There sat Detective Sergeant Black, wolfing down a hot dog in a bun oozing relish and mustard. He rubbed a paper napkin across his face and went on eating. Jessica hoped he wouldn't remember her from the one time he'd been introduced to the class.

But the detective sergeant spoke to her. "Good afternoon. Glad to see you're learning what the police department is all about. I hope this class makes our citizens more aware of all we do for them."

Jessica nodded. "I understand how the police work a lot better. I hope my boss at the newspaper will let me write some crime stories now. By the way, I'm supposed to hide under this table to see if the dog can find me."

He didn't move over but looked at her with a frown. That's all she needed, for him to dislike her. Probably that could make it bad for Michael if the detective sergeant realized how involved they were.

She squeezed under the table. Once the handler released him, the black Labrador retraced her steps, then paused beside the table and barked. The handler strode over, patted the dog, then threw a toy for it to fetch while Jessica crawled out from under the table.

Next Michael and Jessica teamed up for the three-legged race. Standing beside her at the starting line, he slid his left leg into a burlap sack, then held the bag open. "Put your leg next to mine."

She gripped the edge of the sack and lifted her foot. Sliding it inside, she caught her shoe on Michael's pocket and fell against him. Off balance, he tumbled to the ground bringing her body on top of his. His body was warm and hard, all the way down.

He looked sheepish as she rolled off him. He lifted her shoulders off the ground. "You don't want to get that nice shirt all dirty."

He was being thoughtful, but she suspected that wasn't the only reason he lifted her up. She'd felt the firmness of his arousal. Wow, had she caused that? Knowing she stirred him almost as much as he did her made her feel good.

She looked up. There stood Detective Sergeant Black. "That woman did a good job of taking you down, Michael. Better keep an eye on her."

Jessica felt the heat spreading from her chest to her face. Cop instructors and classmates crowded around. Everyone was looking at them. What must they be thinking? She turned away, knowing her face must be redder than her pink shirt.

She felt Michael's hand slide down her side and across her abdomen. What was he doing?

"We can't stand up unless I get our feet out of this bag."

"Uh, right." She leaned away to give him room. He pulled his leg out and stood. As she struggled to stand, he grabbed her wrist and yanked her up—right against his firm chest.

"Oops, I didn't mean to pull so hard."

She backed away, bringing the burlap sack with her. She felt her balance give way, but he grabbed her arms and held her upright.

He steadied her. "Now hold the bag up and let me get my leg back inside."

She held the bag with one hand and braced herself by holding onto his shoulder as he stepped in.

Finally, they were ready. "We'll start on your right and my left foot."

"Get ready, go," shouted the cop in charge of games.

Remembering Michael's instructions, Jessica stepped forward with her right foot. With every step, she felt his firm leg against hers. He gripped her waist tightly as they hobbled toward the finish line.

Barely beating another couple, they crossed it. Jessica felt him falling. His hand still gripped hers, pulling her off balance. She grabbed him to steady him, but the next thing she knew they'd fallen the other way, with him on top of her. Other couples hobbled past.

The instructor walked over to them. "I'll announce the winners as soon as they get untangled. It seems to be a habit with them." He grinned, and others laughed.

Michael quickly extricated himself from the bag and her. Jessica struggled to pull her leg out. He took her hand and pulled her up. "Just let the bag fall."

She did and stepped out of it. Again, heat rose to her face. She wanted to hide.

The instructor handed her a ceramic piggy bank. He gave Michael a pig tie tack. "Might as well live up to the name they give us," he said.

"Yeah, right," Michael said and shoved it into his pocket. "Come on Jessica, let's eat."

Later, as Jessica sat beside Michael licking an ice cream cone, heavy footsteps sounded behind her. She turned. Detective Sergeant Black's gaze went from Michael to her and back to Michael. "What are you doing here with her? You aren't supposed to socialize with persons on a case you are working on."

Jessica tried to stand up, but Michael grabbed her hand and pulled her back down. Jessica faced the chief. "He's been helping Scotty cook. He looked tired of standing so I offered him a seat."

Michael stared at the chief. "I was going to explain to her how things worked in our department. Is that a crime?"

The detective sergeant glared back. "No, but don't sit too close. That wouldn't look good. I suggest you keep a professional distance from now on. And I expect you back at the office as soon as this picnic is over." He turned and strode away.

Michael's lips clamped together. "I don't care what he thinks. My private life's none of his business. And if you hadn't needed police protection, this wouldn't have happened."

Jessica wanted to ask what he meant by "this," but was afraid of what he'd answer. As caring as Michael was, he might just be acting protectively because he worried about her safety.

Michael dropped her hand, grabbed his plate, and rose. Was he going back to help cook?

However, he filled his plate with another hot dog, potato chips and baked beans and squeezed back in beside her.

He polished it off, apparently not worried about the calories. How she wished she would see more of him soon, but she'd have to leave it up to Michael. She didn't want to be pushy.

If he were interested in anything more, he'd have to make the next move—but would he?

She looked up to meet his smile.

"I'm lousy at horseshoes, and I don't relish taking part in another three-legged race. Besides, I don't want to give my boss more to hassle me about. Let's take a walk in the woods. We might see some birds. Looks like the chief is going to make a speech. This would be a good time to sneak away. I've heard what he usually says a hundred times."

"Won't you get in trouble for not staying?"

"Not if he doesn't notice us leaving. Come on."

She followed him into the woods. It was quiet and peaceful there. A squirrel ran up a large oak tree. Further on a green lizard scurried across the path.

Rustling sounded. A crow shot up with wings flapping. Then the air was still again.

Michael looked around, then took her hand. "I want to tell you—"

A muffled shot rang out. Whistled past her head and Michael's.

He shoved her behind some bushes on the other side of the path. "Stay down."

Jessica crouched. Michael took out his gun. Looked around.

Her heart pounded. What if he got shot? "Don't just stand there. We should run."

"Shhh."

She listened. At first nothing moved. Then more rustling sounded.

Michael grabbed her hand. "Stay low." He pulled

her back to the path. "Now run back to the picnic."

She did. Her pulse raced. Her stomach lurched.

He ran too, his head moving from side to side, watching, looking. "I can't see anyone with a rifle."

"The picnic area–we're almost there." Almost breathless, she could hardly talk but kept running.

Another shot blasted by. So close it tore her sweater. "Damn," Michael said, "Another inch–it would have hit me in the chest."

Finally, they tumbled into the clearing. Everyone was cheering the contestants in another three-legged race. Michael urged her into a knot of people. "I'll tell the chief what happened so he can send out a search team to hunt the shooter. We can't have a mad man loose in the area."

"What if they don't catch him? Could be a kid just shooting in the air."

"It's not a kid, damn it. That last bullet barely missed. I think he was aiming for me."

Then his mouth dropped open. "You're bleeding. You were hit. Why didn't you tell me?"

"I thought it only tore my sweater. Must have hit my right shoulder, the one that was hit at the football game. It still hurts from the time I was shot."

He pulled her cardigan off. Pushed up the sleeve of her top. "He did hit you. The others can handle the manhunt. I'm not waiting for an ambulance. I'm rushing you to the emergency room."

"We don't need to hurry. It doesn't hurt more than a cut." But then it did. She felt weak and let him lead her to his pick-up truck. She leaned against it while he explained what happened to the chief. Then he helped her up onto the truck seat and drove like mad to the hospital.

Once there, Jessica waited in pain in the emergency room for half an hour before being examined. They took X-rays. After that, the doctor said, "Your shoulder was only grazed." After the nurse treated and bandaged her wound, it still hurt a lot. Could she have a bullet in her shoulder, hiding behind the bone, and the doctor had not realized it? She said something to the nurse about that, and the woman hurried after the doctor.

Chapter Sixteen

The doctor returned, inserted her X-ray in the display case and pointed. "Here's the dark spot from your earlier shooting, but there's no bullet hiding anywhere."

After the doctor left the examining room again, Jessica was reaching for her clothes when her parents burst in. She hadn't expected that.

"Jessica, darling, how are you feeling?" her mother asked. The worry in her eyes was plain. "I'd hug you, but I'm afraid I'd hurt you."

"I'll be okay, Mom. The bullet just grazed my shoulder. It hurts, but the doctor says I'll be right as rain in a few days."

Her father let out his breath. "Thank goodness for that. I was so worried after Michael called."

Her mother faced Michael. "I'm glad you were with her when it happened and brought her here. It means a lot to know someone is looking after my girl. If you two ever decide to get married, but even if you don't, you'll be welcome at our house for Sunday dinners."

Michael's grin told Jessica that meant something to him. Perhaps now he'd have another mother to give him some attention like he probably never got at home.

Her mother patted her hand. Her mother's suggestions about fixing herself up so she'd attract a man must be because her mother loved her and only wanted her to be happy with a partner, but that didn't mean Jessica had to cater to her every whim or feel guilty when she didn't.

"Look, Mom. You'll have to finish those Christmas cards yourself. I'm not feeling up to doing that for you."

"Okay, dear. I can manage that."

After they left, Michael said, "I like your folks. I can tell they care about you." He held out her sweater. "Let's go. I'll get your prescription for pain meds and take you home."

Her shoulder might have only been grazed by the bullet, but it still hurt. Michael insisted on staying with her that evening. He filled the tub. Steam rose. "Remember, the doctor said not to get the bandage wet."

Standing at the doorway, he grinned. "I'd love to share the bath with you, but you're in no condition for that. Call when you're done, and I'll rub you dry."

She smiled, remembering how they'd been in the tub together during the tornado warning. How he'd set her senses burning. Now she could only soak up the warmth and hope her shoulder felt better.

Having him tenderly pat her dry would only make her want to do more than she should, except he'd wouldn't try anything because of her shoulder.

"No thanks. I'll manage. Don't you need to get home and feed Dog?"

He nodded. "I just want to get you tucked into bed. Then I'll feed him and come back.

Feeling better after her bath, she dried herself, put on pajamas, and snuggled into bed.

He pressed a tender kiss on her forehead. "I'll sleep on the couch. Call if you need me."

She heard the door slam as he left, then drifted off

to sleep.

In the morning, she awoke to the smell of coffee brewing. Padding to the kitchen in her bathrobe, she heard a knock on the door. She glanced in the living room. No Michael.

He called from the front door. "Let me in. I have breakfast." After she unlocked the door, he strode in, carrying a sack. "I have bagels and cream cheese." In the kitchen he popped two halves in the toaster. "Sit down. I'll have these ready in a moment." He poured coffee, then spread the bagel halves with cream cheese, set them on a plate and placed it before her.

"You didn't have to do that."

He smiled. "But I wanted to." He fixed a bagel for himself and sat across from her. "Now you can spend the day in bed resting and tomorrow too."

She bit into the bagel, enjoying the crunch and the creamy spread. "I'm going to work on Monday. My shoulder doesn't hurt that bad. After the pain pill works, I'll be okay." She swallowed the pill, then sipped her coffee.

"You're crazy. Your boss won't hold it against you if you stay home a few days."

"You don't know my boss. She'll claim I'm not really interested in my work and not give me good assignments."

"Did you show her the clip from the station where you talked about women and football?"

She nodded. "Yes, for all the good it did me."

"What do you mean?"

"She holds TV news in contempt. She claimed printed news is more accurate and more in depth."

"So, the whole football assignment didn't do you

any good?"

"Afraid not. but she has given me a few better assignments. I guess she's more confident in my writing ability now."

"That's good, but you're not going into work Monday. You're staying here."

She glared at him. "If you're going to boss me around, you can just leave. I get enough of that at work."

"Should have known you wouldn't take orders from anyone except your boss. If you're bound and determined to work before you're healed, that's your problem, and you'll probably take longer to heal. Enjoy the bagels." He strode to the front door and shut it. The noise reverberated all the way to the kitchen.

She took another bite of the bagel. Had she been too abrupt with Michael? He'd done something nice, and she'd snapped at him. Except he shouldn't have tried to tell her what to do.

She slept most of the afternoon and by Monday afternoon she felt lots better so she drove to the newspaper office. Once there, she walked past her co-worker Debbie's desk and saw piles of paper. "Boss pile too much on your plate?"

Debbie looked up. "I heard you got shot. You okay now?"

"Yes, I'm fine now."

"I'm glad. My little girl is sick again. I can't stay late, and I don't know how I can get it all done before five o'clock, let alone do that interview in the warehouse district at five-thirty."

"What is it?"

"A new business. Miss Sharp asked me to write a profile on it."

"I can do that. Let me have it."

"Thanks a million. Here's the contact information." She handed Jessica a piece of paper.

Jessica took it. She'd thought she was the one assigned to profile new small businesses. Was she back to square one again? Well, she'd do a good job on this one and see what happened. She called to make an appointment and accessed her phone for directions. By 4:45 she was in her car and heading for the address.

****

The black Wrangler wove in and out of rush hour traffic. The driver kept a watchful eye on her Toyota, glad to see the Texas sun transform the dark shade into a bright blue sheen that would be easy to follow. Now that he knew there were two of them, he had plans for Jessica and Jennifer. Jessica's purposeful stride as she left the newspaper office on the way to her car said she might resist. But he knew how to make a woman knuckle under. Bet her fair skin would show bruises easily.

And Jennifer, once he had her in his arms, he'd show her how a real man treats a woman. He'd be better than that namby-pamby boss of hers. He'd awaken her passion, show her the two of them were meant to be. He could hardly wait to run his fingers over her soft skin and squeeze those luscious breasts. She'd be wet, ready, and willing by the time he spent a few minutes warming her up. Then he'd plunge into her. Imagining her moans and shrieks when she came—he had a hard on already. Almost missed seeing the blue Toyota exit the freeway.

Hanging back so Jessica wouldn't get suspicious, he followed half a block away. A squirrel ran into the street. He swerved to hit it and missed, damn it. The squirrel darted back where it came from.

He stepped on the gas. The blue Toyota was stopped at a red light. He pulled up behind her. Glancing through the back window, he could see her blonde hair lifting gently in the breeze from the open window. He couldn't wait to have Jennifer's long blonde hair spread out on a pillow as he lay on top. Maybe he'd do Jessica too, after he got her to call her sister. His hard on intensified.

He could tie them both up and bang them until he was satisfied. Except, he had a feeling that would take days. And after—well he couldn't just let them go. He'd have Jennifer and Jessica call their offices and say they were going on a cruise together. Some trip they'd won and had to take right away. They were good with words. They'd convince their bosses. And he'd have a good time with them.

Maybe he could rent a cabin in the woods and keep them there. He had a little money in the bank, and he could take out a loan from his credit union. Yeah, he could do that.

Jessica was pulling into the parking lot in front of a bunch of warehouses linked together in a long building. She parked at one end. He pulled into a space at the other end.

She got out of her car and strode up the steps leading to the one door with a street number. Good. She didn't even glance his way. Probably didn't even notice him. Well, she would before the day was over. He turned off his engine and waited.

****

Jessica rechecked the number on the door of the long warehouse building. The area looked clean. The white building was one of those hastily put up with concrete slabs. A pick-up had parked in front of the steps to the door and a black jeep was parked at the other end of the building. She looked at her watch. After five. No wonder the place seemed deserted. Hoping the business owner was still there, she knocked on the door.

Finally, a woman opened it and said her name was Lee Brandon. She claimed she was the temporary assistant to the boss, a man who'd started the business in his garage and then expanded. Of course, the man wasn't there. Trying hard to hear the woman over their noisy air conditioner, Jessica got a few facts and arranged to return the next day.

Dreading having to explain the delay to Debbie and maybe to Miss Sharp, she climbed behind the wheel, set down her tape recorder and made some notes.

A knock on the window startled her. A man stood there in a wrinkled sports coat hanging loosely on his lean frame. Slicked back dishwater blond hair hung down below his baseball cap. She couldn't see his eyes through his mirrored sunglasses.

She rolled the window down an inch.

"Please, ma'am, I'm lost. Would you be so kind as to give me directions?"

He looked like Jennifer's stalker, but it couldn't be. This man was too polite.

She reached for her phone. "What street are you looking for?"

She didn't recognize the name he gave her. She leaned over, got a flashlight from her glove compartment, and rolled the window down enough to show him on her phone where to go.

He reached in to unlock the door and jerked it open. He grabbed her arm and pulled.

"Let go of me," she shouted, hoping the woman

inside would hear or at least call for help. No one came. Damn that noisy air conditioner in her office. Or maybe Ms. Brandon had heard her and was calling the police. Jessica hoped so. She struggled, but man was too strong. Maybe she could talk him out of hurting her. She pushed her tape recorder on. "I'll give you money. Just leave me alone."

"I don't want money. I want you." Uh, oh. It was Jennifer's stalker.

"What do you want with me?" She wasn't sure she wanted to know, but maybe she could keep him talking and hope someone would stop by so she could scream.

"To call Jennifer so she'll come."

A lump grew in her throat. "Why would I do that?"

"To make her notice me. And to teach her a lesson. Like I told you before, we double dated with your other sister and her boyfriend. We danced together all night. Jennifer liked me then. Now I work in the same building, and she won't even speak to me except to say 'hello' and 'goodbye.'"

Then it dawned on her. He must be the security guard she'd seen at the desk in the building where the TV studio was. "It must get lonely working that desk. How about I suggest she bring you coffee and a sweet roll."

"Yeah, it does get lonely. But just saying 'hello'— that's not enough. I want to hang out with her. Now shut up. You're coming with me." He yanked her arm. She resisted, not sure how long she could keep him from pulling her out of the car.

"Maybe I can talk her into going on a date with you."

"No. If I can just get her to come to me, I can get my own date with her."

"What if I refuse?"

"I've got a gun. You don't want a bullet in your arm—"

She glanced at her shoulder. Just thinking about the pain sent a jolt down her spine. He wouldn't kill her, would he? She studied his face. His expression made her think he'd just as soon shoot her as not. Her pulse raced, and her heart beat frantically.

He pointed his gun at her chest, its black surface reflecting beams from a street lamp several yards away. Black—like the black coffin she'd be buried in if he shot her. She screamed, but no one came.

She turned her tape recorder off and pulled it into the seat beside her, then edged toward the door. Hesitantly, she stuck her legs out. Slowly, she stood, her legs now weak. She grabbed hold of the car door. She needed her legs to be steady to run. She drew a deep breath to gather energy, but he grabbed her arm and yanked her in the direction of his black jeep.

She dragged her feet, but he managed to pull her a few yards from her car. "Wait. I need to go back and shut my car door. The battery will run down and then the car won't start." If he let go for one second, she could run.

"No. You won't be using it for a while."

She gasped as a misty rain dampened her face, arms, and hair. He pulled on her right arm. That tore at her wound. It hurt. "Let go of my arm. My shoulder still hurts from being shot,"

He dragged her toward his truck. She screamed again. Still, no one came.

She tried to kick him and nearly fell. He stuck the gun in the waist of his jeans, wrenched her arm behind her back, and shoved her forward. Pain shot through her.

She turned to reach behind and hit him with her other arm. He stepped to one side, still twisting her right arm farther up behind her back.

He shoved her closer to the jeep, a black Wrangler, like the one he'd followed her in to her apartment. She screamed again. Again, no one came.

"Shut up, bitch." He clapped one hand over her mouth. She tried to bite him but couldn't get a grip.

He wrenched open the door. Pushed her toward the back seat.

As soon as he let go of her, she tried to back out, but he shoved her leg in and shut the door. An ominous click sounded. He must have pushed a button on his key fob to lock the back doors.

After running around the vehicle, he jumped in, slid behind the wheel and stepped on the gas. She reached over the back of the seat and tried to choke him. The jeep jerked to a stop. He climbed into the back and grabbed her hands. Held them in one huge hand.

Again, he twisted her sore arm behind her as far as it would go. The pain was excruciating. He let up for a moment.

She gasped in a breath. Then he grabbed her other hand and bound her wrists behind her with rope.

****

Michael could hardly wait until his shift was over. Soon as he got in his car, he dialed Jessica. He'd follow her home from her job. Last night they'd been together in bed, and it had been wonderful. He couldn't wait to do it all again.

She didn't answer. She probably kept her phone in her purse instead of her pocket. Maybe she was several steps away and didn't hear it. He'd try again in a couple of minutes.

At six o'clock he tried again. Still no answer. He had to leave a voice mail. Uneasy, he called the newspaper office. They said she was out on an assignment. That didn't tell him anything. He decided to drive there and find out from someone where she'd gone. She'd probably complain, but maybe she might be in trouble.

Inside the newspaper office, he stopped at the desk and found out she'd signed out at 4:45 to drive to interview someone at an address in Dallas. Surely, she'd be through by now. He wrote down the address, someplace near a warehouse area—not a good place to be when it was getting dark. Misty rain and clouds blackened the sky. He'd better drive by and see if she were still there.

The drizzle escalated into a pouring rain with a chill wind. He hoped she wasn't out in it. He hated rain. It reminded him of the night he saw his sister Sophia's body in the alley. Shivers ran down his spine. Mustn't think of that happening to Jessica. Mustn't expect the worst. He drove faster.

He reminded himself he was a cop. A cop who protected people.

He couldn't bear it if something bad happened to her. He hadn't wanted to let Jessica get under his skin, except he feared she already had. She just had to be okay.

It took him twenty agonizing minutes to find the address. Finally pulling into the parking lot in front of the warehouses and small offices, he saw only one car—hers.

It was empty. And the door on the driver's side hung open,

Chapter Seventeen

Jerking his car to a stop in the warehouse parking lot, Michael jumped out and rushed over. The car door was not shut, and the window was open in spite of the rain. The headlights beamed dully as if she had just run in to ask one more question and stayed a while. He pushed the car door shut and ran up three steps to the nearest door of the warehouse building.

No lights were on inside the office, but he pounded on the door. No one answered. He peered into the door's dark window. He put his ear to it. Listened. He shouted her name. Still, he heard nothing.

What if she'd been attacked and locked in the trunk? He clamped his lips together... squeezed his eyes shut...tried to hold back the feeling of dread. He ran back down the three steps and pounded on the back of the car.

He called her name. Heard only the hammering of raindrops on car and pavement. He let out a sigh of relief. She wasn't inside.

Unless she were dead.

He swallowed. He wouldn't go there.

His heart in his throat, he scanned the area. Looked for blood, a piece of cloth, some sign of a struggle. He found her purse and notebook on the passenger seat. She wouldn't just leave them there. The tip of her phone protruded from her purse. No wonder she hadn't answered.

Then he saw it—her tape recorder. Lying on the driver's seat. He snatched it up. The black surface, coated with rain, shone in the beam of a street light. He rewound it. Turned it to play. Heard her voice and someone else's.

Someone was threatening her. He froze. Sounds of a scuffle came next, but no gunshot, thank goodness. He backed the tape up farther, caught snatches of Jessica's words. Then he heard, "...bring me Jennifer." A man's voice—gravelly sounding.

"Why would I do that?"

"... make her notice me."

The man's voice sounded again. " ...double-dated with your other sister....danced...all night,...work in same building...won't speak to me."

"What's your name?" Jessica asked.

Michael listened carefully but couldn't make out much. He backed up the tape. Twice. Then he heard it. "Jared."

Hearing his voice, Michael realized where he'd seen Jared before. He was the security guard at the desk in the building where the TV studio was. But then the guy had his hair well combed and had a neat mustache. Michael called headquarters and told them he feared Jessica had been abducted by one of the security guards at the building where Jennifer worked. If only they could find her in time.

He called directory assistance and got the name and number of the head of building security, a Mr. Thompson. The man claimed they did background checks on all his staff. Michael described the man's gravelly voice, mentioned the name Jared, and that he might have kidnapped Jessica.

Mr. Thompson cleared his throat. "I'm afraid we do have a Jared Bolton. Doesn't talk much, kind of a loner, but I don't believe he'd actually kidnap someone."

"Do you know if he has a gun?"

"I needed a man who knew how to use one. He said he was in the military, and then he showed me his gun. It was so polished it looked brand new. He has a license to carry so he wears it here and probably when he moonlights as a security guard at some high school football stadium."

Jessica's stalker could be the man who shot her at the game, and he had her now. Fear clutched Michael and shook him all the way to his toes. "Just give me his phone number and address."

Thompson did, and Michael snapped his phone shut. He called headquarters, gave them what information he had and asked for back up.

"Just give me the address," the dispatcher said. I'll send the nearest officers. Don't go. Let them handle it."

"Hell, no. She's in danger. I'm heading there right now. Send whoever you have available."

"I repeat, you are not to—"

Michael hung up, his stomach in knots. If something happened to Jessica, he didn't know how he'd feel. He damn sure wouldn't wait for backup. He zoomed out of the parking lot.

Minutes later Michael pulled up in front of the address he'd been given. It was one of those loft apartments in the heart of town. How could Jared afford such a place? He must have another source of funds. No way a security guard could afford this.

He rushed inside. A man at the desk looked up. "Are you here to see someone?"

Michael showed his badge. "Police. I need to talk to one of your residents."

"Name, please."

"Jared Bolton. I believe he's holding someone hostage."

The starched-shirted man at the stylish walnut desk looked affronted. "Our residents may be eccentric, but they are very respectable. We do background checks, including their bank accounts. I don't think one of our residents would do that."

Michael glared at him, wishing he'd stop talking and just give him an apartment number and a key.

"He pays his rent on time and doesn't have loud parties," the man continued. "I don't think—"

"Okay, okay. A woman's in danger. Let me in his place."

"I can't do that. He's out."

"He may be holding a woman there against her will."

"I cannot leave the desk."

"Then give me the key."

The clerk frowned and shook his head. "I can't believe Mr. Bolton would do anything of the sort. Do you have a search warrant?"

"No, but I expect other police in uniform to arrive any moment."

At the sound of cars screeching to a stop, the man turned.

Officer Scott strode in and nodded to Michael. "Have you searched his apartment?"

Michael shook his head. "The gatekeeper wants to see a search warrant."

The man at the desk looked affronted. "I'm not a

gatekeeper. I'm here to protect our residents from unsolicited visitors."

Scott marched over to the desk, then edged closer until his spreading paunch hung over the desk. "What's your name?"

"Spencer, Bob Spencer."

Mr. Spencer, we have reason to believe a crime has been committed. And a woman is in danger. We need to check out the apartment to see if she's there."

Frowning, Spencer rose and pulled out a ring of keys. "Very well, I will unlock the door and show you there's no woman there, but you must assure me that you will not touch anything."

Scott said, "We only want to see if a woman's being held against her will."

Head high, Spencer led the way up a short flight of stairs to a landing. He knocked and called Jared's name. No one answered.

Michael's hands fisted in his pocket. Knots grew in his stomach. "Unlock the damn door. She may be tied up or unconscious."

Spencer tried several keys. Finally, on the third try, the door opened to a neat, sparsely furnished place.

Michael pushed past Spencer, past a brown leather couch and matching easy chair. In the bedroom brown drapes fluttered beside an open window. He looked out. Saw nothing but carports and garbage cans lined up in the alley. If she'd escaped, she was nowhere to be seen.

He hurried into the bathroom and yanked the shower curtain loose. The tub was empty. Where could she be? Then he saw them. Above the toilet eight pictures of Jennifer in different poses were taped to the white painted wall above the gray ceramic tile.

Michael studied the photos. It was Jennifer, not Jessica. He was sure. Just as he was sure that Jared Bolton had a twisted mind. No way would Jennifer be interested in him.

Michael beckoned to Spencer. "See, he has pictures of Jessica's twin. Jessica is the woman he's kidnapped.

The desk clerk ran his fingers through his hair. "I'd say he's a bit obsessed with the woman whoever she is."

He and Officer Scott followed Spencer back to the lobby, Officer Talbot was just walking in. He stared at Michael. "I'm here as back up. I take it she's not in his apartment. Any other ideas where she might be?"

Michael shook his head. He gritted his teeth. For all he knew, Jared could be torturing or killing Jessica right this minute. He turned to the desk clerk. "Thanks for helping."

Shoulders slumping, Michael trudged to his car, a sick feeling gnawing at his stomach. He called the TV station. Lawton Knight told him Jennifer had done her show and left. He told Lawton what had happened, and Lawton gave him Jennifer's cell phone number. Michael tried it. No answer.

Maybe the sick bastard had both of them. Visions of them tied up and being beaten tortured him. Michael pounded his fist against the dashboard. Until he found them, there wasn't a damn thing he could do about it. He called headquarters. No news. He hated being helpless. He prayed Jessica and Jennifer would be all right until he could find them, Scott and Talbot took off down the street, probably on other assignments. Damn, where the hell was Jessica?

****

Jared had driven around and made so many turns,

Jessica couldn't tell where they were. He stopped at a run-down motel, then got out and leaned into the back. He grabbed her and tied a gag around her mouth. Looking askance at the dirty rag, she struggled and tried to kick him but couldn't stop him.

The cloth, smelling of rancid grease, made her want to gag. She drew in air through her nose. Felt as if she couldn't get enough.

Jared slammed the door and walked to the motel office. Her wrists chafed and sore from trying to get loose, she tried to unlock the car door. With her hands tied behind her back, she couldn't get her fingers high enough to do any good. Minutes later, he returned. After driving around back of the motel, Jared grabbed Jessica's arm roughly and dragged her out of the jeep. Holding the gun against her neck, he nodded toward a door with cracked paint. "In there."

She screamed, but the gag muffled it. He slammed the gun against her temple. "Shut up."

The pain nearly blinded her. She cried out but couldn't make much of a sound. She could duck and run, but he might shoot. If he missed her the first time, the second or third shot wouldn't.

She swallowed. He might try using her to lure Jennifer here—and do who knew what to her. A sick feeling overwhelmed Jessica. She didn't want Jennifer to be caught and tortured, too.

He shoved her into a shabby motel room. Her shoe fell off. Her foot came down on a coarse, seasick green shag carpet. She turned and tried to pick it up.

"Never mind the shoe. You won't need it until you get Jennifer to come here. She gasped at the implication. He untied her gag and handed her a phone. Now call her and tell her to meet you here."

"No."

"You're going to stay tied up here until you do."

Jessica slumped down in a chair. "You'll have a long wait, because I'm not going to do it."

"Damn you, bitch. I'll make your life miserable until you do."

"Go ahead." She spat at him and grinned at the wet spot on his T-shirt. She probably shouldn't have done that. She stared at him, her racing pulse making her wrist vibrate on the chair arm.

He scowled. "You're worse than a whore."

What would he do next?" She was afraid to speculate. As weird as he was, no telling what he'd come up with.

"Bitch." He grabbed her and dragged her into a bathroom with peeling linoleum. He gripped her arm so tightly she felt it turning numb. He slammed her against the wall. The towel rack bit into her back, and the ceramic tiles chilled her back.

Colder than the wall, his malevolent gaze locked into hers, froze her for a long instant. What was going on in his sick mind?

Her heart pounded. Knots collided in her stomach. Would he shoot her now? Drag Jennifer here to see her battered bloodied body?

She wouldn't let him intimidate her. She glared at him. Somehow, she'd escape and warn Jennifer.

He let go of her arm. It still hurt. He walked out and slammed the bathroom door. It sounded like he was shoving furniture against the door.

Now she wished she'd done more weight lifting. She'd need all her strength now.

She waited until she heard his muffled footsteps and the outside door shutting.

Most bathroom doors opened in. She backed up against the door. Pulled at the knob. It opened, but a bureau blocked her way. She shoved at it, and a lamp teetered.

She backed away. The damn lamp fell on her bare foot. Owww. That hurt. She squealed and got a bigger mouthful of the gag. Her hands were still tied behind her, so she wriggled her foot to get the lamp off.

She had to climb over the bureau. It would be tough with her hands bound. The bureau was about four feet high, too high to hoist her rear up onto it. But she had to try. And she did. Three times without any luck.

Finally, on the fourth try she managed to slide enough of her body onto it to keep from falling off. She swung her legs up and inched across the top. Her muscles hurt from the effort. She wished she'd taken a pain pill earlier.

Now if she could only swing her legs over the edge. She got one leg over but found herself dangerously close to sliding off onto the floor. Lying down, she caught her breath and tried to steady herself.

She was swinging her other leg down into the bedroom when she heard a noise. Damn, was he back? Just in case someone else was there, she tried to scream. All she could do was squeal.

No one came.

Tired and discouraged, she slid down to the shag carpet and lay there. If she rested a while, and he stayed away for a few hours, maybe she could get free then.

Chapter Eighteen

Feeling stronger now, Jessica hobbled to the door. Backed up against it and unlocked it. Pulled it open. It stopped after a few inches. The chain held it firm. With her hands tied, it was too high to reach.

Then she heard something. Sounded like a cart rattling by with perhaps a maid. The maid chattered to someone else in Spanish. Jessica tried to scream, but all that came out was a squeal. They kept on talking. She squealed louder, trying to make it sound as if she were in pain.

The second woman laughed. Jessica caught the word for bed and was that 'cat'? No, it must be 'pussy.' Then she realized what they were thinking. She squealed again.

More laughter. The sound of the cart rolling away filtered through the walls. They were leaving. Damn. She slid to the floor and hurt her ankle. Damn it all anyhow. She needed to be able to run if she could ever get out of here.

Then she heard running feet.

The two maids came and stared at her. She tried to scream help, but all that came out was more squeals. The two women argued in Spanish. One spoke to her.

Jessica caught only "*la puerta.*" Didn't that mean door? Did they want her to open it? She shook her head. Then she turned around. Showed them her hands tied behind her. More talking in Spanish. Then they left. Had they even seen that her hands were tied? Weren't they going to help her?

****

Michael called Jennifer again. This time she answered.

Her voice shaky, she said, "Some guy named Jared called and said he has my sister. He won't let her go until I meet him somewhere."

"Don't go. It's a trap. Give me the address, and I'll go. I'll make him tell me where she is."

"He said he works in my building. He seems to think I've slighted him. I'll apologize, tell him I'm sorry I've been rude."

"That's what he said on Jessica's tape."

"She tape-recorded him? Where did you get a tape?"

"I found her purse and her tape recorder lying in her car. Look, I don't have time to go into particulars. Just give me the address."

Jennifer groaned. "You found her purse and tape recorder? That doesn't sound good. He must have dragged her away."

"Now, do you realize what type of guy you're dealing with."

"I hope he hasn't hurt her."

Michael's stomach twisted in knots. He knew what guys like Jared did to their victims if they didn't get their way. He didn't want to frighten Jennifer, not yet anyhow.

"Do you think he took her to his place?"

"I've already searched his apartment. She isn't there."

"If I meet him at the place where he said to go, maybe I can sweet talk him into letting her go."

"He's obsessed with you. I saw what he did to your picture in Jessica's apartment. And he has eight pictures of you taped above his toilet."

"Oh, no. That's scary."

"No way am I letting you go there alone. He's probably stashed Jessica somewhere nearby. Tell me where he wants to meet you."

She gave him the address.

He checked it on his phone. "Thank the lord it's a coffee shop. Park about a block away. Tell me what kind of car you have, so I can find you. You'll be safe inside the restaurant, but you have to get him to tell you where your sister is."

"I'm driving a 2023 Camaro. I'll meet you there."

"Whatever you do, don't go inside before I get there."

"Okay." She sounded anxious but determined.

Michael slid his phone inside his pocket. Damn. It would take him at least twenty minutes to get there. That weighed heavy on his heart, but he couldn't hand this over to another cop. He just had to make sure neither twin got hurt. Especially Jessica.

Except it wouldn't hurt to have help. Stopped at a red light, he called Talbot and explained.

"Can't help you," Talbot said. "I've been called to investigate a domestic assault. The wife sounded terrified on her 9-1-1 call. They relayed it to me on my car computer. I'm almost there. Besides, you may be going on another wild goose chase. Whatever you do, watch your back."

The traffic crawled. Michael tried Scotty but couldn't get through. Michael was on his own. He turned on his siren and sped up. Traffic seemed to melt away and let him through.

Getting closer, he strained to see numbers on businesses. The place was sandwiched between a bowling alley and a tobacco shop. Several letters on the neon sign were not lit up. Now it said, "CO EE HOP. A blonde in a tight miniskirt and skinny high heels climbed out of a red Camaro parked in front of a small church. He jerked to a stop beside her. "You couldn't have picked a more obvious and isolated place to park."

He looked around. "Jared could be hiding in those overgrown bushes waiting to nab you. Just how far can you run in those shoes?"

Jennifer stood, legs apart and glared at him. "As far as I need to. I've been here for ten minutes. I hope that man is still waiting."

He stepped out of his car. "Better let me handle this."

She took a step toward the street. "I'm going inside. I'm not letting any man mess with my sister."

He grasped her wrist—slender like Jessica's. Her fragility struck him. "Look, you can't just burst in there. We need a plan."

"What's to plan? I'll ask him where my sister is and what he wants. Then you can send the police there to rescue her."

Maybe she wasn't as flighty as he'd thought. "Well, that's the general idea, but what makes you think this Jared will tell you where she is?"

"Can't we promise whatever he wants and then go free her?"

"This guy may not be so easy to fool. I've dealt with some clever types." He looked Jennifer in the eye. "He wants you, not Jessica."

Her eyes opened wide. "Me? Why me?"

"After listening to Jessica's tape, I believe he's obsessed with you. He works at the front desk in your building and claims you never even notice him."

Jennifer frowned. "That guy? He's a nerd. What's he expect? For me to ask him for a date? No way. But I do nod to him sometimes. I've said, 'Hello' to him once or twice."

"Did Jessica tell you about the knife stuck in your picture at her place?"

Jennifer's eyes opened wide. "Yes, but I try not to think about that. If he's the one who did that, it looks like I was right to ignore him." She straightened her shoulders. "But if he's got Jessica, I'll talk to him. We've got to get her away from him."

"Okay, now here's what you need to do."

She fastened her green eyes on his face, looking intent and vulnerable. "I'm listening."

"Play up to him. Treat him like a boyfriend and flirt a little. Make him think you'll go with him to wherever your sister is, but insist you'll go in your car. Ask him for directions. Tell him you'll follow him, but you might get separated. Get the address. I don't have a uniform on so he won't realize I'm a cop. I'll enter the café after you and ask to be seated nearby. Be sure you repeat the address loudly enough for me to hear."

With shaking hands, she reached up to push a dangling curl behind her shoulder. Then she smiled. "I can do that. What else?"

"Ask what kind of car he's driving. Offer to follow him. Whatever you do, don't get in his car. Walk out to your car normally and follow him. I'll tail the both of you."

Michael watched her walk across the street, graceful despite those impossibly high heels. He moved his car to a side door of the church and hoped Jared would think it was a workman's car. Ducking down, he waited until she went inside. Then he strolled into the coffee shop.

A sign beside the cash register said, "Seat yourself," so he slid into a booth across from the table where Jennifer and Jared sat. He snatched a menu from the waitress and told her he needed time to think.

Peering over the edge of the menu, he noted Jennifer was leaning toward the guy and smiling. She even patted his hand. She was a good actress.

Jared leaned back. "I'm not telling you where your sister is, but I'll take you to her."

"I'm not getting—I don't want to leave my car here. Someone might steal it. I can follow you there."

"No way. I don't want you calling the police."

She shook her head. "I promise I won't do that."

"I can't be sure. Give me your phone."

"What if we get separated? I need to be able to call you."

"Just give me your phone and stay right behind me. I'll return it after I take you to Jessica at the motel where she is."

Michael watched her hand him the phone. Damn. She needed to keep it, but he couldn't interfere.

Jennifer leaned forward and placed her hand on his arm. "Can't you be a dear and tell me the name of the motel so I can watch for it?" she pleaded in honeyed tones.

"Hell, I don't remember exactly. Easy Resting Place or something like that. Do you know where it is?"

She shook her head.

A waitress handed Michael a menu as she passed by his booth. Noticing Jared laying a bill on the table, Michael hoped he could get to his car before the perp noticed where he was going. He handed it back and pointed to his phone. "I've got to leave."

Outside the restaurant, he ran across the street to the house next door to the church. Damn, that hedge along the side of the yard had no break in it, even at the back of the yard. And it had thorns. Finally, he found a place where it wasn't so thick. Squeezing through, he pricked his leg and scratched his arm.

Seeing Jared and Jennifer walking into the parking lot, he walked over to the nearest building and hid behind the drainpipe running down the side of the building, hoping Jared wouldn't notice the thin row of red and blue lights on the roof of his car.

As he held it, the pipe from the roof's gutter pulled away from the wall. He'd have to come back and fix it later. He watched as Jennifer got into her car and Jared slid in beside her.

Damn. He thought she was going to follow him, not let him ride with her. An uneasy feeling inside made it hard to wait until she pulled out of the parking lot.

As soon as she pulled into traffic, he jumped into his squad car and pulled to the edge of the driveway of the parking lot. He wanted to arrest the guy right now. For all he knew Jared might be holding a gun on her. But if he wanted to find Jessica, he had to tail them without being noticed.

He let a couple of cars get between her red Camaro and his car. He pulled out into a line of cars. His stomach knotted, and his hands sweated, dampening the wheel.

In and out of traffic Jennifer wove. They slowed at

an intersection with a traffic light. Jared pointed, and Jennifer turned left. The light was yellow. Michael followed, keeping a little distance behind. The light turned red. He turned. An eager beaver at the intersection slammed on the brakes. Michael swerved and barely missed being hit.

Now Jared was pointing back at him. Michael pulled into a driveway and stopped. He called headquarters and asked for back up. No one was available. Damn. "Well, if you can't find anyone, at least get me the address of any motel that sounds like Easy Resting Place.

"Give me a moment. I'll get back to you."

He backed out into the street again. Maybe Jared wouldn't notice him this time. Driving down the way he'd seen them go, he looked in vain for Jennifer's red Camaro. At every side street he paused and looked both directions. Nothing. How could they have disappeared in such a short time?

His radio phone beeped. "Steel here."

"The nearest motel with a name like you mentioned is on Highway 360 near Sublett Road."

"Thanks. If anyone's free send him there." He turned on his colored lights and siren and headed to the freeway. On the highway he thought it best not to call attention to his car and switched off the siren and colored lights. His gaze roved from side to side looking for the motel. Finally, he saw it on the other side of the freeway. Damn, he'd have to exit and make a U-turn. Seeing the red Camaro ahead, he slowed and let another car come between them.

****

Peering through the crack in the motel room door, Jessica heard footsteps. Sure and steady, they sounded

233

like a man's. Was Jared coming back? Could she slide her hands down behind her back and get them in front of her? She tried and got stuck at her hips. Shouldn't have put on those last five pounds. But at least, she'd gotten the gag partially loose.

The footsteps came closer. Her heart beat faster. A lean man with dark hair passed the door. It wasn't Jared, but he didn't look her way. She squealed and pounded her head against the door jamb. The footsteps stopped. The man came back.

"What's wrong?"

"I'm being held hostage." She turned so her tied wrists were visible to him.

"Oh. Who did this to you?"

She cleared her throat. "Help me."

"Is someone behind you with a gun?"

"No. He's gone. But my hands are tied. I can't open the door."

"Maybe I should go get the manager."

"But the man who tied me up might come back any minute."

"Turn around. I've got a pocket knife." He sawed at the ropes binding her wrists. It seemed to take forever, but he finally got her hands free. She snatched the gag off.

"What the hell are you doing?" shouted Jared as he ran to the door. "Don't let her loose. She's crazy. She might scratch your eyes out. I tied her up to protect others."

"That's a bunch of bull," Jessica said and stepped outside. "You tied me up so you could lure my sister here. She turned her head and saw Jennifer in her red car, with her hands tied. She was gagged like Jessica had been a few minutes ago.

Jared glared at the other man. "Get the hell away from her. This is none of your business."

"The man pulled out his cell phone. "I'm calling the police."

"The hell you will." Jared snatched the phone, threw it on the sidewalk and stomped on it.

Jessica tried to push past him. He grabbed her arm. His meaty hands squeezed so tight it hurt. The next thing she knew a gun was pressed to her temple.

She gasped.

She stopped struggling.

Damn, why hadn't she signed up for karate lessons?

Chapter Nineteen

The hard metal gun barrel pressed against Jessica's temples. Slowly, she turned. Expected to be blasted any moment. "Jared, you'd better let me go. That guy will call the police."

The man in question was edging away. Damn. He probably thought them both crazy. Would he go call the police or just leave? Jared pointed the gun at the other man. "You'd better leave or I'll shoot." The man ran toward the motel office. Jared kept the gun against her forehead.

Time to try a different tack. "Jared, you've got Jennifer there in the car. She's the one you want. Why don't you let me go?" She held her breath, hoping he wanted her sister alive, not dead. Maybe he wouldn't hurt her—at least not until help came.

He glanced at Jennifer, then back at her. Maybe if Jessica could distract him, Jennifer could get loose and go for help. Jessica put a hand on Jared's arm. "Maybe if you talk nice to her, she might be more interested in you—you know, go on more dates with you. She might even get you on her TV program."

He glared at her. "She never has men on her show." He scowled. "She's given me heartaches. Well, now I'll give her one too."

Jessica watched his intent look. Held her breath. What was he thinking?

His eyes grew cold, his expression grim. "I'm going to kill you…and let her watch."

Jessica gulped. Her heart pounded furiously. Her pulse raced. Visions of herself lying bleeding on the pavement, gasping out her last breaths. Jennifer standing over her body.

She couldn't die now—not with her ambitions and dreams stopped in midstream. She hadn't done anything worth putting in her epitaph. All they'd say at her funeral was that she was a reporter—and dead.

She couldn't die now—not now she'd found Michael. Not now that she loved him. What a time to realize that—when she was about to die.

She'd thought Jared was crazy, but she hadn't realized how Machiavellian he was. Never in her wildest imagination had she thought he'd go this far.

She couldn't stop trembling. "You can't shoot me." she insisted, her heart in her throat. "Not out here in plain view of everyone."

Her tormenter frowned. "What do you take me for? An idiot?" He grabbed her arms and pulled. He was going to drag her inside. She couldn't let him.

She planted her feet firmly on the ground. As long as she stayed outside, he wouldn't dare shoot. Her brain whirled, racing to find a plan, any plan to stop him. What could she do now?

****

Ten feet away in the Camaro, Jennifer stuck one bound foot out of the car. A lump the size of Mount Everest lodged in Jennifer's throat. She couldn't let him shoot Jessie. She'd take a bullet herself before she let him kill her sister. Where was Michael? He was supposed to follow her, but there was no sign of him. She had to get away and get help.

Maybe if she moved over to the other side of the car, she could get out easier. With this door open, he could shoot her, then kill Jessie too. She couldn't shut the door without making a noise. But she could pull it to. She squirmed on the seat. Hard to do with her hands and feet tied. She turned her back to the door. Then edged her bottom to the end of the seat.

Hands behind her, she reached for the handle. And missed. Reached again and slid onto the floor. Damn. Feet in the air, she groped behind her. Her arm ached. If she could just stretch a bit further, she could reach it. She tried again. Stretched 'till her wrist got chafed by the rope.

Tried again. Couldn't quite reach it. She couldn't give up. Any moment he might shoot Jessie. Jennifer took a deep breath. Raised up and stretched until her arm felt like it would be wrenched from its socket. She managed to wrap two fingers around the handle. Tugged the door toward her with two fingers.

She'd almost closed it when something stopped it. She frowned. What was holding it back? Then it dawned on her. It was her own body. Curling into a circle, she scooted away. Barely held onto the handle. By now, even with the window open, her hands were sweaty and slippery. The door handle slipped from her grasp.

She backed closer. Finally got a good grip and pulled until she got the door closed. She hoped the faint click didn't alert Jared to her actions. Rising to look out, she saw Jared aiming a gun her way. She ducked and fell with her legs stuck up in the air.

Jared shot right through the open window. "Stay put or I'll shoot your sister, Jennifer. I'll deal with you later."

The bullet passed right over her head. It zapped the heel of her dangling shoe. Jolted her foot. Damn, the bastard ruined her favorite pair of Jimmy Choos. She wanted to give him a piece of her mind.

Couldn't think about that now. She had to get out. Had to get help. She'd find someone braver than that passerby who tried to free Jessie. Damn coward had disappeared when Jared brandished a gun.

Where was Michael? Why hadn't he come and brought more police? They needed someone here now. Jared was crazy. She couldn't even guess what he'd do next. She held her breath. If she screamed, he might shoot again. Keeping her head low, she crawled between the seat backs and scraped her cheek on the gear shit hump. Her hands were still tied. Would she be able to run when she got out? She shook off her remaining high heel.

Now on her knees, she had to get one hand on the driver's side door handle. Finally, she grabbed it and shoved the door open. She squirmed around and shoved her feet down. She stood, then hobbled away from the car. She crouched beside her Camaro. Careful to keep her head down, she looked around. No cover anywhere. Nowhere to run.

Instead, she screamed as best she could with the gag in her mouth.

A car screeched around the corner. Gun drawn, Michael jumped out but stood beside his car. "Police," he shouted. "Put down your gun."

Jared stood with a gun to her sister's head. Michael strode between the cars and faced Jared. "Put your gun down."

Jared shook his head. "Put yours down, or I'll shoot

you."

Michael kept his gun aimed at Jared. "You don't want to do that. In Texas you'll get the death penalty for killing a cop."

Jared inched toward the motel room door, still holding a gun to Jessica's temple. He jerked her against him and backed into the doorway.

Seconds later, he slammed the door.

Jennifer gasped. "You let him pull her inside." She glared at him. "Now what are you going to do?"

"Hope for back up. Then we can surround the place."

She frowned. "You mean you're just going to stand there and wait? What if he shoots her in there?"

"It's you he wants. Can you talk to him?"

"I could if I wasn't tied up."

"Oh. Come here."

She hopped toward him. He pulled out a pocket knife. "Stick out your hands."

She did. He sawed through them. Rubbing her wrists, she let out a breath. "What about my feet?"

"Turn around."

He soon had her feet free. "Now, see if you can persuade him to trade your sister for you. He'll have to open the door. Then I'll grab him or shoot him if I have to."

"I don't want him to hurt her." She didn't want to think about what he'd do to Jessie. She swallowed. "I'm not sure I can persuade him to open the door."

Michael met her gaze. "You're the best hope for avoiding bloodshed. Now stand over here away from the door and the window. He might try to shoot through one or the other.

Jennifer took a deep breath. If she failed, life would never be the same without Jessie.

Chapter Twenty

Jennifer inched toward the motel wall, careful not to stand in front of the door or the window. So much was riding on what she said next.

Why, oh why, hadn't she been more friendly to Jared? Should she lie and pretend to like him now? Would he see through that? She faced Michael, and whispered, "How should I play this?"

He shrugged. "You're the one he's obsessed with. Flirt with him."

Jennifer swallowed. "That won't be enough," she whispered. "He wants me to fall for him."

Michael whispered back. "Didn't you ever take acting?"

"Yes, but we never did anything like this." She twisted her fingers together.

A knock on the window startled her. Jared peered through a crack in the door. "Well, aren't you going to beg for Jessica's life? Don't you love your sister?"

Jennifer moved closer to the window. "Of course, I do. Please don't shoot her."

"That's more like it. Now what can you do to make me change my mind?"

"I'll-I'll go out with you. To a movie or dinner. I'll even pay for it."

"Not good enough. You let me kiss you good-night on that last date we had. But you were kind of lukewarm. I want you to kiss me like you mean it."

"Our last date?"

"The senior prom. Don't you remember how wonderful that night was? I never wanted it to end."

She swallowed. She'd wanted to wipe that night from her memory. It was a wonder she hadn't recognized the new clerk when she passed the security desk at the building where she worked. He was older now, more muscular, and had grown a mustache. "I remember now." She recalled it being wild and crazy—and wishing she'd never gone to the lake with him. After her mother had shamed her so, she didn't even want to think of that time.

Jared's eyes darkened, his expression dreamy. She swallowed and took a deep breath. "If I give you some really great kisses, will you let Jessie go?"

"Maybe. What I really want is some hot sex like you give your boyfriend at the TV station."

"You mean Lawton, the news director?" She didn't want Lawton being a target. "We don't have sex."

She hoped Jared would buy that. She wanted to be an actress. She'd have to convince him. "Lawton's just a guy I go out with once in a while. He likes to go places with an attractive woman on his arm. Makes him feel important. And he's my boss, so I have to keep him happy." Even as she said it, she realized her relationship with Lawton was lukewarm. She should let him find a new girlfriend. But she wasn't going to tell Jared that.

"He's not man enough for you. I'll show you what a real man's like."

"Man, I can't wait to hold your boobs in my hands." His gaze seemed glued to her chest.

She trembled. She wanted to slap his face.

"Bet you wear a double D bra."

"Actually, I don't, but my bra size is none of your business."

Michael shook his head as if warning her not to anger Jared.

"You sure look that big in those sweaters you wear. Baby, we could have some really hot sex."

Jennifer cringed. Just thinking about him touching her brought bile to her throat. Except she had to play along to get him to release Jessie. "We could go to the lake and—" She lingered over the words and smiled. "If you'd just let Jessie come out."

"I'm not doing anything with that cop standing there. He'll have to go."

Jennifer gulped. She didn't want Michael leaving her alone. "What should I say?" she whispered to Michael.

"I'll get out of sight. I can hide nearby," he whispered back.

"I'll tell him to walk away."

"Not good enough. I want to see that fucking pig drive out of sight. Don't want to see his damn car anywhere near."

Jennifer looked at Michael. "What now?"

"Tell him 'okay.' "

She stepped closer to the window. "Jared, he says he'll leave."

"I'm waiting."

"Michael, please go."

"You called him by his first name. Do you sleep with him too? That's pathetic."

"No, he's just a cop I met after you broke into Jessie's apartment and stuck a knife in my picture. That wasn't very nice."

"Well, I was mad at you. Here I am wanting you, and you don't even act like you want me. That's not nice either."

"I can do better. Michael's leaving now."

"He'd better because I feel like shooting him." He waved a gun.

He could shoot Jessie. Her heart pounded, sounding like a kettle drum.

Michael slid behind the wheel and gunned the motor. He pulled down the street out of sight of the window. Jennifer stepped back. She was alone here. Even though Michael wasn't far, shivers ran down her spine. What if Jared tried to hurt Jessie now?

"Jared, open the door and look. See. Michael's left."

He opened the door a crack and peered out. "Good. That bastard needs to be gone. Now, maybe you'll be reasonable."

Jared's idea of reasonable was to give in to his demands. She took a deep breath. "Jared, please, let Jessie go. I promise I'll be nice to you, even go out with you, and kiss you like I mean it." She held her breath, hoping he'd believe her lies.

"And sex too? I want lots of sex. Maybe a marathon worth of sex."

She shut her eyes. "You can't compare sex with a marathon. That's twenty-six miles. Last I heard, the Boston record was two hours and three minutes."

Jared laughed. "I can last longer than that in bed—well maybe ten minutes in between to get another hard on. Hell, I want more than two measly hours with you."

Trying to keep her revulsion from showing on her face, she said, "I guess I could manage that. Except that might make me a little sore."

"Nah, it wouldn't. I'm a great lover. You'd be so excited you'd beg for more. And I can give it to you. But you might be exhausted by the time I finish."

"Let me in, and we can get started. Except, you'll have to let Jessie go. We don't want her watching. This is between you and me."

"Don't you want her to be green with envy, to know what she's missing? Hell, I might even nail her too. If she's half as good as you, that wouldn't be bad."

Jennifer gulped but tried not to let her revulsion show. "I don't think she'd go for it. She has her own ideas about who she wants in her bed. Just because we're twins doesn't mean we think alike or go for the same guy. Leave her alone. This is between you and me."

"Keep talking," whispered Michael off to the side.

Jennifer kept her eyes straight ahead. Breathed in the scent of honeysuckle, so sweet and harmless as opposed to the evil lurking inside. She should be smelling sulfur and brimstone.

"So, are you going to open the door and let me in? I kiss pretty damn good."

"Stand beside the door."

Her heart in her throat, she moved closer to the door. Out of the corner of her eye, she could see Michael behind the honeysuckle bush. If Jared let Jessie go, Michael could grab Jared, and this would be over. But if Jared didn't release her, he might shoot Jessie or Michael.

Jennifer took a deep breath. No one else seemed to be coming. And heaven knew what he'd do to Jessie. She'd have to chance it. "Okay, open the door. I'm coming in. You'll get that kiss I promised. And more."

Jared opened the door a crack. "You can come in, but I'm not letting your sister out until after you kiss me. And it better be terrific."

Jennifer bit her lip and glanced at Michael. He shook his head. "No, you have to let my sister come out before I'll come in and kiss you."

"No deal." He slammed the door shut.

Michael shook a finger at her. "Don't go in, whatever you do." He held a finger to his lips, then whispered. "I'm going to get a key." He strode toward the motel office.

Minutes later, Michael returned with the manager. His gun ready, Michael planted his feet in front of the door. "Police. Open the door and come out, or I'll shoot."

"No. If you come in, I'll shoot Jessica."

"If you do, I'll either kill you or take you to jail. Want to spend the rest of your life in prison?"

"I won't have to if I kill you. Cops are bastards. One less will be a good thing."

"I've got the manager here. He can unlock the door. You'd better come out peaceably with your hands up."

"No way, man."

****

Michael was sweating now. Where was the backup he'd called for? He wasn't supposed to be handling this alone, but he couldn't wait for backup. His heart beat furiously. Just the thought of Jessica being shot brought a bleak picture of life ahead. He didn't want to face a life without her.

He swallowed. Couldn't think about that. He had to save Jessie. Had to do whatever worked. Except with crazy fools like Jared, who knew what would work? "You can't win, Jared. Come outside. Maybe we can cut a deal." Michael gripped his Glock 19, his hands sweating.

"What sort of deal?"

What could he say? It had to sound realistic or Jared wouldn't buy it. "Maybe I could get you probation." He wasn't lying exactly. Except there was no way in hell he'd recommend that.

"Why would I want friggin' probation?"

"It beats going to jail."

"But I haven't done anything."

"You call kidnapping and attempted murder not doing anything?"

"Suppose she's here of her own free will."

"I know damn well she isn't. I heard what you and Jessica said before you dragged her away. It was on her tape recorder."

"Shit. What did you hear?"

"I heard plenty. Along with what you've said here in front of witnesses, it's enough to make a kidnapping charge stick."

"Hell, I can get a lawyer to have that tape thrown out of court."

Michael glanced through the window. Jessica was edging near the wall, away from the door. "I'm giving you one more chance to open the door and let Jessie go."

"I'm not surrendering to a fuckin' pig."

Michael pointed toward the keyhole and spoke in a low voice to the manager. "Unlock it, then step away. If you hear shots, call an ambulance."

The manager did. Michael, his gun ready, grabbed the doorknob and pushed. The door only opened an inch or two. Damn, the bastard had the chain on.

Michael kicked the door. It didn't budge.

"You come in, and I'll shoot you."

Jennifer stepped closer, touched his arm. "You could get killed. Aren't you going to wait for back up?"

Michael shook his head. He slammed his body against the door. His shoulder hurt but the door gave way. The splintering sound was followed by a shot.

Oh, God. It couldn't be Jessica. He'd kill the bastard.

Michael's gut tightened. He surged around the door. Fired at Jared.

Jared stumbled but got off a shot.

Michael felt the jolt and shot again. Intense pain crumpled him to the floor.

"Michael, you're hurt." Jessica's voice sounded far away.

Her soft hand grasped his shoulder. "You can't die now." She sounded desperate.

The last thing he saw was the shine of tears in her eyes.

Then he blacked out.

****

Jessica glanced at Jared. He lay curled up on the floor clutching his chest. His gun lay beside his hand.

Jessica snatched it. Pointed it at him. "If he dies, you'll get the needle. Killing a cop gets you the death penalty."

Jared scowled at her. He raised his head, then let it fall back down. He lay there without moving.

She held the gun in one hand, out of Jared's reach. After making sure Michael's gun was also out of Jared's reach, she patted Michael's shoulder. "Michael, you've got to wake up." She bit her lip, afraid to think what her life would be like if he were gone. She squeezed her eyes to keep tears at bay.

She looked up. Jennifer peered through the crack in the doorway. "Quick, Jenny, call 9-1-1. Michael's hurt, and I don't have my phone with me."

"Michael already did," her sister answered. "I think I hear the sirens now."

Jessica listened. Sirens were sounding, but they were faint. Were they even coming here? "Call again. Tell them we need an ambulance."

"I can't. Jared took my phone. Are you hurt?"

"No, but I'm worried about Michael. He's unconscious." She leaned close and checked his neck for a pulse. She couldn't feel one. Oh, lord, what could she do now?

She shut her eyes. "Please, God, don't let him die."

Should she try CPR? She leaned over his face. A slight puff of cool air fanned her cheek. She let out her breath. "Thank you, God," she murmured.

She needed to check for injuries. He must be bleeding somewhere. She hadn't even looked. She patted his clothes. No wet spots.

Maybe his back was bleeding. She dared not turn him over. She ran her hand along his side. There, just below his waist, she felt something wet and sticky. She pulled her hand up.

A red smear stained her finger. He hadn't moved since he blacked out. What if a bullet hit his spinal cord, and he were paralyzed? He'd hate being stuck at a desk job.

She shut her eyes. She wouldn't care what he did as long as he lived.

His skin felt cold. Was he going into shock? She rubbed Michael's chilly left hand, then his even colder right one. His face and neck were cool too. She grabbed a blanket from the bed and laid it over him. She stole a glance at Jared. He still hadn't moved.

A train whistle sounded nearby, then the rumble of its wheels. Damn, she couldn't hear the sirens now. She waited until the train passed. Heard a quick blast of the sirens, then nothing.

Footsteps sounded outside. She looked up. A tall lanky paramedic rushed through the door. She pointed to Michael. "Take care of the cop first. He's been shot. The other man kidnapped me, but he's been shot too."

The emergency medical technician examined Michael. "Found the bullet entrance. It's probably still inside. We need to get him to emergency."

Another paramedic, shorter and somewhat stocky, wheeled a gurney in. They slid a board beneath Michael and lifted him onto the gurney.

The second paramedic grabbed Jared's wrist. "Pulse is weak," he said. After pulling out a stethoscope, he listened to his heart. "We need to take this one too."

"Let's go then." He glanced at Jessica. "Do you want to ride with us?"

"May I?" Jessica asked.

"Not in the back, but you can sit beside the driver," said the first paramedic. "Get in quickly."

More sirens blared. "We need to leave before police cars block the street."

Three police cars jerked to a stop, their sirens silenced. Cops scrambled out, guns drawn.

"The shooting's over," Jennifer said. She hugged her sister. "You go on. I'll talk to the police." She slid on her red high-heeled shoes.

A second ambulance arrived. They loaded Jared

inside. A policeman told Jessica, "We'll question him at the hospital, then post a guard at his room. As soon as he's well enough, he'll be transported to jail to await trial."

Her heart beating wildly and her hands shaking, Jessica watched them load Michael. Then she climbed into the passenger seat. One paramedic got behind the wheel. With sirens blaring, the driver took off. Seconds later they were racing through city streets. Some cars moved to one side, clearing a path, but others didn't. The driver zigged and zagged, weaving in and out of lanes. She was jerked to one side as he careened around a corner.

A muffled call came from the back. "Hey, take it easy."

Jessica clenched her hands together and prayed. If only Michael came through alive, she'd learn to live with his tendency to flout the rules. Maybe she could persuade him to do it less often. He didn't break the important ones, but he always seemed to get the job done.

She wondered if she could stand knowing Michael could be shot again and maybe die. Except she knew he loved his job just as much as she loved hers. She couldn't ask him to give it up.

At the hospital Jessica walked beside the gurney as they wheeled it toward the emergency entrance. She held Michael's hand. Limp and cool, it chilled her heart.

Then he opened his eyes and looked at her. Her heart beat furiously, but she tried to look calm. "You're going to be all right. They'll take good care of you."

"Love you," he said and closed his eyes.

She held her breath. What did that mean? Was he afraid he was going to die?

The paramedic pushed the cart faster and faster until he was running.

Jessica gasped. Was Michael taking a turn for the worse? She ran to keep up, afraid to ask what was happening.

The door opened automatically. One paramedic pointed to the right. "Go to the desk and answer questions. We need to get him to an examining room. The gurney wheels whispered as they rushed Michael down the hall.

At the desk smiling attendant asked, "May I help you?"

Jessica took a deep breath, barely noticing the attendants now pushing another gurney with Jared on it down the hall. As Jessica told the woman at the desk what she knew about Michael, she realized she didn't know very much. Except she knew what was important—who he was inside, what he loved to do— and that he'd said he loved her.

"Is that all you can tell me?" the woman at the desk asked.

Jessica nodded.

"You may sit over there and wait. We'll let you know when you can see him."

Two uniformed officers rushed in. "Where's Steel? Is he still alive?"

Jessica pointed to the desk. "They took him to an examining room, but the desk needs more information."

Jessica sat. Oh, dear, she hadn't told him she loved him. Maybe that would have been the difference that spurred him to fight to live. She didn't even know how seriously he was hurt. They probably wouldn't tell her. Damn privacy regulations. He wouldn't be able to sign anything to allow her to get information.

What if he died? She couldn't bear the thought of him dying without her telling him that she loved him. Why hadn't she? She must not have been thinking clearly.

How could she go on without him? She'd enjoyed all their times together. And especially their times in bed. Could any other man ever make her feel the way he did? Would she ever feel as close to another man?

She looked at the clock. It moved interminably slowly. No one came to tell her how he was. She wished she had something to do to take her mind off him.

His family. She should call his family. Except she didn't have their phone number. How would his parents feel if they couldn't be with him before he died? She knew hers would want to be at her bedside.

She walked over to the policemen at the desk. "What about calling his family?"

"Shit, I'd hate to be the one to do that?" said another officer.

The desk officer frowned. "Somebody's got to."

Jessica said, "I never met his folks, but I'll do it if you just get me the phone number and lend me your phone."

In a minute, the taller officer handed her a piece of paper. She dialed the number. A woman answered. "Is this Mrs. Steel?"

"Who-who are you? Why you're callin'?" The woman's words slurred. Had she been drinking?

"My name's Jessica Ballard, and I'm a friend of Michael. He's been hurt. I thought you'd want to know."

"Oh, no. Where is he?"

"Arlington General."

"Lessee, that's on what street?"

"Genesee. Why not call a cab? The driver can get through traffic faster than you can.".."

"Good idea. I might jus' do that."

Jessica hung up, hoping his mother would follow through. She sat down to wait. Time dragged on. With each passing moment she feared Michael had died and they weren't telling her.

She prayed. Vowed to go to church more often. Vowed to help out some charity.

"Miss Ballard," the woman at the desk called. "Someone wants to speak to you. Make it short We need to keep the phone lines open.

Jessica grabbed it and listened.

It was Jen. "How's Michael?" her sister asked.

"I don't know. He was still alive when they rushed him to an emergency room. He didn't look good. I'm trying to stay calm until I hear something."

"I hope he comes through okay."

"What happened with Jared?" Jennifer asked.

"I don't know. They rushed him down the hall too. If he dies, he deserves it for shooting Michael."

Jennifer sighed. "I hate that he used you to get me. I could have at least smiled at him, said 'hello,' and talked to him. Then I might have recognized him as my prom date."

"Maybe not. People change as they mature."

"If I'd only been more friendly, maybe he wouldn't have been so obsessed with me."

"I'm not sure that would have been enough. He's sick."

"I should have realized that sooner."

"Why? You're no psychologist."

"Maybe now I'll remember to be more tactful with guys when I turn them down. I know you're waiting to see if Michael's okay. I'll let you go." She hung up.

Jessica caught herself biting her nails. She stopped and clasped her hands together instead. Finally, a man in scrubs came and stood before her. "We've got Michael Steel in room 208. You may see him now. Don't stay too long."

"Is he going to be all right?"

"I can't tell you that. Most likely they'll operate as soon as there's an operating room and a surgeon free."

She followed him down the hall to a small examining room with pale green walls. A gray tube ran from a metal IV stand to Michael's arm. He lay there, pale and subdued.

She took his hand. It was cold, but his firm grip reassured her a little. He wouldn't die—he couldn't.

She gazed into his eyes, hoping he could see how much she cared. "Michael, I was so worried. I feel better now that I can see you. How are you feeling?"

"Like a Mack truck rolled over me." He smiled, a wan smile, but a smile never-the-less. "Seeing you're okay ..." He let out a breath. "I can stop worrying."

"I wanted to tell you I love you. I couldn't bear it if you died."

He smiled. "I won't die. I'm going to hang around until you agree to marry me and live with me and all my cranky moods until I die."

She blinked. "Is that a proposal?"

He grinned. "Not very romantic, but I couldn't wait. Hell, I might still die. But I'll buy you a ring as soon as I'm able." His smile broadened, warming her heart. "Well, are you going to say 'yes'?"

She squeezed his hand. "Yes, yes, yes." She turned to the doctor standing behind her. "Is it safe to hug him?"

The doctor rubbed his chin. "I wouldn't go as far as to say that, but a kiss wouldn't hurt, he said on the way out of his room."

Jessica bent down, cradled Michael's dear face in her hands and kissed him gently.

He reached up and pulled her closer. He grinned. "You can do better than that." His lips met hers in a long lingering kiss that set her head spinning and her heart pounding.

He grabbed the phone on the bedside table. "Now I'll call my mother and tell her the good news."

"I already called her. She's on her way, in a taxi I hope."

His smile vanished. "Had she been drinking?"

Jessica's lips tightened. "Maybe a little. She sounded worried about you."

Michael's smile returned. "I'll be fine, and she'll be happy for us. No matter what she did in the past, she's my mother, and I know she loves me.

He grinned. "Now, even more important, ask the good doctor when they're going to let me out of here so I can make love to you properly."

"But you need to rest and recuperate for a few days until you get better."

He grasped her hand and squeezed it. "Nothing else will speed my recovery more than the promise of a little R and R." The amber glow in his eyes shone with love. Golden sunlight lit up the room. She squeezed back, thrilled with thoughts of spending all her days with him. Love filled her heart and overflowed. Life was wonderful.

Epilogue

Michael's mother blew into the room in a good mood. She hugged them both, then waited with Jessica through the night and during Michael's surgery. It went well. Michael insisted on claiming the bullet they removed.

As soon as Jared was out of danger, he was sent to jail. With the shirt he'd ditched at the stadium with his name badge attached to it, the shell with his fingerprints, and the bullet from Jessica, the police had more than enough evidence to convict him. Last she'd heard, Jared couldn't make bail.

Michael and Jessica's wedding was lovely with Jennifer as maid of honor in pink satin and Angela in paler pink as a bridesmaid. Her dad smiled as he handed her to Michael at the altar. "You're lucky to get such a smart woman," he whispered, then sat beside her mother. Michael's mother was sober, gracious, and lovely in a cream and blue lace dress. Jessica's twin caught the bouquet of pink roses and baby's breath.

Jennifer offered to take care of Michael's "Dog" his name now changed to "Doug" while they honeymooned in Hawaii. Jessica insisted she owed her that after taking care of her rambunctious Sheltie puppy.

After they got back from Hawaii and moved into his house, Michael patted the plastic encased bullet on top of his bureau as he got ready for work. "I'm strong enough to survive battles with the bad guys and smart enough to catch them."

"You could do that without breaking department rules? What makes you do that?"

"Not what, who. The way my boss puts me down brings out the rebel in me." He looked thoughtful. "Guess I can follow rules and still be the best detective in the department no matter what he says." He took her in his arms. "I only care what you think of me."

"I want you also to care about not taking dangerous risks. I want you coming home to me every night."

"No one can keep me away from you. I will always come back." Then he grinned. "No way will I miss out on making love to you."

Jessica smiled and kissed him, her friend and lover for life.

Dear Reader:

If you enjoyed *Double Jeopardy,* I'd love it if you would post a review on your favorite site so readers will know about this novel.

To receive notice of new books coming out and to get a free story, sign up for my newsletter by e-mailing me at carolynrwilliamson@charter.net. Put "Get free story" in the subject line.
Carolyn Rae

Also by Carolyn Rae

Searching Series

Searching for Love, (The Wild Rose Press) Valerie Trumbull reluctantly teams up with her ex-fiancé's brother to hunt her missing sister in Mexico, but she didn't expect to spend a night with him in a jail cell.

Searching for Justice (The Wild Rose Press) Attorney Kayla Walker fights for justice for her client, but the opposing attorney, Joe Morales fights her in court and kisses her in private.

A word about the author…

Carolyn Rae follows her passion, writing romantic suspense where bullets are flying, people are dying, and lovers are resisting attraction until they can escape the danger following them.

On a long road trip, she entertained her younger sister with stories. As a teenager, Carolyn Rae told stories to kids she babysat.

She taught home economics and family living in Michigan, Illinois, and Texas, where she earned a master's degree and also taught English. In Illinois, she worked as a researcher for a mincemeat company and met her neighbors by bringing samples of mincemeat pies. She was a teacher and supervisor of ironwork, painting, and carpentry residents at the Fort Worth Federal Correctional Institution in Texas. While there, she also wrote and directed videos on nutrition and fair fighting for married couples

Carolyn Rae wrote the text and many recipes for There IS Life After Lettuce (Eakin Press, Fort Worth), a cookbook for heart patients and diabetics. Her profile and travel articles have appeared in the Romance Writer's Report, Fort Worth Star Telegram, The Dallas Morning News, Positive Parenting, and AAA World, Hawaii and Alaska. She has worked as a paralegal.

http://carolynrae.com

Thank you for purchasing
this publication of The Wild Rose Press, Inc.

For questions or more information
contact us at
info@thewildrosepress.com.

The Wild Rose Press, Inc.
www.thewildrosepress.com